MW00736718

BELINDA

ALSO BY MARK ZVONKOVIC

A LION IN THE GRASS
THE NARROWS

BELINDA

A NOVEL

MARK ZVONKOVIC

DOS PERRO PUBLISHING

Belinda
© 2022, Mark Zvonkovic. All rights reserved.

Published by Dos Perro Publishing
An Imprint of Dos Viejos LLC, Denver, Colorado

ISBN 978-1-7352751-6-1 (hardcover)
ISBN 978-1-7352751-4-7 (paperback)
ISBN 978-1-7352751-5-4 (eBook)

Connect with the author at www.MarkZvonkovic.com

This book is a work of fiction and, except in the case of historical fact, any resemblance to actual persons, living or dead, is purely coincidental.

Without limiting the rights under copyright reserved above, no part of this publication may be reproduced, stored in or introduced into a retrieval system, or transmitted in any form or by any means (electronic, mechanical, photocopying, recording or otherwise whether now or hereafter known), without the prior written permission of both the copyright owner and the above publisher of this book, except by a reviewer who wishes to quote brief passages in connection with a review written for insertion in a magazine, newspaper, broadcast, website, blog or other outlet in conformity with United States and International Fair Use or comparable guidelines to such copyright exceptions.

Dos Viejos believes that copyright encourages an author's creativity. Thank you for supporting authors by buying an authorized edition of this book and, by complying with copyright laws, supporting authors generally.

For
Nancy Boden Davis

Do I dare
Disturb the universe?
In a minute there is time
For decisions and revisions which a minute will reverse.

From "The Love Song of J. Alfred Prufrock"
T. S. Eliot

1.

THE TWENTY-SIXTH OF OCTOBER, 2017, Houston, Texas, a red glow was on her office wall from the setting sun. A bank of clouds had moved to the south, which made visible the Williams Tower, an exclamation point on Houston's western horizon. Belinda Larkin sat at a desk, her back to the window, the rims of her shoulders glowing from the sunlight as if they radiated heat. She bent forward and her face was shadowed, her wavy hair short, curling beneath the jawline, a frame for her sharp features.

She normally turned around to watch the sunset through her window. But today she ignored it, struggling to finish a draft agreement. Her mind wouldn't stay focused, which annoyed her. Every few minutes, the text on her monitor disappeared, like a ship sailing into a fog. The words were sharp, and then they were dots in a gloom. She considered whether to close the document, turn off the lights, and go home.

Her office was more her home than her house was. She'd never had a husband. Her career was her life. The law was her husband. It'd been a happy marriage for three decades. Then, a month ago, she'd started to lose interest. This faithlessness was hard to deny. She wanted to run out the door into the night, not sure where to go, but certain to never return. The law was no longer exciting, like it'd been when she started her career. Just like that, it had started to be a burden.

A woman in Texas chose to ignore age after sixty. But the managing partner of her law firm had sent her a reminder that the partnership agreement required her to submit a retirement schedule. It was meant to be a gentle process, easing herself away from her practice over several calendar years. That meant the best she could hope for was the end of 2020. She didn't like easing into anything, particularly if it promised to be a slow descent into oblivion. A plan for aging was nonsensical. Age was just a number. Burden or not, the law was still her life. What would she do without it?

She stopped her attempts to draft and let her mind wander. Her restlessness would wear itself out, she thought, and her focus would return. When she was a girl growing up in Corpus Christi, she'd ridden a bicycle faster than the boys, thrilled by the wind pushing back her pigtails. The memories of hitting a softball over the fence and kicking a soccer ball into the goal thrilled her, the accomplishments still feeling fast and raw. She'd hated the fair skin on her arms and had tried hiding it with long sleeves. Her mother had said she had a colt's long legs and called her by her proper name, Belinda, when she was strong minded. She'd worn jeans, never shorts, and she'd gone snake gigging with the boys, her eyes sharp to the movement of grass along the creek, her reactions swift, her aim deadly, never feeling remorse for the creature. It was a skill that continued to serve her well as a lawyer, given all the sideways-sliding men in suits.

It was late. Her head ached. At this rate, she would be there all night. There were so few provisions left, no more important sections to write, only continuity items, like straightening the napkins and silverware on the table before a dinner party. Not that she had many of those. They bored her, especially the men in suits, always talking about themselves. It was such a nuisance to get them to leave once it was clear they wanted to get her in bed. She'd slept with several men over the years, but only in locations from which she could easily depart. Her nights were precious. She wouldn't squander them for a few moments of pleasure. One didn't stay in the theater after the show ended.

There was a man whom she'd wanted to spend an entire night with, many nights, in fact. Jay Jackson had been a law partner of hers for many years. He left the firm to take over his family's ranch. A few years later, on October 30, 2015—she remembered the exact date—they slept together. And then she hadn't seen him in almost two years. She didn't know where he was. But she didn't much care. It was her habit to move on after disappointment. Life was short. She didn't waste time with regrets.

She didn't want to retire. A future without her career was unimaginable. She would fight it. The chance of winning was slim, she knew. The managing partner, a woman in New York who shamelessly ingratiated herself to the male partners, would be unsympathetic. If nothing else, Belinda resolved to go down swinging.

2.

THE TWENTY-SIXTH OF OCTOBER, 2017, Baja California, Mexico, a pelican was fishing, gliding in a semi-circle and then plummeting into the water, its body rotating and flashing black and gray. The sun was just above the western horizon, reflecting red in the windows of the beach houses at Los Pelicanos, a community overlooking the Pacific Ocean, fifty miles south of the border that divides San Diego and Tijuana. Except for the man standing on his patio watching the pelican fish, no one was around. It was Thursday, and the vacationers from California wouldn't show up until Friday afternoon. The revelries would then begin, and the atmosphere would be different, until Monday morning when they all went home.

Jay Jackson had grown up on a ranch in Texas, and for him, ocean life was mysterious. The pelican's flight was a right awkward-looking dance, he thought, although not much different from a calf lurching backward after you've roped him and stopped your horse. It made him nostalgic for his ranch in San Saba, Texas, where he'd not been for two years.

He was a tall, gaunt man who wore his clothes loose, what was sometimes called a *relaxed fit*. Tight-fitting clothes revealed his strong muscular build, and given that he'd once been a spy, it'd been important to him that others underestimate his prowess. During that time he'd also been a lawyer, a career that had provided his cover, and his suits had been full cut from Brooks Brothers. In 2012, he'd left both those professions behind to become a rancher. The cowboys he knew always wore loose-fitting clothes out of necessity, except in the evenings at the bars, when they wore T-shirts that fit them snugly and showed the taut muscles in their chests so the women would look at them. But Jay didn't much care for being looked at.

It'd been easy to leave the law. His partners had called it early retirement, but he saw it differently. The law firm was unsavory. Herding cattle, checking the fence lines, and brushing his horse were true, honest endeavors. Practicing law, he'd told his partners, was worse than kicking shit around a pasture. His partners were probably still kicking shit at each other.

Hunting bobcats was safer than spying. But retirement from the Agency wasn't as easy. Soon after he'd told his law partners he was leaving, Jay called his Agency handler, Ben Lufkin. Ben's cover was as the managing partner of a boutique private equity company, Branoble Partners, which invested in international energy ventures. Branoble had also been Jay's law client.

"I'm all done, Ben," Jay said. "I'm going back to San Saba to run the family ranch. It's time for me to come in from the cold."

"That could prove difficult," Lufkin said.

"I'm sure you'll get along fine without me."

"You're too talented to retire, Jay. You'd make a fine teacher. Not have to go out in the field as often. I have a young agent who would benefit from your experience, the same as you did with Raymond Hatcher."

"Kind of you to say those things, Ben, but you have plenty of others with talent. I'm putting myself on gardening leave. And it's permanent."

There'd been several moments of silence. "I need to remind you about your secrecy obligations," Lufkin said.

"No reminder needed. I've forgotten everything already. I won't be writing any books. Just riding my horse and mending fences. No secrets there."

"Once you close the gate, you probably can't come back," Lufkin said.

"I know what it means to close a gate, Ben."

"You know a lot of people in the business, Jay. You may be bored without them."

"With all respect, Ben, if I'm going to hang out with snakes, I prefer the ones under the rocks at my ranch."

"Okay. We'll need to do a debriefing."

"Fine by me. Send me the time and place. I'll bring all my papers."

"You're sure about this?"

"Look, Ben, I've had enough of practicing law, and of sneaking around the world, and of leaving my cowboy hat at home to pretend to be someone I'm not. I can't do it anymore."

"You've always been good at pretending, Jay. And I'm not sure you know who you really are."

"Maybe. But I'm sure I'll find out soon enough, once I stop the pretending."

"Let's stay in touch, at least," Lufkin said, after a pause.

"Whatever you say, Ben. Call me anytime to talk about old times. Just don't be asking me to do any more pretending."

The ranching life was comfortable for Jay. As he'd expected, he kept his own counsel, required only to be polite to the ranch hands and his neighbors, of which there were only a few. It was a big ranch, and visitors rarely appeared. The change came in late October of 2015 when he began a romance with Lyn, who'd been his law partner, listed on the law firm website as Belinda Larkin. He'd held his feelings in for more than a decade, and he'd continued to do so for a while after he left the firm. Then he had a weak moment when he saw her in Austin. The old reasons to refrain were gone. He was no longer her coworker, and all the dangers of clandestine operations were behind him, including the risk that he might inadvertently put her in harm's way. Of course, he couldn't tell her he'd once been a spy. But that was irrelevant, as far as he was concerned. He was just a lucky man.

Until his luck failed. His mentor from his early years at the Agency, a man named Raymond Hatcher, was murdered. Continued separation from his spy practices became impossible. A reparation was due. It was in his heart. So he'd left the country, gone away for two years, left his budding romance behind. Spies knew how to do that.

Now, standing on his patio in Mexico, convinced that his grief for Raymond was behind him, Jay wanted to believe that it would be safe to return to Texas and to call Lyn. But he couldn't decide how to do that, and he'd been dragging his boots up and down the malecón in front of his beach house for a month, trying to make sense of all that had happened, not wanting to go home to his ranch until he felt closure. There wasn't much sense in this. He had a good enough cover story. *It was the strangest thing. Just got to traveling and couldn't stop.* But the bullshit would show on his face. The foreman, who'd been at the Jackson Ranch even before Jay's last brother died, would know "something weren't right," as would the ranch hands. And Rosie, the housekeeper, didn't miss a thing. She'd been at the ranch since she was born. Her father, a young local boy and World War II veteran, had been a ranch hand who'd fallen for a Mexican girl in 1950. Jay's mother had given the couple sanctuary from the town's ostracism. Jay just couldn't face them until he was sure that the turmoil inside him had settled, until he could stand before his mother's grave and tell her his bad episode was behind him.

The sun dropped below the horizon, and Jay got honest with himself in the gloom. He missed Lyn, their one night together still smoldering in his chest. Sentimentality normally irked him. Sugar was meant for coffee, his father had once told him. His brothers had all married. That was what you did. And they'd all gone to Texas A&M, then back to ranching. Jay hadn't married. He'd gone to Princeton, and he returned home only to see his mother before she died. But, maybe forty years late and even as old as he was, a relationship with Lyn Larkin was possible. It would cleanse him of all the lies and bureaucracy. At least that was what he hoped.

Now it was dark, only a glow on the horizon. The pelicans were all gathered on a jetty a hundred yards below, reminding him of cows hanging their sleeping heads above a paddock. He sat down and took out his phone. It was two hours later in Houston, but he tapped in Lyn's office number. He expected that the call would roll to voicemail, and he could make a brief howdy, say that he'd just been pondering old times and would be right happy to talk to her, should she want to call him back. It was putting his toe in the water.

Lyn knew she'd dawdled away the evening, unable to make more corrections to her draft. The indemnification provisions were so intricate that they made her dizzy. She felt as if she was in a maze of hedges in an English garden, going forward, then backing up, searching for a way out. Every phrase looked like the one before it.

The phone on her desk rang. Her shoulders sagged. She could listen to the voicemail tomorrow. When the ringing stopped, she gave up her vigil with the agreement. There would be no more drafting tonight.

A message from the night receptionist appeared on her screen. The caller was Jay Jackson, the message said. She became flustered. It had happened so fast, like a gust of wind blowing a tumbleweed into her path on the highway.

They'd been lovers that one night. He'd called five weeks later, on the seventh of December, 2015, to invite her to his ranch in San Saba. And a week after that, he'd reneged, not even having the guts to talk to her himself, just leaving a message with her assistant.

The Hold light on her telephone blinked, insistent. Her fluster became anger. She'd finally reconciled herself to his absence. But she mustn't lose perspective, she thought. His call might arrange the last pieces of the puzzle of why he'd jilted her. Although why she wanted to know that, she wasn't sure.

She picked up the receiver. Her greetings were habitually positive. And in difficult circumstances, she overflowed with energy, like a poodle leaping to catch a tennis ball.

"Well, hello there, stranger!" she exclaimed.

"Give me a chance before you hang up," he said immediately.

"I'm an open-minded woman. You have ten seconds."

"I know I should've called long before now."

This apology, if that was what it was, sounded hollow to her. His voice wasn't apologetic. The words were spoken too politely, thrown out as a perfunctory expression of regret. She held the phone away from her ear for a few seconds. He was not to be forgiven easily.

"That's a start. But not good enough," she said.

"It's no excuse, but a lot has happened to me since I saw you last. I want to see you, to tell you in person."

"You can make an appointment with my assistant. But I'm pretty busy."

He laughed. But she wasn't joking. Her statement was a preparation for hanging up the phone.

"Okay. Just think it over," he said, after some moments of silence. "I'm on the West Coast. The weather is beautiful. The beaches are fabulous. Can you get away for a couple of days?"

No would be the best answer. It was nervy for him to ask her so unexpectedly after all this time. A truly repentant man would've sent a dozen roses in advance.

"I'm quite busy, actually. Some of us still have to earn a living."

"I'm sorry. I know I surprised you," he said.

"Yes, you did."

"I should've sent you an email telling you I was going to call."

The line became silent and she wondered whether she could hear the ocean in the background. That he was on the West Coast, and not at his ranch, was strange. Then her shoulders sagged again. She wasn't comfortable being strident. And her life had been going sideways. Boredom made her want to be imprudent. So much so, that she might run away to a beach with a man who'd ditched her for two years. She did live in Houston. Pacific weather would be a relief.

"I could probably get away for a day or two," she said, hesitantly.

"Good. Fly to San Diego on Saturday. Send me the flight information. I'll be there waiting."

"That's too quick!"

He was not the one to be dictating the terms. She was pissed about his disappearance. A trip to the beach wouldn't make that go away.

"Aren't we too old to put things off? Come on," he said.

She wasn't old. How dare he say that! And what about the two years that he'd put off their relationship, that he'd just squandered?

"You've been incommunicado for two years, Jay. And now you're in a hurry? Forget it," she said.

"Okay. You're right. But I want to explain. Two years was way too long. Why make it longer?"

Two years was only too long because now he'd called and made it so, she thought. The draft of her agreement seemed to flash in front of her. An upcoming trip to the beach would motivate her to finish it.

"That's a fair point. I'll send you an email when I sort out my schedule," she said, after a few seconds.

It was an impetuous decision. Trepidation washed over her and she thought about slamming down the receiver, pretending she hadn't said what she had. But she didn't.

"Great, I'll be waiting for it," he said, and hung up before she had a chance to say any more.

⁓

The conversation unsettled Jay. He should've left a voicemail. He felt like he was galloping his horse and the saddle was slipping.

He went inside and fixed himself a Grey Goose martini. He didn't like to drink alone, but he was rattled. A martini wasn't a proper cowboy drink, he thought on the first sip. It was a drink for lawyers and spies. But he took another sip. The truth was that a martini was his favorite drink, even at the ranch. He was a Texan, but he'd been infected with the outside world.

Upstairs on the porch outside his bedroom was a blue bench, a good place to think. There, above the malecón that stretched a mile from his house to the other end of the community, the stars were bright, even if not as bright as out in the middle of a meadow at the ranch. It perturbed him that the beach communities along the ocean were scrunched together like they were. He could see their lights for miles up and down the coastline of the bay in front of him. You could fit ten of these bays within the boundaries of his ranch. On a night at the ranch when there wasn't a moon, he could ride out to a meadow, turn in a circle, and not see a single spot of artificial light, just a dark blanket rolling out over the hill country under the stars. His horse liked to go out at night, which was unusual for a horse. Her name was Patsy, after a character in a novel he liked.

As he often did when he drank alone, he thought about Raymond, who'd recruited him for the Agency during law school. Jay had met Raymond through his college roommate, the son of one of Raymond's friends from World War II. Raymond had taken Jay under his wing, become his mentor, and become a father who was a man of the world, not the narrow-minded, hill-country rancher that was his real father. They'd worked together on clandestine operations for the Agency for four decades, until Raymond was forced to retire. Jay had been happy to focus on his law practice after that, moonlighting occasionally when an interesting opportunity was offered to him by Ben Lufkin, until he retired from both lawyering and spying in 2012. He made a mistake in 2015, embarking on that one last spy mission in Bilbao with Raymond, when Raymond was ninety. It was on account of that excursion that Raymond was murdered.

Jay expelled all the air in his lungs and gazed out at the dark Pacific. Almost two years had elapsed since he'd gone to the Hatchers' farmhouse after the murder. He was the Hatchers' executor, and he'd done nothing except file extensions in the probate court in New York.

Out on the ocean horizon, a cruise ship moved south toward Ensenada, its lights glittering on the water. Jay sighed. He was reluctant to do the estate work, to distribute the cash and the property. It was necessary, but so final. After Lyn's visit, he would have to face it. His glass was empty. And so was his soul, gone into the night. He went inside, took off his sandals, and put on his boots. He wore his boots at night, when he took some comfort from walking in them to the other end of the malecón and back. He missed riding Patsy out to a meadow at sunset, and he much preferred crickets and cicadas to the roar of the ocean.

As he walked, waves pounded against the rocks and gave power to his sorrow. He walked faster after he turned back toward his house at the malecón's end. There was a waxing moon, which made him anxious about Lyn's visit, as if she were a light becoming brighter. He feared it might show what was in the dark room inside him.

3.

ALMOST TWO YEARS EARLIER, THE eleventh of December, 2015, Hudson, New York, Jay sat in a rocking chair on the porch at the Hatchers' farmhouse, studying the line of spruce trees about two hundred yards away across a hayfield to the north, its grass a brown blanket glowing faintly red from the setting sun, the scene an omen of winter. The Hudson police had called him the day before, when he'd also been sitting on a porch in San Saba. A terrible accident, the police chief said, his voice shaky; Raymond and his wife Megan, dead from a stray hunter's bullet. Jay had gone to New York and had now sat for hours on the Hatchers' porch, paralyzed with grief, knowing that once he began to look for a reason, their deaths would become real. The early night air became colder as the sunlight faded. There would be a frost overnight. But he didn't go inside, only zipped up his jacket.

Jay wasn't looking forward to the next day. It was protocol, but it was going to make him angry. He would try to be cordial, but he knew himself well enough to expect that his patience would be lost. Someone from the Agency always showed up after the death of an agent to check for any restricted documents or other Agency materials in the house. Of course, the Agency had required Raymond's retirement more than a decade before. So Raymond's secrets were all old and cold, certainly. At least, as far as they knew. Maybe they wouldn't bother.

They came the next day. "Mr. Jackson," the man said, holding out his credentials. "I've been sent to liaise with you while you wind up Raymond Hatcher's affairs."

Jay stood in the doorway, his face hard as stone, and didn't let the man in. "Not sure what you're talking about, sir. I'm only a rancher. Don't know squat about liaising."

"I'm sure you remember that the Agency insists on reviewing the disposition of an agent's assets."

"It was a long time ago that Hatcher was an agent. And I don't work for the Agency any longer. Ask Ben Lufkin."

"I don't know a Ben Lufkin." Agency bureaucrats never acknowledged active members of the clandestine service.

"Of course you don't. When you see him, tell him I refused to cooperate."

"We know you're the Hatchers' executor. But you signed an agreement with the Agency to cooperate."

"For my own affairs, I did. Not for my client's. I am Mr. Hatcher's executor. You're right there. But I have no obligation to tell the Agency a thing about the Hatchers."

"No need to be hostile, Mr. Jackson. Both you and Mr. Hatcher served your country admirably for many years. Our inquiry is only a routine formality."

"Murder is never routine. Why don't you tell me what really happened here."

The man kept his face flat. "It was a hunting accident," he said.

"Right. That's bullshit," Jay said.

"Do you have a copy of the police report?" The man began to open his briefcase.

"No need," Jay said. "I have my own. It was a perfect coincidence, I was told. The Hatchers were standing at exactly the right place together at exactly the time when a single bullet, fired from a difficult angle, killed them both. Got it. What kind of bullet was it, by the way? That wasn't in the report."

"I have no idea. The police have handled everything."

Jay looked at the man carefully for a moment. Was it possible he hadn't been briefed, that the real investigation was being kept above him? "Mysteriously, they didn't find a bullet. It went right through them both, which was rather extraordinary for a hunting rifle. I'm guessing you were here before and you have the bullets. Surely there was more than one." His anger rose, the image of them gunned down on their porch.

"I'm very surprised at this, Mr. Jackson," the man said, his composure now rattled. He looked behind and to the side quickly, as if worried someone else was listening. "What I was told is that the police handled it. Perhaps we could go inside and talk about all this in a civilized manner."

"I don't know why you're here. Clearly, I don't know anything," Jay said, and gripped the door harder. He didn't care, suddenly, what this man knew. "I don't work for the Agency and I don't care to·be civilized."

"I'm sorry you feel that way. We must insist that you turn over any materials relating to Mr. Hatcher's service with the Agency."

Jay laughed. "So you didn't find anything when you looked yourself. Before I got here. That's why you're bothering me."

"What are you saying?" the man asked, surprised again.

"I'm saying that I have no obligation to give you a damn thing. My only obligation is to hold my client's matters in confidence. You don't like that, you can arrest me, or whatever you think you can do. Tell Lufkin that when you see him."

Jay slammed the door in the man's face. It wasn't the man's fault, but he didn't care. Someone at the Agency had to know it wasn't a hunting accident. That made all of them culpable. And then he started looking for what the Agency was worried about, items bearing witness to one of the "off the books" operations he and Raymond had done. The Agency hadn't known where to look, but Jay did. What he found astonished him, much more than ticket stubs or handwritten notes. It was a journal begun in World War II, the last notation made the day before his death. *Talked to Unuka.* Who was Unuka? It was prohibited by the Agency to write things down. But that's what Raymond had done. For sixty years.

The rest fell into place quickly. The cleanup guys had found the bullets in the two holes in the porch wall but hadn't bothered to fill them in. The holes were deep, too deep for ammunition used to hunt deer. A shell casing was under a bush on the other side of the hayfield, sloppy of them not to look for that. The casing was from a sniper rifle. Their entire cleanup operation had been poorly done. That made Jay angry. The Agency he'd known was more professional than that.

The next morning, just after dawn, Jay stood at the window, looking out over the porch and the scene beyond. His phone vibrated and the name Ben Lufkin appeared on the screen. A sheet of frost hung over the field. That meant it was still dark in Denver. Jay's anger had been sandpapered with a wedge of despondency, and he set aside the blame for the present. It was inevitable that Lufkin would call him.

"It's a mess, Ben. A stray hunter's bullet is a joke. The cleanup was poorly done. The man who came yesterday hadn't been briefed."

"I was afraid of that. It all happened fast, and it wasn't an experienced team Langley sent out there. The police chief wanted an investigation, and an appeal had to be made to his patriotism." The tenor of Lufkin's voice was puzzling. Was it chagrin or lament? Jay couldn't tell.

"I don't care much about cover-up and damage control. Raymond was my friend," Jay said, his voice cracking slightly at the last two words. A cardinal stopped on a feeder hanging near the corner of the porch and then flashed away with seed in its bill. He remembered Jay telling him that cardinals didn't migrate south in the winter. Soon the feeder would be empty.

"Langley only briefed me," Lufkin said. "And reluctantly at that, only because they're worried what you might do. I told them you wouldn't be one to call the newspapers."

"The judgment I care about isn't a public one. The Agency is probably worried there's something here that needs to be destroyed. It looks like their team only did a half-assed search."

"And?"

"There's nothing here," Jay said without hesitation. Raymond hadn't trusted Lufkin, and for the time being, Jay wasn't going to, either.

"Okay. Nothing to suggest who the assassins were?"

"I don't need a suggestion, Ben."

"I expected that you would suspect it was Piquart."

"You discounted Piquart in Bilbao, Ben. And you were wrong. If it weren't for Raymond, the entire dock would've exploded, along with several Branoble businesspeople, I might add."

"You and Raymond did a good job there, I have to admit that. But it was an unsanctioned operation. So, it never happened, good outcome or not. I assume you've found nothing there about that?"

"So you never told Langley?"

"Only at a very high level, Jay. And we left it at that. But I took a lot of grief about it. Shit, you guys were retired."

"My friend was there. And his daughter. On Branoble's behalf, in case you forgot. So it makes no fucking difference to me that I was retired."

"Okay. I admit it was my mistake not to heed Raymond's warning about Piquart. And I see how you might suspect he sent the assassin to murder Raymond."

"We should have gone to France and killed him after Bilbao."

"You know I couldn't sanction that. And, in case you're wondering, the Agency won't sanction that now."

"I don't need anyone's approval, Ben. I'm retired, in case you forgot."

The men were quiet for a few moments. There were two smaller birds on the feeder. A chickadee and a titmouse. In the distance, Jay could hear the cardinal calling his mate, and a *peter-peter-peter* from another bird. Raymond had taught him the calls.

"It sounds like you may be heading to France."

"I'm not saying anything, Ben. You can deny that I told you anything."

"You haven't told me anything. But I have a young agent who needs a vacation and she wants to go to see her grandmother in Europe."

"I don't need any help."

"Who said anything about help, Jay. I just thought you could have dinner with her in France and give her some travel tips. You are certainly a veteran traveler. And she is fluent in French."

Jay laughed. He was fluent also. Not just in French, but in Spanish, German, and Russian. He didn't need Lufkin's novice agent watching over his shoulder. But it was better to know who Lufkin would send. Jay had no doubt that Lufkin was going to do that, regardless of whether he refused the help. "Okay. But dinner only. What's her name?"

"Anna Stegineo. She's a Branoble analyst on the energy side."

"Give her my number."

Lufkin laughed. "Do you think your Texas cell phone will work in France? I guess you don't have the old phone we issued you. I had to call your ranch for the new number."

"I threw that phone away. My new plan has international roaming."

"I'll have her bring you another Branoble phone that works in Europe. You can send it back to me when you return. And call me when you get back."

"Sure."

"Safe travels," Lufkin said, and hung up.

The frost was gone now, and the day was clear and bright with morning sun from just above the tree line. The farmhouse was on a hundred acres, with beautiful views of the valley and the Hudson River. The Hatchers had moved to Hudson when Raymond retired and Megan had bought an old storefront in town and opened a bakery. Her father had been a baker in Catalina, California, where she and Raymond had met when he trained there at a secret facility in 1944. Megan had named her bakery *OSS Bakery*. Inside, a sign said *Oh So Sweet Bakery*, but Jay knew the OSS really stood for Office of Strategic Services, where Raymond first became a spy in World War II.

It took several days to get the farmhouse secure for the winter. Jay didn't know when he would be back. He also met with the Hatchers' local lawyer to file the will for probate and request a delay in additional filings on account of the deaths being unexpected. But Jay couldn't bring himself to read the will carefully, or the other papers. That would only add to his grief. He shoved the papers into a pocket inside his suitcase, along with Raymond's journal. He would go somewhere remote after France, a place where no one would find him, and then he would deal with his grief and the papers.

His last act was to lease the bakery to the woman who'd worked for Megan for years, the only conditions being that she not change the name and that she go out to the farmhouse once a week and put more seed in the birdfeeder.

4.

PRESENT DAY, THE TWENTY-EIGHTH OF October, 2017, Houston, Texas, Saturday morning, time to go to the airport for her departure for San Diego. But Lyn set out for downtown Houston by a route that passed Rice, the Hotel ZaZa, and the museums. The Southwest Freeway was the direct route, but the calm of the less-traveled streets was better to wash away her truculence.

The day before, she'd finished her draft agreement without too much struggle, as she'd predicted while she was talking to Jay, and sent it to her client. Next, her travel plans were made and an email sent to Jay. By that evening, she was in high spirits, sipping from a glass of wine and stuffing beachwear into her suitcase. Holding up a blue skirt, she pictured it swinging around her hips while she pranced in the ocean shallows, her hands above her head, wrists flexed, reaching for the sky. And then the phone rang. It was a man from her client, Global Oil Trading Corporation, referred to by the press as *Global Trading*. Global Trading always wanted things done *yesterday*. So the meeting had to occur Saturday. And that was that. She rebooked her flight to the afternoon and sent another email to Jay.

Now the cars in front of her stopped. Her plan to show up a minute late as a small personal protest was foiled. A pedestrian had been hit by a METRORail train on the Red Line. She had to detour around a road block on Main Street. It meant she was ten minutes late when she got to the Chase Tower garage. In the elevator up to the opposing law firm's offices, she slumped against the back wall in despair. This was going to be another long, frustrating, and fruitless shuffle fuck, just like the last meeting.

The elevator rocked and she briefly lost her balance. As if released by this movement, a doubt about her commitment to her career arose. She pushed it away, like she was blowing a strand of hair away from her eyes. It was damn silly, thinking she might quit the law on Jay's account. She was only off for a fling in San Diego. Nothing had changed. She would refuse to retire.

She stepped off the elevator into a dim vestibule with a closed sliding door. This law firm, Stewart Baines LLP, represented ERIS, the seller of the oil company her client wanted to buy. She looked through a window for Will Baines, the partner from this firm who represented ERIS. He was young but could be stodgy. That sometimes dampened her enthusiasm and made her feel old. But many men did that. She was damn sick and tired of stodgy men.

She waited, impatient. Global Oil Trading Corporation had hired an advisory firm from New York because, despite the *Oil* in its name, the company only knew about trading and shipping oil on world markets, nothing about finding or producing it. But the knowledge of the advisory firm in those matters was superficial, as Lyn had known it would be when she learned they were from New York. Worse, the men they sent were haughty and obstinate and generally ignored industry advice, particularly from a woman. They were always late to the meetings. She wasn't in the mood for it.

~

William Bennett Baines III was the grandson of one of the founders of Stewart Baines LLP. He was six feet tall, with graceful shoulders, long arms, a fluid golf swing, and a stream-lined face—the quintessential handsome, white-shoe Houston lawyer. The year before, he had turned forty, but one could easily mistake him for fifty. Or older even, when he was being dour and cranky. He stood at the window of a conference room, from which he'd just watched the morning sun creep up from a flat, urban plain through which Buffalo Bayou meandered to the Ship Channel. The refineries there looked like stick figures, cloaked in a swirling petrochemical mist. It was a rather squalid scene, which suited him.

Will worried that the sun was burning holes in his retinas, and he turned back to the conference room table. Eleanor Sorel sat there looking at the draft agreement that had been sent over the day before by Belinda Larkin, the counsel for Global Trading, the prospective buyer of the ERIS oil and gas company. Eleanor was young, a second-year associate. She was a petite woman, not too many inches over five feet, which, Will thought, made her breasts look bigger than they probably were. He always stopped himself from looking at them too closely. It would be insensitive. Eleanor was very intelligent but also disarmingly pleasant. Will was drawn to her because she was an only child, the same as he was, and she'd returned to Houston after law school to be close to her parents, who'd retired there after living in many places around the world. Her father had been an oil company executive, again, the same as his. Both had graduated from Ivy League schools. Eleanor had graduated at the top of her law school class, Order of the Coif. Her credentials could have made her stuck-up, but she was instead demure—too much so, Will sometimes thought. The outfit she was wearing today was quite modest, dark slacks and a sweater, even though it was a Saturday.

"They've put that title warranty back in," she said, as he sat down.

"Yeah. I saw. Eleanor, it was really okay for you to skip this meeting, you know. It's a Saturday and I really doubt, based on that draft, that we're going to make any progress." He'd told both of his associates, Eleanor and Nick, a fifth year, that the meeting was a waste of time. But Eleanor had really wanted to attend.

"As it turns out, this is the most exciting thing I have for today. My boyfriend was supposed to come for the weekend, but he had to cancel. He's made friends with some private equity guys who he hopes will become clients, and he's going out with them. Sometimes his ambition gets the better of him, in my opinion. He has big plans for success."

Will had met Eleanor's boyfriend a couple of times, and hadn't liked him. He was a very self-assured (or maybe self-promoting was more accurate) associate at a large Denver law firm. The young man had asked questions about the Global Trading transaction, and Will later had told her she shouldn't have told him the names of the parties. But she was young. He understood that. Many things about Eleanor he understood because he had twin daughters who had just left for college. They were his only children. He also understood why Eleanor was in Houston near her parents rather than Denver near her beau. Will had returned to Houston after law school to be near his parents. But Will was nothing like his father. Bennie Baines was a legend in Houston, having founded and built up an oil and gas company, Baines Resources, that he'd then sold for several billion dollars. Bennie was a garrulous, larger-than-life man. Will, like Eleanor, was self-effacing to a fault.

"I'm sorry for that. But I can still think of a million more interesting things you could do," he said.

She laughed. "Yes. I know. But you're not a young lawyer who craves experience. And, you should remember, experience can be exciting."

"Okay, I'll give you that." He looked at his watch. "I suppose I should go look in the lobby. No receptionist today, and the Global Trading guys probably won't think to look for the phone near the door."

"You know, Will, that Ms. Larkin's associates like to disparage their client's advisors, who don't know a thing about the oil and gas business."

"We're going to keep that to ourselves for the time being. Just be polite," he said, and stood up.

Will left the conference room and walked around to the west side of the elevator lobby, where he discovered Belinda Larkin from the law firm Wanasas & Kindres, known as *W&K*, just stepping off the elevator. She hadn't seen him through the hallway window, and he watched her pace the lobby for a moment, probably unhappy to be there, as he was. He liked how her cheekbones were prominent and set just below her eyes. It didn't matter to him that she was twenty years older than he was. She looked younger, and besides, being older made her alluring. The rules that applied to his not looking at Eleanor didn't apply to Belinda, particularly since she didn't know he was there.

Will's client was a large, New York-based private equity outfit called ERIS, an acronym based on the last names of its four founders. Belinda's client, Global Trading, was the highest bidder for an oil and gas company ERIS wanted to sell. But the negotiations had stalled on account of the buyer's obduracy about contract terms. ERIS was losing patience. Their principals wouldn't attend the meeting. Will's instructions were to say no to the Global Trading demands one more time.

He opened the door. "Belinda, welcome. Your client didn't tell me you were coming," he said, after looking behind her to make sure no Global Trading people were lurking in the dark lobby.

"Maybe I should just turn around and go home then," she said. "If you're disappointed, I mean."

Her eyes sparkled. Closer to her now, he was quite attracted to her, and then felt foolish, like a boy smitten by his friend's mother. His face reddened slightly.

"I didn't mean that," he said hastily.

"My client's advisors will be disappointed also," she said, and looked up at Will with wide eyes. "None of the Global Trading executives are coming, but one of them called me last night. He said he didn't care whether the advisors invited me or not. 'Tell them to call us if they have a problem,' he told me. They won't like it, but that's the story."

"I'm not disappointed. I'm happy you're here. You weren't here for the last meeting," he said.

"I wasn't invited that time either. Anyway, not sure what good I'll be, but, hey, what else would I have to do on a Saturday?"

Will customarily played golf on Saturday, which he'd had to cancel. It distressed him to break his routine. When he dressed in the morning, he put his right leg into his pants first, and in the evening, he folded his soiled clothes before he put them in the hamper.

"Maybe they'll be receptive this time," he said.

"Don't hold your breath," she said.

He did hold his breath. She'd come closer to him in the doorway, and he became distracted by the tilt of her head, the blue in her eyes, the delicate, translucent veins in her temples, and the soft downward curve of her lips. A tightness gathered in his chest. There was no sense in this, he thought. He could be having a stroke, his heart rate became so elevated. With a great exertion he stepped away from her, as if to slap some propriety into himself.

"Let's go back to the conference room," he said quickly. "My associate is there, and she'll come back and check for your clients in ten minutes."

In the room, Lyn dropped her bag on the floor and pulled back a chair for herself at the head of the rectangular table. He watched her bend her long legs and smooth the back of her skirt as she lowered herself into the chair. His pants began to feel tight. So he sat down, quickly, in a chair two places away. Eleanor was watching him.

"Belinda, this is Eleanor Sorel. She's working with me on the deal."

"Lovely to meet you, Eleanor. I'm sure you're both wondering why I'm wearing a skirt on a Saturday. I was supposed to fly to San Diego first thing this morning, and I'm hoping this won't last long, so I can catch a noon flight," she said.

"I wear jeans when I fly," Will said, blushing at the suggestion that she'd noticed him looking at her legs.

"I always dress nicely," Lyn continued. "If the plane goes down, I want to look nice when they pull me out of the rubble."

"Oh," he said. And Eleanor laughed.

"I'm pulling your leg, you know," Lyn said. "I want to look good for the gentleman who is picking me up at the airport."

"Ah. Makes sense."

Will was sure she would look good in jeans, but he didn't say so. Several minutes elapsed. And then she was looking at him, waiting, which made him nervous. Eleanor was looking, discreetly, at the draft.

"I'm missing my Saturday morning golf round," he said, because it was the first thing he thought.

"Do you wear jeans to golf?" she asked.

"And my boots and hat, of course," he replied.

"Oh, I bet you have a pair of those precious golf slacks and white shoes," she continued. "What color are the pants? Pink or yellow?"

"They're bright orange, like the vests that hunters wear. You don't want the idiot behind you teeing off while you're still within range."

"That wouldn't be good at all," she said, and turned to wink at Eleanor. "Golfers seem to think of everything."

Eleanor laughed again. Will got up and retrieved his briefcase from the corner. He'd already looked over the papers twice. There wasn't much to say about her client's demands. Except no.

"Belinda, before they get here, I want to let you know that there's a good chance I'm going to be abrupt with your guys, maybe even rude. I don't want you to think it has anything to do with you. You've been nothing but reasonable and helpful."

He knew it was a strange thing to say. What kind of lawyer apologized before he'd actually done something wrong, before he was caught? Some lawyers did this, apologizing before malfeasance, like a mugger who said, "Sorry for this," before bashing his victim's head with a pipe. But Will wasn't one of those. And he wanted to set a good example for Eleanor. Civility was dying in the legal profession, and it shouldn't be.

"One thing first," she said, holding up her hand. "You persist on calling me Belinda. Quit."

"Okay. But we're in the office." He didn't see why she wanted him to address her informally. They weren't sitting in his living room. In truth, he'd called her Belinda there as well.

"Fine. In the meeting I can be Belinda or Ms. Larkin, or whatever. But it really makes me feel old when you call me those things. I've told you this before. I'm *Lyn*. And that goes for you too, Eleanor."

"Okay," he said. Then he added, quickly, "You're not old."

"Good. Then you can call me Lyn with no problem?"

"Yes. I can do that."

"And one more thing, Will," she continued. "Being rude to these guys may be an act of kindness. I've tried everything for the past few weeks to get them to understand how the business works, and they still don't get it. I know they're my client's advisors, and I shouldn't be telling you this, but you're not going to make progress by being nice. I don't think they're even going to listen unless they're afraid you're going to pack up your toys and go home. You may need to be an impatient professor and explain everything to them in first-year-college terms. Know what I'm saying?"

"I think so."

"Good. They work for my client so I have to be polite to them. You don't. And I'm not going to let them make a bad deal. Also, at this point, the worst deal would be no deal at all."

"Thanks. I plan to be very direct with them," he said, and then looked at his watch. "It's been twenty minutes. I suppose Eleanor should go back to see if they're in the lobby."

"If she must, but it's a shame to ruin the morning."

When Lyn turned back to her papers, she bounced in her chair, pulling it closer to the table, and her chest moved noticeably. An image of her breasts in a sheer bra sliding against the inside of her blouse was in Will's head suddenly. His face reddened yet again, and he turned quickly to watch Eleanor go out the door. The lobby was empty when Eleanor got there and she returned to the conference room alone.

⁓

Waiting always made Lyn jumpy, so she said she would check the lobby about ten minutes after Eleanor returned. The advisors were there, circling the elevator lobby like a school of fish, frequently changing directions. She paused, her hand on the door handle, wanting to turn away and leave them there, walk up the interior staircase to the next floor, take an elevator down, and drive to the airport. No, she would soldier on. A deep breath. She turned the handle and presented herself.

"Welcome, gentlemen," she said. "Great to see you again." Then she saw the disappointment on their faces at her presence and said, with less enthusiasm, "Follow me. I'll take you to the conference room."

They sat down across the table from Will. The sun was bright through the windows they faced. They appeared to be posing under a photographer's light for a club portrait.

Gerald Kent had blond hair, combed back along the sides of his head, held in place by a hair gel that reflected the light. He was too well groomed to take seriously. New York was an incubator for men like him. He had a Hamptons tan and a very good dentist. The others kept looking furtively at Eleanor, who appeared to Lyn as trying to be invisible.

"William, thanks for the quick meeting," Gerald said. "You're probably missing a golf date."

"No problem," Will said.

No one spoke for a time. It was a tactic they taught in business school. The one who spoke first revealed what was most important to him.

"You see, William," Gerald said finally. "We were confused by your last draft. You deleted the guaranty that you own what we are buying. We told Belinda to put that back in the draft she just sent to you. It seems like we keep putting it in and you keep taking it out, and we thought it was best to talk about the issue before you cross it out again. I hope you understand that we must know the value of what we are purchasing."

"It's not customary in the oil business to make promises about ownership, Gerald. The first thing I plan to do is delete it again."

"This is a big problem for us. We are paying a lot of money for your oil."

Will looked at him, then straightened his back and folded his hands together, balanced on the edge of the table. "Let me try to explain again. You're not buying any particular quantities of oil, Gerald. You're only buying whatever rights we own to look for oil on the lands and to produce and sell the oil reserves under that land, however much that turns out to be. There are estimates of how much oil is in the reservoirs on the lands from which we're producing. Those were prepared by an independent engineering company. You have them. But the value of that oil changes every day with changes in the market price of oil. We don't guaranty that value. No one does. The engineers report is what you get. If you want, you can get another engineer to audit that report. But how many barrels of oil are ultimately produced from those reservoirs is your risk, not ours. And it's your risk whether there is any oil at all on all the other lands that are not yet producing."

"But how can we be sure you really own the rights to look for or produce oil on these lands?"

Will looked at Gerald for a moment. Was he really that dense? Will had gone over the basics of ownership several times. It wasn't rocket science. "Gerald, the simple answer to that, as I've said before, is that you can't be sure. The rights to extract minerals on lands in Texas can be traced back to grants from the sovereign owner of the lands before Texas became a state, hundreds of years ago. Sometimes those rights are held by the same person who owns the land, the rancher who has his cattle grazing around the oil derricks, for example. But the oil rights can sometimes be owned separately. A person can sell his ranch but keep the oil rights under it or he can keep the ranch and just sell the oil rights. Generally, buyers of the oil rights get legal opinions about their ownership, particularly on the lands where oil is currently being produced. That's what we did. All those opinions are in the company's files we gave you access to months ago. Your lawyers can audit those opinions. Or you can get your own lawyers to issue new ones. Up to you."

"That's not exactly comforting that we're getting anything for our money. Those opinions are only worth as much as the lawyers who wrote them."

Will laughed. "Which I'm guessing you don't think is very much."

"Yes, to be blunt," Gerald said, not smiling.

"Gerald, you can only be as sure as the diligence you do, as I just said. You're getting what we have, what we acquired when we bought the properties. By the way, we do represent that we've done nothing to compromise the rights we acquired when we bought the properties. That's the customary promise in a deal like this. Beyond that, ERIS won't take the ownership risk for you."

"Then all you're saying is that you own what you own," Gerald said.

"Precisely. No one does any more than that with oil properties."

"And no insurer will give a title policy on oil rights. We've asked."

"Exactly," Will said. "For the very same reason we won't. Caveat emptor, and all that."

"And we could end up with nothing, and look like fools!"

Will laughed and leaned forward. "You mean like you've bought a pig in a poke?"

"That's a clever way to put it, William. I know you all like witticisms. But this is an important issue to us."

"Gerald, if you knew the oil business, you would know that a deal like this requires that you do your own investigation about ownership of the properties. In the offer memorandum we provided you before you made your bid, we stated specifically that we will not guaranty ownership or value. Do you want to do this deal or don't you?"

"That's hardly in the spirit of good-faith negotiation, William."

"Gerald, there is nothing to negotiate," Will said, sitting up straight, his hands now forming fists on the table. "The answer to your request for a guaranty is no. It's not going to change. If you want to buy the company, you do your own diligence."

And that didn't take long, Lyn thought. These were boys on a playground. She wanted to stay quiet. Gerald was arrogant enough to allow Will to walk out. Then she would make the flight to San Diego. She saw that Eleanor had put down her pencil and was wide-eyed that this whole deal could collapse right before her eyes. Lyn remembered being that young and naïve. She was envious. Ahead of Eleanor was a golden path paved with the excitement from learning and experience. The sun went behind a cloud in Lyn's heart. Was she at the end of that path? She pulled herself up. This deal was what mattered right now. Time to intervene. A duty to her client.

"William, could you please excuse us so we can talk this over among ourselves?" Lyn asked.

"Of course," Will said politely. "Eleanor and I will be in our offices. Call me when you're ready."

5.

THE TWENTY-EIGHTH OF OCTOBER, 2017, Los Pelicanos, Baja California, bright morning sunlight stabbed into Jay's eyes. He hadn't slept well. The consequence of drinking alone. A gulp of strong black coffee he'd just brewed made his stomach jump, as if he'd seen a rattlesnake. He added cream, put on sunglasses, and went out onto the patio. A breeze blew off the ocean, and the air was clear. The palm trees down near the beach were flapping their long skinny leaves, like they were about to take flight. He stood for a time and watched a fishing trawler on the horizon.

At eight o'clock, he walked down the malecón to the home-owners' association's office to get a visitor's permit for Lyn. He'd not seen her recent text until this morning. It was a bad idea to check messages just before bed. They sometimes set off a thinking rodeo that could go on for hours. So it wasn't until an hour ago that he learned that an unexpected meeting had been called, and her trip was in doubt. She would arrive later in the day, if she came at all. But he decided to proceed as he'd planned. Storm clouds on the horizon didn't mean you shouldn't ride out to check a fence line. He would run errands in San Diego. He needed more Grey Goose. It was hard to find in Mexico.

Near the office, a man Jay didn't know stood on a promontory, gazing at the ocean. He saw that the man noticed him. But the man didn't acknowledge doing so. He kept looking into the distance, a good imitation of a statue.

On the way back from the office, the man was still there. His hair was almost white, but he was a young man, very well groomed and wearing a polo shirt that broadcast affluence. He didn't look like the contemplative sort. Not that a young affluent man couldn't be contemplative, but his gazing over the ocean, Jay thought, was saying that he was too important to be bothered by the residents. It was unfriendly. A simple nod was all that was necessary.

"Howdy," Jay said. "Pretty nice day it's turning out to be, isn't it?"

The man turned his head slightly to look at Jay. His eyes were a flat brown color. After a moment, his mouth curved into a half-assed smile. "Good morning," he said, and looked away.

"Okay then," Jay said. "Y'all have a nice day now."

Jay went back to the house, got his wallet and his passport, and then drove to the exit. The community had only one gate, always staffed by a guard. Jay waved to him as he turned onto the road that would take him to the highway. It took about an hour to drive to the border in Tijuana on Mexico Highway 1D, a well-maintained toll road until it turned into the Border Highway, which was narrow and pot-holed. The border road didn't go directly to the border crossing. A series of turns on several local streets was next, and then came the line and the waiting, inching forward toward a booth. Jay was rarely asked any questions or required to open the compartment on the back of his truck, but he still had to wait in line.

There were hawkers who walked in between the cars selling food and drink, churros, blankets, cheap jewelry, and all manner of other paraphernalia. Jay ignored them and thought about Lyn's arrival. She was going to ask what he'd been doing for two years. He couldn't tell her much. Not that he was a spy, not about what happened to the Hatchers, not that he'd left their farmhouse two years before to find the man who'd hired the sniper. So what the hell could he say? He felt dejected. It would be more lies, what he'd hoped to put behind him when he retired. His law career had been a lie. Basically, he'd lived his life in a house of mirrors, adding rooms to it as his lies compounded. How would he ever tell her that? It would've been easier never to have called her.

He had no regrets for what he'd done after he left the Hatchers' farmhouse. So many borders he'd crossed, and here he was almost two years later, next in line at the United States border. He rolled down all his windows so the agent could glance inside, a polite way to cross the border.

"Where you headed today?" the agent asked, without opening the passport.

"To the airport to pick up a friend."

The man handed back the passport and nodded him into California.

6.

ALMOST TWO YEARS EARLIER, THE eighteenth of December, 2015, Ortaffa, France, the day after his flight from New York to Paris, and then a local flight from Paris to Perpignan, France. Jay made his way to a small hotel, several miles north of Château Bernard. The château was owned by the old Frenchman, Georges Piquart, the former French Sûreté agent. For three days, Jay drove the roads in and around Château Bernard, judging time and distance to remote areas in all directions, particularly toward the higher elevations of the Pyrenees to the southwest, on the other side of which were several Spanish highways leading to Zaragoza and then further west to Bilbao. Across the Tech River from the château was a secluded wooded area, accessible by foot, an opportune location, Jay thought, from which to access the house without attracting attention. It wasn't perfect because it was winter, the trees were bare, and the water was cold.

On the night of the fourth day, Jay sat in the hotel bar and studied the way the light reflected off his martini glass. France was the homeland of existentialism. The vodka in the frosted glass was simplicity and complexity, he thought, a demonstration of Husserl's *epoché*. He chuckled to himself. He was an old cowboy and a Princetonian amateur philosopher, about to murder a dastardly Frenchman up the road, a man so old he would die soon without any help. He asked the bartender for two more olives.

A young woman sat down on the stool next to his. She was Anna Stegineo, he was sure, the Branoble analyst Lufkin promised to send. After studying her in the mirror behind the bar, he was sure she was more than just a young analyst on a trip to visit her grandmother. He felt his ears go back, the same as Patsy's did when trouble was nearby. Lufkin was sly, and Jay was sure he wasn't going to get rid of this woman easily.

"Howdy, ma'am," he said.

"Hello, Mr. Jackson," she said, her voice polite.

"Call me Jay," he said. "You just don't call an old rancher 'mister,' even in France."

She laughed. "Okay, but it won't come natural."

A minute went by, no words between them, he just watching her as she sat turned to him, as if posing for a portrait. She was a striking woman, green eyes, a lithe torso, long legs, small breasted, strong shoulders, a body balanced for combat. She wore black pants and a dark-blue tailored blazer.

"Can I buy you a drink?" he asked.

She laughed. The bartender put a glass of wine in front of her. "A bit late on the draw, pardner," she said. The accent was all wrong, but he suspected that was intentional. He shrugged. Her eyes didn't give a thing away.

"I know you were Raymond's friend," she said. "I'm very sorry."

"It's kind of you to say so. I guess Mr. Lufkin told you he died."

"Yes. But I knew Raymond also. He met my grandmother in Italy in 1943. Her name is Vera. She lives in Croatia."

A memory kicked in. Vera worked for Tito when Raymond met her in Italy during World War II. And working for Tito's security service, she reunited with Raymond on several occasions. Jay had once met her, a long time ago, when he went with Raymond on a trip to Zagreb in 1999 to visit Pavletić.

"Mr. Lufkin told me you were going to visit your grandmother. But he said she was in Europe."

"The Croatians consider themselves part of Europe. You're not with the times, Jay."

"No. I'm but an old rancher. Does your grandmother know you're stopping to see me? I met her once, actually, a long time ago."

"Yes. She remembers. Actually, she knows all about you. I told her I was meeting you in France."

"Right. I suppose she might be worried that this old cowboy is going to get you drunk in all the French wineries."

Anna laughed. "Nice story, Jay. But you don't care for wine. What you like are martinis," she said. A nod at his glass. "My grandmother told me that. But I like the old cowboy story."

"So, how thick is my dossier?" he asked.

"Dossier?"

"That bundle of papers that Mr. Lufkin gave you."

"All he told me was that you know your way around Europe."

"Okay, Anna," he said. "Let's stop kicking the horseshit around the barnyard and get to the point. I'm not a travel agent. Why are you really here?"

He'd played his high card too soon, but he had no patience with the Agency, or with Lufkin, who would probably be happy if Anna told him Jay went back to the ranch. Lufkin certainly didn't want to have to explain to Langley that his old renegade cowboy retired agent was loose in France looking for revenge.

"I only want to help," she said. "Mr. Lufkin told me to give you whatever assistance you would take. If there are any items you require for your tour, I can probably obtain them for you. A camera, maybe?"

He supposed that was better than her saying she wanted to talk some sense into him, that it was ill-advised to do what he planned, that it was best that he return to Texas. How would she know what he planned?

"I'm much obliged for that, sweetheart," he said, "but I don't need any help."

"Really?"

"I've gotten along just fine on my own in this game for many years. No reason to change now. So, you can go on to Croatia and then back to the office and tell Ben that I was just as ornery as he expected."

Anna was pretty. He had to give her that. Her grandmother had been a beauty in Vis in 1942, according to Raymond's journal, where there was a description of Vera that showed Raymond had been quite taken with her. Did Anna know that Raymond had kept a journal?

"Jay," she said quietly. "Mr. Lufkin doesn't know I knew Raymond as well as I did. My assignment, to be blunt, is to keep you from getting caught by the French authorities. He would rather that you go back to Texas. But I mean to help you with whatever you plan to do."

"That could make you a rogue agent, I think. You're a bit young for that, don't you think?"

"Look who's talking."

"Honey, I know I keep repeating myself. I'm only a cowboy on a personal trip. Mr. Lufkin told you, I can tell from what you've said, that I once worked for the Agency with him. It doesn't matter. I don't work for anybody now but myself."

"With all due respect, Jay, in all your difficult operations, you had Raymond with you. Bilbao, for example."

"Lufkin also told you about that, I guess."

"No, Raymond did. I was there with the Branoble team attending the closing ceremony. I didn't know at the time that you and Raymond were there."

"Lufkin wasn't happy about that."

"He never said that to me. He never even said what happened."

"Forgive my skepticism."

"Raymond told me what happened right after I got back to New York. Look, I may not be as good as Raymond, but I'm damn good. You may not want to hear this, but you need me."

"Do I? To do what, exactly?"

"Kill Piquart, of course."

Jay laughed. "And how did you come up with that?"

She looked at him. "Raymond told me you would do this."

He thought to make a joke about talking with ghosts, but he had no words. Raymond had always anticipated Jay's reactions. He would put his hand on Jay's shoulder in those times, and Jay would have to pause. Think again, Raymond would say. The memory made Jay's hands shake, and he put down his glass with the olives.

"When?"

"At his farmhouse. After Bilbao."

"Why?"

"It was advice from my nonno."

"What?"

Anna looked at him for a moment, as if debating whether to describe the cat that had just jumped out of the bag. "You don't speak Italian? Raymond was my grandfather. Illegitimate, I guess. He and Vera slept together in Budapest in 1957. Her husband wouldn't let her keep the baby, so my mother was born in a convent in France and later adopted by a French family. Raymond didn't even know I existed until my mother was killed in 2005, and Vera decided she had to tell him. There was no father in my life, either. My mother didn't marry, and she never told the man who'd made her pregnant. Like mother, like daughter? Anyway, once Raymond found me, everything came out. He trained me like he trained you, and then I went to the Agency. Raymond didn't mention any of this to you, I guess."

"No. I'm sorry. I didn't know."

"Our background is Croatian but from a part of Croatia very close to Trieste. So there's a lot of spillover from Italy. He called me his unuka, or granddaughter."

"Hell, he never told me about you. And I thought he told me everything. I loved him like a father." Something squeaked in Jay's head, but he couldn't say why.

"I felt the same way about him. He was a very private person."

"He was always one step ahead of me. So he predicted I would go after Piquart if something happened to him?" Jay was upset, all these words just seeping out. His head spun. He had so many questions. But it wasn't a good time to ask. It was likely there would never be a good time.

"He did. Last October, my grandmother came to New York and Raymond told a story about you being rash, how you'd once run off to East Germany after an assassin. My grandmother then mentioned that Piquart had been the one who hired the East German assassin. For her it was only the gossip of old spies. It disturbed Raymond terribly. And later, he told me that I shouldn't let you be rash again if anything happened to him."

"As in go off to France after Piquart."

"One could argue this is rash."

"I'm too old to be rash."

She smiled at him. "I know. Just an old cowboy."

"Glad you remember. I'm tired of saying it."

"Maybe your old lawyer self can remember a man named Parnell?"

Parnell was a former law partner of Jay's. He'd sexually accosted a young woman associate in New York. Jay had tried to have him expelled from the firm. But the firm refused and only sent him to the Paris office.

"Wish I didn't. Don't care for him much."

"So I've heard. It doesn't matter. Do you know he is Piquart's nephew?"

"Yeah, I know that."

"He was in New York at one of the meetings. I'm sure you know it was Branoble's portfolio company, Global Oil Trading, that sold the LNG terminals in that deal. The closing ceremony was in Bilbao, but he wasn't there, so you wouldn't have seen him."

"Yeah, I know that too. But I wasn't there doing legal work. I was on a bird watching trip."

"Right. Just trying to save some seagulls from a harbor blowing up."

"I'd retired, in case you forgot. Just an old cowboy, looking at Spanish birds."

"Whatever. Parnell knew I was in Bilbao and he sent me an email inviting me to his uncle's château in France after the Bilbao ceremony. Lufkin told me to go."

"Why?"

"He was curious about the people connected with the buyer after you and Raymond found the bombs. Piquart was one. When I got to his château, I discovered that he was somewhat unhinged in his old age. He'd hated the Wrights, Raymond's friends from the OSS, because he thought them anti-French. He had them murdered in Vietnam, but their son was rescued. And then Piquart later became fixated on killing the son also. Not sure any of this is in the Agency records. Lufkin never said he knew any of it when I gave him my report about Piquart. He told me to forget it. And Raymond wasn't much help when I told him about it. I think the murder of the Wrights still hurt him, even after seventy years."

"I know the details. But did Piquart talk openly about these things?" Jay knew that Lufkin was aware of Piquart's history with Raymond, so he'd not been telling Anna everything. Or

Anna was covering for him. It wasn't clear, but he decided not to challenge her.

"No. I overheard a diatribe about the bombs not exploding in Bilbao. The men were in the library for cognac and cigars after dinner, but I could hear Piquart from the living room. Raymond told me that the Wrights' son was your college roommate."

"More than that. We worked together at the law firm until I retired. And now he works for another Branoble company, I think."

"Yes. Parnell also told me at the château that Piquart planned to make another attempt to kill the Wrights' son, this time at your ranch the following week."

"He and his daughter come to the ranch sometimes. But how did they know when?"

"I didn't know at the time. But after I found out, I went to the ranch to intercept them. I wasn't smart enough to figure out that they'd go after Raymond at the same time. Parnell didn't even mention Raymond, but I should've known. It was a bad mistake." Pain showed on her face and she looked away.

"Hard to be in two places at once," he said. "And Raymond's relationship with the Wrights was complicated."

"I could've called you."

"Or Lufkin."

"Raymond didn't trust Lufkin. He asked me not to tell Lufkin that I was going to your ranch. As far as I know, he doesn't know what happened there, or, if he does, he thinks you were responsible. I honored Raymond's request not to tell him anything, even after Raymond was murdered."

Jay sat up straight. "You told Raymond you were going to the ranch."

"Yes. He was the one who told me the exact dates the Wrights' son was visiting you."

Jay wanted to ask, *Did Raymond tell you not to call me also?* But he didn't. He remembered that he'd ridden Patsy out to the rise above the picnic spot because he'd had a feeling something was wrong. There he'd spotted the assassin in the tree, but before he could react the man had fallen to the ground with an arrow in his neck.

"It was you who shot the arrow," he said.

"Yep."

"You could've waited around and introduced yourself."

"Nope. Raymond didn't want you involved."

"I dragged the corpse down into the gulley," he said, not knowing why he needed to explain anything. "Left it for the buzzards."

"Appropriate."

"My grandmother used to take us out there for picnics. Didn't seem right to leave a body there."

"I'm sorry, Jay. I should have stayed to explain."

"I don't understand why Parnell told you their plan?"

"He was drunk." She paused a moment. "And I was fucking him at the time."

~

Two days later, the twentieth of December, 2015, Ortaffa, France, Anna and Jay drove to Argelès-sur-Mer, parked on Allée des Pins, walked up and down several small streets to Rue des Roses, ate breakfast, and looked at the beach. A cold wind easily breached the fabric of Jay's coat, making him shiver regrets he'd not brought the leather one he had at the ranch. Anna didn't seem to notice the weather. She chatted as if they were tourists, comparing the rocky coasts near Dubrovnik. Raymond had been a legendary spy on account of his ability to blend into a venue, his language mimicking the local vernacular. Anna was like him in so many ways. Jay marveled at her skills but was saddened to be reminded of Raymond, whose training in her was so apparent. He was still somewhat suspicious of her, that she might not have told him about other Lufkin instructions, but as the day went on and he observed her more, chatting with the shopkeepers and flirting with the waiters, he felt better. They stopped for lunch at Café Durand in Elne.

"I don't think you're going about this the right way, Jay," she said, enjoying her frites. "You should stroll in, rather than make an assault. Not hang out in a tree across the river and wait for the old man to pass a window. You're a very good shot, Raymond told me. But you would need a rifle. Have one, by any chance?"

He didn't, of course. It wasn't something you took with you on an Air France flight. She could probably obtain one. After all, Lufkin had meant for her to provide him items for his tour. But killing the old man from a distance wasn't an option. His desire for vengeance was too personal for him to do that.

"No. I was planning to use a knife," he said.

She laughed. "Right. Raymond's OSS knife, I suspect."

Of course Raymond would've told her about that knife. He'd treasured it, a reminder of his good fortune to survive the Indochina jungles during World War II. But Anna's knowing about it made Jay felt less Raymond's confidant now.

"I didn't know anyone else knew about the knife."

"Oh, I came across it one day looking at his old stuff, and he told me about it. I'd just found a grandfather. I wanted to look at everything in his house. And I'm a real snoop. Anyway, my plan for the château is that you're just going to walk in there. I know how," Anna said.

"I'm going to ring the doorbell and ask for an audience. Is that it?"

"Something like that. But I'm going to be inside and I'm going to let you in. They know me. I'm Parnell's lover, in case you forgot, being the old cowboy you are."

———

Several more days went by before the right time came. Anna learned that the servants were given a holiday the Christmas weekend. How she found this out, he didn't know. And the old man's longtime girlfriend, Sandrine, would go to Paris that weekend, Anna was sure, because Sandrine always tried to avoid staying with the old man, made all the more horny by the absence of the women servants, who he frequently tried to fondle. It would make Anna's surprise visit all the more exciting.

"I made a copy of the key when I was there, and I know the alarm code," Anna said. "They don't change it anymore. The only guard on site is in a room in the basement, and he's always drunk and watching TV. I can take care of him. The security is sloppy. I think everyone is just waiting for the old man to die. His grandson lives in Paris. As does Parnell."

———

The night before they went to Château Bernard, they met in Anna's room at the hotel. As she laid out the plans for what seemed like the hundredth time, she cleaned a Walther pistol, her hands nimble and quick, sliding the chamber, unloading and reloading the magazine, screwing and unscrewing the Omega silencer. It was as much an aerobics exercise as gun maintenance.

"Darlin', I hope you got a big purse to carry that in," Jay said. "But it is a nice-looking pistol."

She laughed. "Oh, no, cowboy. This is for you."

"I don't know," he said, taking the gun and weighing it in his hand. "I never cared much for pistols. And I have Raymond's knife, in case you forgot."

She pulled a Sig P365 from the small of her back and began to clean it as well. Jay shook his head. She'd taken his place as Raymond's protégé. He had to give her that. But he didn't care for being babysat.

"It's always good to have a backup weapon," she said, and winked at him. "And that reminds me. Not to be too personal, Jay, but would you happen to have some Viagra on you?"

He wasn't sure he heard right. The woman was so young, she could be his daughter. There weren't words in his vocabulary that he could use to respond to her question. Then, she laughed, her eyes twinkling, clearly having great fun over his discomfort.

"Didn't think so. Not to worry. I have another plan for that," she said, and walked quickly to the door. "Be back in a few."

~

The twenty-seventh of December, 2015, Château Bernard, Ortaffa, France, early morning, the wind was gusty and cold. Jay was glad Anna had talked him out of swimming the Tech River. She'd gone over to Château Bernard the night before. Jay showed up at the door, feeling awkward on account of the clothes Anna had insisted he wear: a black bomber jacket over a black T-shirt and black jeans, clothing quite foreign to a self-respecting cowboy. The pants were very tight and the black leather boots perplexed him. They only covered his ankles and they had zippers down the sides. He'd wanted to wear his black suit, which he'd brought with him from New York. Everyone would notice him in that, she'd said. The bomber jacket did hide the pistol well. He had to give her that.

She came to the door wearing a rumpled nightgown, not much in the way of cover. The material was sheer and the darkness of her nipples was visible beneath it. But her hair was pulled back tight into a ponytail with a rubber band, her nod to being ready for combat.

"Shouldn't you be dressed by now? Or am I too early?"

"We have to move quickly," she said, ignoring the questions. "I'm going to run down the hall to the guard's room and turn off the cameras. The old man is up this staircase and at the end of the hall to the right. I loaded up his coffee with Viagra to hinder his movement, if you know what I mean. He won't be springing out of bed to defend himself. He may even be dead, I gave him so much. You go up and say your piece. It's all the way at the end of the main hall. I'll be right there."

A massive marble stairway extended from the entryway to the second-floor landing, which was fronted with a balustrade carved from pink marble. Giant portraits hung on several walls. One of them Jay recognized as General Jean de Lattre, who served under General de Gaulle in World War II. Three surveillance cameras were visible.

"I'm sure it's too late on the cameras. There are quite a few pointed at us now," he said.

"The man back there is a drunk, and it's unlikely he's even watching the video feed," she said. "Trust me, Jay. There will be no video of us. I disabled the recording device last night."

"Okay. It's your rodeo."

She laughed. "Yes, it is. You go on, cowboy. I'll be there in a minute."

Piquart was propped up in his bed with an erect penis projecting upward through the slot in his pajamas. A grin on the old man's face, ear to ear, his eyes focused on his penis, not his visitor. The room was bright, all the lights on, one even appearing to be pointed at the man's erection.

"Mon dieu. Regarde ça!" he exclaimed.

"Enjoy it, monsieur. It will be your last," Jay said, as calmly as he could while pulling Raymond's OSS knife from his belt. So many times during his career, he'd killed without a trace of emotion, but now he was riddled with rage. Here was the man who murdered Raymond.

Casual, unconcerned about the man with the knife, Piquart leaned over and pushed a button on the side table. His eyes moved back to his erection, followed by his hand, and he cackled. "You're that old CIA cowboy. Are you wearing a disguise? Do you plan to cut my throat with that knife?"

"It isn't your throat I plan to cut," Jay said, moving toward the bed.

The old man's eyes focused, pools of hatred. He showed no fear, only clutched his penis with both hands, as if it were a weapon. "I would put that knife away, if I were you," he said. "My man will be here momentarily and I would rather you not be dead when I ram this up your ass after he gets here."

Jay thought Piquart was bluffing until Parnell burst into the room, wearing pajamas and waving a shotgun. Anna had been sure Parnell wouldn't be in the château. "Where's Anna?" Parnell shouted, and then looked over at his uncle. "You were fucking her. I know you were. I'm going to kill the bitch."

"I was certainly hoping to," Piquart said. "But she ran out before I got the chance. And there's no reason to shoot her. That man there with the knife. He's the one to shoot."

"And this would be your nephew?" Jay asked Piquart.

"My idiot nephew," Piquart said, and started pushing the button on his bedstand like a madman.

Parnell stumbled toward Jay, who raised his hands, the knife still gripped in one of them. He needed just a little time, a distraction before Parnell pulled the trigger.

"Howdy, Parnell," Jay said.

Amazement dawned on Parnell's face, eyes wide, the barrel of the gun moving slightly down. "It's you! Jackson. What are you doing here?"

"Just came by to say howdy. I was in the neighborhood."

"Shoot him, you fool!" Piquart screamed.

Parnell moved the shotgun up to his shoulder, trying to aim it, a pointless exercise for a shotgun at close range. Anna burst into the room, marched to Parnell, locked in surprise at her return, and surrounded him with her arms, her hands on his wrists. "You bad boy," she said, as calmly as if she was speaking to a child who'd misbehaved. Whirling him around, the gun was pointed now at the old Frenchman. All so fast.

The gun's blast surprised Jay. Piquart's face became a bright-red circle, hair and brains making a shadow on the wall behind him. Parnell's eyes bulged, Anna's arm having slid up across his throat, until he collapsed to the floor, unconscious.

"I don't remember this part of the plan, honey," Jay said, his hands still in the air. Why hadn't she said Parnell was there when she met him at the door? He felt like a piece on a chess-board, the next move disguised.

"No. Parnell wasn't supposed to be here. I had to improvise," she said, squatting down, checking his pulse, pulling back an eyelid. "He's alive, but I'm sure his blood is barely moving."

"How much Viagra did you give him?" Jay asked, trying not to think about her possibly fucking Parnell again the night before. It made his stomach churn, and he considered shoving the OSS knife, which he was still holding, into Parnell's chest.

"I gave him midazolam last night in a cocktail. Not enough, evidently. He shouldn't haven't been walking around, never mind waving a shotgun. He won't remember a thing. Or no one is going to believe it."

She wore gloves when she arranged Parnell's body on the floor and laid the shotgun in his arms. This tactic, a shotgun and strange drugs, hadn't been in Jay's training. But he wasn't curious. Raymond's murder was avenged, for what that was worth. He didn't feel good, didn't really feel anything. Anna looked him, and nodded at Raymond's OSS knife in his hand.

"I suppose you still have a few minutes to use that thing, cowboy," she said.

"Too late," he said, and secured the knife back in his belt. "The bull's already left the pen."

7.

THE TWENTY-EIGHTH OF OCTOBER, 2017, Houston, Texas, an atmosphere of frustration in the conference room; they'd squandered most of Saturday morning talking about the ownership issue. It was almost noon when Gerald finally told Lyn that he would tell Global Trading not to buy the properties without ownership promises from ERIS. She had to work hard not to say what she thought. He didn't know what the fuck he was doing. She wanted to tell him again that he could hire an army of landmen and title attorneys to check the ownership, which should've already been done. If she was a man wearing a bowtie, with Ivy League credentials and a New York office, he might listen to her. She was only a Texas woman. He hadn't hidden his hubris.

"Look, you may not believe me, but you're taking a risk that Baines is going to bid you farewell if you make the demand again," she said. "He'll call his client and they'll terminate the negotiations. In case you've forgotten, their acceptance of your offer letter has expired. They're free to put the properties back on the market."

"I'm not stupid," Gerald replied. "We're paying a high price. If they want it, they can take all the risk that the value isn't what we think it is. Oil prices have dropped. They won't find another buyer at our price."

Actually, he was stupid, but she didn't say so. This was an oil deal, not an IPO. "Why don't you call the VP at Global Trading.

When I spoke to him last night, he said I should recommend to you to call him if we got hung up on an issue."

Gerald looked surprised that the VP had called her. He grumbled something about making the call, even if not needed, and Lyn excused herself to go to the restroom. Make it easy for him by not being in the room when he called.

From a visitor's phone booth in the hall, Lyn called Will, and they met at a window on the other side of the building. Below was Jones Hall and Tranquility Park. Buffalo Bayou twisted west between Memorial Drive and Allen Parkway until at Shepherd Drive it disappeared into trees on the backside of the River Oaks Country Club. The Williams Tower was to the southwest, where Baines Resources, Will's father's old company, occupied two high floors.

She'd worked as an associate for Will's father, Bill Baines, what he was called when he still worked at the firm, and she'd also known the grandfather, Colonel Baines. If Will knew that, he'd never mentioned it. There'd been a dramatic kerfuffle between Bill Baines and the firm's partners the year she'd made partner. She'd departed to W&K shortly after. Then he'd left the firm to form Baines Resources, where he was called Bennie.

"I've stood in this very spot hundreds of times," she said. "You know that I once worked at Stewart Baines, don't you?"

"Yes, of course," he said.

"And that I worked as an associate for your father?"

"He mentioned it once."

"Well, I hope I got an honorable mention," she said.

"He didn't go into detail."

"Okay," she laughed. "I'll just assume the best. Did you know your grandfather very well?"

"Yes, I did. He's a legend around here."

And so is your father, she wanted to say. But she let it go. She was only making small talk, looking for a connection to be friendly about. They gazed out the window for a time. It was awkward, being quiet. But it didn't seem to bother him.

"I have a good story about Colonel Baines. Do you all still have the Colonel's Council?" she asked.

"Of course."

"In my early days, it wasn't a formal thing. No name or anything. The Colonel just took out associates for cocktails on Fridays. He didn't drink much, as you probably know. He would ask for an empty glass, a second small glass containing a shot of gin, neat, a third glass with tonic, and a fourth glass with ice. These he lined up and then doled out to the empty one a cube of ice, a teaspoon of gin and some tonic. It was his way of being collegial without really drinking."

"I've heard that. Our managing partner, Ed Reid, says those were the good old days."

"Yeah, I'm pretty old."

"I didn't mean that."

"I know Ed. That's how old I am. We were associates together."

"I didn't realize that. But I guess I could figure that out on account of you working for my father."

"My god, I'm not as old as your father!"

"I didn't mean that either."

"Yeah, I guess I'm closer in age to him than to you. But what's a few years anyway?"

He didn't respond to that. She knew he was an only child, which made him hard for her to understand. Her sister was often difficult and probably should've been an only child. At times she would walk away in the middle of a conversation.

"What time is your flight?" Will asked.

"I've missed it." She sighed.

"I'm sorry. I guess there's always tomorrow."

"It's not the end of the world. There are later flights."

"Frankly, I see no reason to keep beating a dead horse," he said.

She paused, feeling her lips curve down and her eyebrows push together. Was he saying that she shouldn't have any hope of making it to San Diego, that she was beating a dead horse? Maybe it was true, but he was a dick to point it out.

"I mean the negotiations," he said immediately. "Not your trip. Sorry."

"I hope we can give the negotiations a bit longer," she replied.

"I'll give it more time," he said.

"I heard your daughters are home from college for the weekend. How are they surviving their first year?"

"It's good to see them."

"There are so many college vacations now. It sounds like a boondoggle, if you ask me."

"Yeah. The colleges in New England have a lot of what they call study days," he said.

"Maybe every other Monday should be a study day for law firm partners."

"I'm planning to go to Goode Company with them tonight for BBQ. They miss the place. Nothing like it in Boston."

"Just thinking about it makes my mouth water. What do you usually get?"

"Sliced brisket. I don't like to get my hands greasy with the ribs."

"I know what you mean! But I can't resist them. What's your favorite side?"

"Okra and tomatoes."

"I like the collard greens."

One of Gerald's coterie interrupted, asked them to come back to the conference room. Gerald sat at the table, his head tilted back slightly, sunlight angled through the windows making a vague shadow on the wall behind him. The man next to him wrote furiously on a yellow pad, like an athlete running in place, preparing for a race.

"William, we are unable to accept your position. Even if not customary, we must have an ownership guaranty. We cannot agree to go forward without it."

Gerald glanced at Lyn. He was gloating that he wasn't taking her advice, she thought. Had he called the Global Trading VP? It made her furious. Her trip had been interrupted for nothing.

Will leaned forward, his hands on the arms of his chair, ready to stand up. "Fine. I will let ERIS know our negotiations have terminated."

Gerald's confident expression faded. His bluff had been called. The adjacent man stopped writing so quickly that his wrist twitched like the body of a decapitated snake.

"Please, William, we don't intend to terminate negotiations," Gerald said.

"Gerald. There is nothing more to negotiate. ERIS won't insure ownership or value for you. End of story. What more is there to say?"

"Give me a couple of days to talk this over some more with my client," Gerald said. "Then, we'll call you."

Will leaned back in his chair, entwined his hands behind his head, looked at the ceiling, and exhaled a long breath. Was it an act? Lyn wasn't sure. She thought about Goode Company BBQ. Okra and tomatoes. The smoky smell, sharp and sweet at the same time. Then Will stood up, smiling. She envisioned his hands greasy, breaking his rule and getting the ribs, and she had to press her lips together to fend off a smile.

"Fine, Gerald. Just be sure to tell them ERIS will not take the risk that ownership of the minerals is compromised by anything other than what we've done. Nor will you be given any assurances of value of the minerals," Will said. "Our oil company will be back on the market on Monday."

Gerald sat, looking at the bright windows. Maybe disappointed. Maybe not. It was common with guys like him. Easy come, easy go. There were other deals. She would give him some time to call Global Trading. It was his responsibility to give the bad news. She would call them on Monday from San Diego. Still Gerald sat.

"Can I call you gentlemen a cab?" Will asked.

"No thank you," Gerald said and stood. "We have made our own arrangement."

There was handshaking, not particularly friendly, no eye contact. In the lobby, Gerald went inside an elevator hurriedly and then turned to glare at Lyn. A sore loser blames someone else. Well, she'd been blamed for things by better men than he.

"I'll get the next one," she said, as the doors closed.

"Can you make a flight today?" Will asked.

"You bet I can!" A forlorn look was on his face. "Will, this isn't your fault. You gave them a chance. I expect my client will rein them in."

"Maybe. I hate to see a deal go south over an unreasonable demand. I had no room to compromise. ERIS was clear."

"Give it a couple of days. It's not yet time to mourn this one."

"Fine. Enjoy San Diego. Call me if you hear something," he said.

"Of course. I'll call my client on Monday. They won't let the deal die," she said, as the elevator door closed between them. She wasn't convinced that was true, but there was nothing else to say.

8.

THE TWENTY-EIGHTH OF OCTOBER, 2017, Millbrook, New York, at six in the evening, Patrick Brashner stood on his terrace. He was a short man in his mid-fifties, not fat, but with the physique of a pipe, arms too long for his body. The mansion behind him was shaped like a Stealth Bomber, the cockpit the mansion's entrance and its fuselage fanning out behind fir trees, opening onto a terrace and then a manicured lawn, a large swimming pool, and tall green hedgerows. Preparations for a dinner party were in progress, caterers bustling about, spreading linen and silver cutlery on dinner tables on the lawn, the scent of wealth in the air, wafting over the scene from the estate's thirty acres of fields and trees. The grounds were screened by trees along the Millbrook town road, a half mile away, creating an impression of cloistered elegance.

Brashner was disturbed by the small army of caterers. It was a blotch on the idyllic setting that he'd so carefully sculptured. They were necessary for a dinner party, but a shame they couldn't be invisible. He saw that a bar was situated incorrectly and he charged down the steps to the pool area. At the bottom step, he tripped and was propelled forward, his arms rotating awkwardly, the pool looming, until he was grabbed by one of the men setting up the bar. He immediately shrugged off the man.

"Be sure you've cleaned up all this mess," he said, looking for but not finding catering gear.

"Yes sir."

"And I told you I want the bar over there," he stated, pointing across the pool.

"Yes sir, you did. But there is not an electrical outlet there."

"Then use a damn extension cord."

"Yes sir."

"And get it done quickly. The guests are arriving."

Back on the terrace, Brashner's annoyance increased when he eavesdropped on his wife speaking to the first guests. *Yes, it's a lovely spot but too ostentatious for me*, she was saying, or something like that. She'd built a place for herself, down a path from the house, stables and living quarters bucolic and unpretentious. These provided her a retreat from her husband. He wanted to interrupt, to say he was a perfectly charming husband, and she had no need to flee his company. But he greeted another guest instead.

He circulated among the guests, shook hands, said what a beautiful night it was, all those pleasantries, and pointed out how carefully maintained the landscaping was, thinking all the while that a bit of ostentation was necessary with some people. Clients wanted their lawyers to be affluent. No one trusted a commoner. You couldn't have a backyard party with a rusty grill. Without his clients, his wife wouldn't have the horses in her stables.

Brashner walked to the bar to say hello to Max Regaleme, the "R" at ERIS, a big client of Brashner's law firm, Stewart Baines. Max's wife was a horse-riding buddy of Brashner's wife. The Regaleme's had a week-end house in Millbrook for equestrian events, and spent most of their leisure time at their house on Long Island when they weren't at their penthouse on Fifth Avenue.

"Good weather for the weekend," Brashner said.

"Perfect for the beach," Max replied. "All this damn horse stuff. I don't know why she likes it."

"There are great trails through the woods here. And the foliage is turning."

Max wasn't a hiker, and Max liked a show, his parties at his beach house in East Hampton always a performance. Prominent men always attended those. If he'd had his way, Brashner would've built his mansion on Long Island, near the Regaleme place. But his wife loved the countryside, her horses, the trails, and all the mundane people who lived around them. She hated the beach. Brashner's happiness for the Hudson Valley was feigned, lest anyone think his wife made the decisions.

"I don't know why my wife wanted another house up here," Max replied. "They have some horse farms on the north shore. It would be a shorter drive. But she wanted Millbrook. Now she drags me away from East Hampton for these big riding events, like this weekend. You know, the people here are so damn boring."

A din made by bugs emerged in the early twilight. Brashner didn't like the sound. The song of crickets was monotonous.

Brashner considered himself the Stewart Baines partner in charge of ERIS, a kind of traffic-control officer on all ERIS matters. It irked him that Will Baines in Houston was doing all the work on a current ERIS transaction, especially since it was being directed by the ERIS principal, Larry Sutter. Sutter was invited to that night's dinner party but had sent regrets the day before, dashing Brashner's hope to create some goodwill with him. And Will Baines wasn't giving Brashner any information about the deal.

"How's the sale of your oil company going?" he asked Max.

"Difficult negotiations," Max said.

"It's taking a long time."

Max was about to say more when Wallace Sesame—pronounced se-SAH-mae, unlike the seed—joined them. His appearance irritated Brashner, the invitation to the ERIS general counsel given only on account of a standard law firm practice when a client's principals were attending. Lawyers working as employees of a client weren't held in high regard by law firm partners.

"Hey, Wally," Max said. "Patrick was just asking about our Global Trading deal."

Sesame smiled broadly, the look of a critic happy to find a mistake. With his right index finger, he pushed his glasses up the bridge of his nose, the eyes behind them a flat gray, like nature had forgot to add gloss. The hair on his eyebrows was dense, here and there a curled loop springing out. "Now Patrick, don't you have an ethical concern about talking to Max about this? You know better."

A smile was also on Brashner's lips, but he was angry. Sesame was referring to a legal formality, a technicality, that a lawyer who'd represented both parties in the past must refrain from engaging with either party about a transaction between them. Brashner was representing several defendants, all Global Trading affiliates, on a matter involving alleged stock manipulation and insider trading two years before in shares of a company to which Global Trading was selling its marine shipping terminals.

"That sounds like a legal problem," Max said. "Maybe we should consult a lawyer or two. See any around?"

Sesame laughed. "They're everywhere, Max. Watch where you step."

"I asked an innocent question, Wallace," Brashner said. "Do you think I'm going to run inside and call my Global Trading friends to tell them what you tell me?"

"With all due respect, Patrick, you're missing the point. Innocent or not, discussion of the deal with you is improper. Neither we nor Global Trading should talk to you about it. It could appear to violate the conflicts agreement Stewart Baines signed."

"I was only asking whether the deal had closed, Wallace. We can skip it."

"One could construe that you were soliciting information. Not good for us to have even an appearance of impropriety."

"Come on, Wallace. It was just an innocent question at a cocktail party. You're making it out to be a Supreme Court case."

"Boys, how about we talk about something else," Max jumped in. "Something that's not legal. Did you know I just got a new boat? It's nothing much, only ninety feet, but it's still the best way to get to Bermuda."

A good opportunity to change the conversation before Sesame said more. "That's great, Max! How many bedrooms does it have?" Brashner asked.

"Four, in addition to living quarters for the crew. And a giant living room."

"Does it bother you, Patrick, that your partner in Houston is handling the matter?" Sesame asked, a dog with a bone. "Larry Sutter said he has a great reputation for doing oil and gas deals."

"I'm sure he does, Wallace. I don't know him well. We're a big firm, and I don't keep up with what we do in our smaller practice areas."

Sesame laughed. "You might take a look, Patrick. It's a pretty big practice, and probably the best in the country. I'm happy I got Will Baines on board before Global Trading contacted him."

"I'm sure you're right, Wallace."

"And isn't he the grandson of the founder of your firm?"

"That makes no difference at all."

"Ah. In any case, this deal is a long way from a litigation matter, your specialty."

"I'm well versed in transactional practice, Wallace. And my litigation experience makes me more effective."

"Is that so? And you know about oil and gas exploration and production? The litigation matter you're working on for Global Trading has nothing to do with oil and gas."

"That's irrelevant. Drafting and negotiating transaction agreements are the expertise, whether it's oil and gas or manufacturing. We handle everything in New York."

"It's too bad Larry Sutter didn't make it tonight. You and he certainly have different opinions about that."

"I wouldn't know."

Sutter knew the oil business. A lawyer wasn't going to fake his way into representing ERIS, which Brashner would've had to do. And Brashner hadn't wanted to expand future ERIS representation to the Houston office. That was why he'd refused Sesame's inquiry, rather than recommend Will Baines. It was always better to take the shot yourself. Why pass the ball to a teammate? And Brashner had wanted to represent Global Trading in matters other than litigation. Their principals knew nothing about the business, and he could've fooled them, using a young partner to do the corporate work in the background. Understanding the oil business made no difference; all he needed to know was how to compromise. And that would've made ERIS happy also, that Brashner as Global Trading's counsel was easy. But Sesame had retained Will Baines before a pitch to Global Trading could be made by Brashner after he'd learned about the deal from Sesame.

"It doesn't matter anyway," Sesame said. "Max, you can't be talking to Patrick about the deal. He's on the other side of what we call a *Chinese wall* until the deal is done."

"Whatever you say, Wally," Max said.

"Tell you what. We can have a BBQ closing dinner in Texas. You and Patrick can talk all you want then."

"Sounds good," Brashner said, smiling and sounding pleasant, but wanting to punch Sesame.

The sun was hidden, like Brashner's anger, behind the red-rimmed black silhouettes of the nearby hills. It frustrated him not to know how the deal was progressing, because in exchange for some off-the-books legal work, he'd received equity in an entity affiliated with Global Trading two years before—a little incestuous, but that's how things were sometimes. That entity was the principal defendant in the insider trading lawsuit. Next week, Brashner planned to call the Global Trading chairman's nephew, with whom he'd ingratiated himself by arranging a membership in the New York Athletic Club. And if he had to, he would call the chair of the parent company of Global Trading, a private equity company named Branoble Partners, a man who'd made him some promises about recovering some of the losses incurred on account of short sales of stock that were also a subject of the lawsuit. If any of this came to the attention of management of Stewart Baines, Brashner would be asked to withdraw from his representation of the Global Trading affiliates and divest his ownership. But he'd hidden his ownership carefully, and he didn't care what law firm rules it violated. His partners owed him anyway, for all the fees he'd collected for them over the years.

Brashner ate very little at dinner. Night fell, and the evening insects sounded like a truck's grinding gears. Max left early, still complaining that he wasn't at the shore.

9.

THE TWENTY-EIGHTH OF OCTOBER, 2017, on her Saturday afternoon flight to San Diego, Lyn sat in the front row. First-class cabins were all the same, the seats leather, not as narrow as in the back; a dedicated and attentive steward to deliver food and beverages, the uniform a bit too tight around his paunch; the engine noise coming from behind the cabin soft, the sound of whispering death. She refused the beverages, her nerves too much on edge. And the food looked worse than being hungry.

The space between the seats protected her arm from being rubbed but provided a wider view area for a seatmate. The man next to her leaned forward, rummaging through his bag on the floor, availing himself of a low angle view up her skirt. She pulled the thin airline blanket over her legs, put on an eye mask, and pretended to sleep, fighting a battle to keep from moving. He was watching her chest, she guessed, but at least she couldn't see him doing it.

In the dark behind her eye mask, she wondered what made so many men desirous. The men at her firm weren't lecherous, but she often felt her body was on display. No sense in it, that she could figure, her chest not large, no alluring makeup, her clothes never provocative. Her eyes were pretty, more interesting certainly than her breasts, covered by bra and blouse, but they were still always their focal point. Sometimes, she wanted to pull up her shirt and flash them, solving the mystery for them, freeing them then to attend to who she was. But she knew it wouldn't work.

On the escalator down to baggage claim in San Diego, her legs were cold, her hose stripped off in her car at the Houston airport. Hose were only worn in business settings or outdoor events in Houston, mosquitos swarming. She saw Jay watching her from the bottom.

He leaned against a wall, legs crossed, arms folded, and head tilted in amusement, she guessed. He was tall, his blond hair lightened from age, his stature that of a lifeguard or rugby player, she couldn't decide. Not a lawyer, certainly, wearing a T-shirt and flip-flops and not jeans and boots, despite his claiming to be a rancher. Did cowboys go to the beach?

He pulled her close and hugged her tightly, testing her balance, her face becoming hot from a blush, requiring that she pull her blouse away from her chest when they separated. Her blood was up, a memory of how hard his chest and arms had been when they'd slept together. Embarrassed to be aroused in an airport, she fought to control her breathing as she leaned back to see his face, her hips still in his grasp.

"I've missed you," he said.

"You're one to talk, Jay," she said. "I didn't go away." She sighed to herself, now that she'd let him know how much he'd hurt her, a failure by her to be unemotional, as she'd intended. He'd made no promises, after all, their night only a moment of passion, a fast fuck of a sort. No sense mooning over it.

"I have been a stranger," he said. "But I can't say I'm sorry. I was doing something I had to do."

"That's bullshit," she said, pushing herself away from him. He was a dick to say he wasn't sorry, to offer such a lame explanation, and she didn't care that she was now making a scene. Her face was red again, but this time from anger.

"I deserved that," he said. "What do you say you give me a couple of days to do better? The weather will be perfect this week. It will clear the head and heal the soul."

One night and a flight back to Houston tomorrow would work for her. A ceasefire for now. And what was *soul healing*? Was it like popping back into place a dislocated joint? Would it hurt?

"As long as I'm all the way out here, I guess it won't hurt. For now, anyway."

"Good. Let's go over there and find your bag," he said, nodding at the baggage claim area.

She pushed her carryon into his arms. "You said beach. All I thought I needed was a bathing suit and tee shirts. If I'll need more for your soul-therapy plans, we'll have to go shopping."

"You won't need anything fancy," he said.

They went out the door, across a pedestrian walk, and through a nearby parking lot to a recently washed white Toyota four-door truck, not a sports car or a fancy German rig, the kind of cars Houston men drove. She watched him toss the suitcase into the backseat as if it was a pillow. He wasn't dressed like a Houston man. His shorts weren't from Norton Ditto.

A breeze slipped around her. The air was warm, not hot. It was a long way from Houston, where parking lots were indoors. He kicked off his flip-flops and started the car.

"From the way you were looking at my clothes, I suspect you think I've gone native," he said, putting his bare foot on the brake pedal but turning his head toward her instead of putting the vehicle in gear.

"Have you?" She looked out her window, not at him. It was apparent he'd noticed her looking at his shorts. And the rest of his body.

"Of course I have. One learns a lot by getting into the local customs. If you stick out, people become wary, even suspicious of you. Don't you think?"

"I suppose. I've never really thought to do so. I think I'd feel like I was spying on them, wearing a disguise."

"It's nothing like that," he said, putting the car in gear.

⌒

The twenty-eighth of October, 2017, San Diego, California, Jay drove on North Harbor Drive in the direction of the downtown buildings. The late-afternoon light made huge navy vessels appear to lurk in the distance, their gray silhouettes amplifying the silence in the car. Before downtown, he turned uphill on West Grape Street, then drove over trolley tracks, past India Street, San Diego's Little Italy, to the south entrance of Interstate 5, and still she'd not spoken. The well-known beach communities were north, the opposite direction. When zipping by the Coronado exit, he wondered why she hadn't asked him where they were going. Maybe his little surprise was a bad idea.

"This highway reminds me of the Gulf Freeway," she said.

"We're not going to Galveston, in case you were curious," he replied.

"Where are we going?"

"Baja. I did say to bring your passport. Right?"

"You did say that. But it's been a long day and I didn't think we would cross the border the first day. It will be night soon. Why go now?"

"We're going to my house."

"Your house is in Mexico?"

"Where did you think it was?"

"California! Where was I supposed to think it was?"

"You didn't know I was living in Mexico?"

"How would I know that?"

"Rumor, perhaps."

She didn't reply. The atmosphere in the car turned heavy with her irritation, her glaring at exit signs flashing by, her teeth clamped together. H Street. Palomar. Palm. Had he ever seen her bad tempered? Not that he could remember.

"Don't worry. You'll like it," he said, as they passed the last exit before the border.

"I'm not worried. I just wish you'd told me before now."

"You're right. I thought it would be a fun surprise."

"But I haven't seen you for two years. How do I know where you've been and what you've been up to? Maybe you've changed. In a bad way."

He laughed. "I still have all my faculties."

A sideways glance. A tiny smile on her face. Cautious optimism in his chest. They reached the border, where Interstate 5 funneled into a few lanes separated by concrete barriers, traffic crawled past inspectors, who ignored them, and he turned onto the border highway, a rusty wall along it, next to a high fence, surveillance cameras on top, and nothing to see beyond. After curving through a canyon and up a long hill, there was a fork in the highway, *Playas* to the right and *Ensenada Rosarito Cuota* to the left, the way he went, and soon the Pacific Ocean spread out beside them, as blue as the sky and speckled by white random flashes on its surface, moving, it seemed, in a disjointed march toward the shore.

People ran across the cuota now and then, climbing over the barriers in the center. Every few kilometers were gated communities or patches of dwellings in various states of shabbiness. A few high-rise condominiums.

"I don't like them running across the highway," she said.

"There aren't too many ways to get across."

"Still."

"View of the ocean is beautiful," he said.

"I'm not sure. Where are all the boats? I only see a few oil tankers. No pleasure boats. It makes me wonder what's out there, maybe lurking beneath the waves," she said.

"Baja doesn't have marinas like San Diego. It's really just an inexpensive vacation destination. You'll see when we get further down. There are no big resorts."

"Okay. I don't need glitzy. But do they have Grey Goose in the bars?"

"No, but I have a couple of bottles in the back. My porch is much better than a bar."

"And you have ice?"

"Believe it or not, electricity works the same down here."

"Ha," she said.

The bantering made him feel better. But it wasn't solid. He could still hear an edge in her voice. He was moving too fast, he guessed. They needed to get to know each other again. Until then, she wouldn't relax, acting like a horse approached by a stranger, walking away from him sideways so she could keep an eye on him.

The highway curved inland north of Rosarito and passed a Home Depot, a Walmart, and a cinema complex, just like a Texas town. The road angled back to the coast and they passed a huge Jesus up on a hill above the highway, looking out to sea. Lyn looked up at it for a minute, her head turning as they passed below.

"He won't be watching us all night, will he?" she asked.

"Oh, no. My place is too far away for him to see anything."

From the Puerto Nuevo exit, he doubled back a kilometer on a local road. A guard admitted them to Playa de los Pelicanos. The entry road descended, in front of them the Pacific Ocean framed by palm trees, and then, turning left, a street made with large uneven paving stones. At its end was a large iron gate, behind which was a covered parking space with a blue tile floor.

"You park on tile?" she asked.

"Why not?"

"It's just unusual."

"It's Mexico. Many things are unusual."

They left the car and entered a courtyard, palm trees and lemon trees in the corners, a guest house on one side with a bougainvillea on its wall. At the main house, they descended stairs to a great room and kitchen, pots and pans hanging over the stove, a television remote next to a fanned-out set of magazines on a coffee table, everything orderly, no knickknacks, the mantle over the fireplace bare. Clean counters and clean lines made him comfortable.

He led her out to a veranda, the beach below them, a hundred yards down a wide path, made of various sizes of flat stones, that curved by other houses. Waves roared, the ocean stretched as far as they could see, late-afternoon sunlight glittered on the water, and sea birds hung aloft, magically. The atmosphere was soothing.

"We're actually facing south because we're on a large bay," he said. "Most people find it confusing when they first arrive, that the sun doesn't set straight out over the ocean."

She nodded her head, but still a frown was on her face. What was causing her uneasiness? It wasn't right for the view in front of them. If she was pissed, she should say so, even take a swing at him. That, he would be able to interpret. He was much better reading enemy agents than he was this woman. It was his fault. He should've called her right after he left France, but he hadn't known what to say then, either.

The ocean was blue, not the fecal brown of the Gulf of Mexico. He thought he might remark on that, but he remembered that she was from Corpus Christi and he was nervous she would think he was being critical of her home. A long rock jetty stretched out perpendicular to the beach. A group of pelicans perched along it, looking like pensioners at bridge tables.

"Are those statues?" she asked, pointing at them.

"Nope. They're pelicans, and they just sit still like that for a while. They're why this place is called Playa de los Pelicanos."

"But they're sitting on rocks, not the beach."

"So what? We should call the place Rocas de los Pelicanos?"

"It would be more accurate."

"I suppose. I hadn't thought of it that way."

"I'm tired, I guess. And being contrary. I shouldn't, in front of all this," she said, motioning toward the ocean.

"Precision is a lawyer affliction, I suppose. I've been trying to get over it myself."

"Maybe you're right. I don't know. Why not just 'Los Pelicanos?'"

"That is, in fact, what everyone calls it. Let's take a walk down the malecón."

"What's a malecón?"

"It's a boardwalk with stones instead of boards."

They walked along the malecón, on the left, ice plant and other blooming succulents carpeting a hill down to the beach, and at one point a giant century plant, its heavy waxen spiked leaves arranged methodically. The malecón flattened close to the ocean, atop a thirty-meter embankment of sandstone, its fingers protruding out into the ocean waves, causing occasional showers of ocean water they had to dodge. Ten minutes of walking, a clubhouse and pool area, where they sat on a bench facing the ocean. Hovering pelicans fished, plummeting into the water, looking awkward, then pausing to swallow what they caught.

"What a beautiful place!"

"It's pretty nice. Some days I like it more than others," he said.

"So what? You've been here two years and the thrill is wearing off? You're a fickle man."

Her old self emerging: feisty and challenging. It made him happy, her voice no longer edgy, but not yet playful either. The wind blew her hair back from her forehead, and he pictured her making a pelican dive. This candid side of her made men at the firm uncomfortable, he knew. An unpredictable dynamo in a pretty package.

"You're right, I suppose, about the thrill wearing off," he said, after a minute. "But I don't know about being fickle. I've always liked you. And I haven't been here but a few months, darlin'. I visited several other places since I last saw you."

"Don't give me that cowboy talk. *Darlin!* I know you're a stuck-up Ivy League guy just pretending to be a rancher. And you can quit patronizing me. I don't like it."

He laughed. She was right. A pelican splashed into the ocean nearby and then floated over a wave with a long part of a fish hanging out of its bill. How to explain what he'd been doing without telling her what he couldn't tell her? He didn't want to lie. That would make him a liar again. But he'd been a spy. So he would always be a liar. No changing that. And a lie was often what you didn't say. No changing that either.

He clearly hadn't thought it through, when he'd asked her to come see him. A lover shouldn't be a liar either. He was in a gully, not sure how to get himself out. On the seawall near him, an empty beer can and a cigarette butt, a sorry sight with ocean and sky just beyond them. It depressed him.

"It was a long time ago that I went to Princeton," he said. "But I don't think I was stuck-up. I'm sorry you think so. And I'm trying hard to be a rancher. You just don't go from lawyering to ranching in one easy step. It takes some work."

She looked at him and her eyes softened, the ocean taking her irritation down a notch again, he hoped. "Maybe I was exaggerating," she said. "I do that when I get nervous. I'm a long way from home, and you've tricked me into going to a foreign country."

"It's not that foreign. They have a Walmart."

"It's probably because you're being so mysterious that it feels foreign here."

"I'm not trying to be mysterious. Anyway, I've missed you."

"So where was it that you missed me from, if, as you said, you've not been here for two years?"

"I'm happy to tell you, but it's a long story. Not sure where to start."

"It can be as long as you want, cowboy. Where am I going? I'm a prisoner here. I wouldn't know how to get back to the airport. There's even a guard at the gate."

He laughed. "He keeps people out, not in."

"How do I know that? How about you tell me where you went first, after you stood me up."

"My old friend and mentor died. His name was Raymond Hatcher. I didn't want to cancel your coming to the ranch, but I had to."

"I remember the message you left me, that someone had died. I'm sorry. But after a few months and you didn't call, I felt jilted. Skip that. Just tell me, where first."

"France. Perpignan, France, to be exact. Near the Mediterranean. I spent a couple of weeks there. There was a man I went to see. He'd been in Indochina at the end of World War II, the same time as Raymond."

"And you went to Perpignan to tell him about Raymond?"

"Not exactly. He and Raymond were enemies of a kind. I went to confront him. But as it turned out, I hardly spoke to him."

"Okay. You're being mysterious. Enemies from Indochina during the war? Must be a story there. You went to confront him? Did you punch him, or what?"

"Not exactly. Raymond and I never talked about him. I read about him in a journal Raymond had written. Raymond's dealings with him were way before my time." The best lie is based on the truth, he knew. Murder was confrontation in a way.

"How old was Raymond?"

"Almost ninety."

"Ninety! And his enemy?"

"Older than that, I think."

"That would make them old enemies! So Raymond was really old. You couldn't have been too surprised that he died."

"Well, that's not exactly true. He was in good health. I was surprised," he said. Rage bubbled up in him. Even if he could tell her, he wouldn't be able to make himself say Raymond had been murdered, gunned down by an assassin.

"Okay," she said. "I'm being insensitive again. I'm sorry about Raymond. Nothing like that has ever happened to me. My mother died from cancer, but we knew for quite a while it was happening."

"I've not been so lucky," he said. "My father ran over himself with the tractor."

"That's awful."

"He forgot to take it out of gear and then tripped in front of it."

"I'm really very sorry," she said.

Wind gusted off the ocean and he stopped talking. It was frustrating, his attempt at veiling the truth gone wrong, banging his thumb with a hammer while trying to repair a fence railing. It was time to head back to the barn.

"I think maybe we got a little off the path of my story," he said. "We might both do better if we went back to the house. It's way past cocktail time in Texas."

"I suppose," she said.

He stood up, but she didn't move for a moment, only looked at him intently. What was she thinking? Not a hint coming from her. He always knew what Patsy was thinking, the way her nose and ears twitched, the look in her eyes, the stamping of a foot. But he couldn't interpret Lyn's gaze. A large wave crashed against the sea wall, and a bit of its spray blew over them.

~

The twenty-eighth of October, 2017, Los Pelicanos, Baja California, the sun poised at the horizon, a golden path on the ocean before it, gulls flapping silhouettes over it, Lyn sank into a lounge chair on the veranda. The horizon would soon swallow the orb, the long strands of light sucked into the deep. She thought of a meatball on top of linguine spread on a blue plate. A strange but pleasing thought. He returned with two glasses packed with ice and brimming with vodka, olives set on top.

"Saludos. Grey Goose en las rocas, lo mismo que los pelicanos," he said, grinning.

A tangy olive, vodka ice cold, the glass slippery with sea-air condensation, she felt better. Warmth ran through her chest as the sky turned red. Her shoulders relaxed. The spine between her shoulder blades quietly released. More than twenty years of friendship with him, always with Grey Goose and olives.

"Good?" he asked.

A stupid question, she thought. No answer necessary. Where they'd been two years before. Was it returning? Too fast, or not fast enough? It didn't matter. Another sip, and she closed her eyes. In that Austin hotel room, she'd turned off the light and put her arms around him.

"So how about I start again about Raymond and where I've been?" he asked.

"Not necessary," she said quickly, holding up her hand.

"Sure. But I'd like to tell you what happened."

"It ain't broke, so don't try to fix it."

"What?"

"I've decided it's not necessary for you to tell me anything. I'm just happy to be here. Grey Goose and olives. Ocean. Sky. Why risk messing it up?"

"Then you don't want to know?"

"I didn't say that. Only tell me if you want to."

She sat back and sighed, waiting for his decision. His gaze upon her was alluring. She wished he would look at the sunset instead. It made her nervous to be studied, like he was doing.

"You're a mystery," he said.

"Maybe to you. Besides, you're the mysterious one, cowboy. But it's your choice. You can tell me. Or not," she said, shrugging.

"Okay, I'll do that. What I didn't say before is that both Raymond and his wife died together on their farmhouse porch near Hudson, New York. And it wasn't a coincidence."

The sun clicked down a notch. She watched his face, her intention fixed. His temple twitched, as if a memory was scared to become vocal and was struggling to get back in.

"What was it?"

"I'd just been to Spain with him. He was an avid birdwatcher."

The incongruity settled on his face, a mask. How was birdwatching relevant? The golden path to the sun glittered manically. She waited for as long as she could.

"So what? They were attacked by birds?"

He laughed. "No. Although that was close, in a way. They were struck by a stray bullet shot by a hunter in the woods near them."

"That's awful." She couldn't think what else to say. He'd laughed, but his grief remained on his face. Was tragedy lessened by blame? Was the hunter found? She wanted to ask but decided not. He was blaming himself, it was apparent. She looked away from him, back out at the darkening horizon. Something as personal as blame, he wouldn't be easily dissuaded, and it was best to wait for him to continue.

"Raymond had been a mentor to me. I worked for him at the State Department before I joined the law firm."

"I forgot you worked there. How come you never mentioned Raymond all these years? All the times we were drinking Grey Goose in all those out-of-the-way bars?" She turned her almost-empty glass around, looking for an ice cube that would fit in her mouth. Doing so was perhaps a request, and she shouldn't have another. But it made her anxious, his talking about his dead mentor. A long way from his two years of travel, the reason he hadn't called her, and her consequent indictment of him for his failure, something to get behind her so she could get to like him again. Enjoyment of the beach was best done with someone you liked.

Jay took her glass with him into the house. It irritated her, his promptness. Screaming red clouds now flanked a half-submerged sun, looking like a red blotch of blood. A bird attack? It was funny. She planned to just sip the second drink.

She kicked her flip-flops off the side of the lounge chair and looked at her toes while she flexed and stretched them, hoping that the joints would crack. She'd painted the nails green. That had been when she'd thought she was going to lush San Diego, not to a desert-rimmed beach in Baja. He came back and held out a martini this time, a V-shaped glass with no ice. In it were several olives the color of her toenails.

"I'm sorry," he said. "Raymond's death is not really the point of my story."

"Fine with me. You were in France. Start there."

"Yeah, but my journey was a bit like traveling back in time through Raymond's life. I found a journal at Raymond's house, which covered just about his whole life. So rather than return to

Texas, I decided to go visit all the places Raymond had been. It was chasing a wild hare. I know that's what you're thinking. But I had to go."

"No, I can see why you would do that. It might bring some comfort," she said, but thinking it was ludicrous to do it for two years. Forgetting was the best way to close a door. The sun was gone, a waxing moon was above them, and toward the horizon on the ocean plain, a shining line from a planet, she couldn't remember which one. The stars were white paint splattered on a black canvas. In Houston, smog and rain clouds often hid the stars.

"Yeah. But in hindsight it seems strange. I mean, I wasn't looking for anything in particular. I only wanted to see what would happen when I went to all the places, thinking that it might bring closure."

"And was the trip useful? Did it make you feel better?"

"Have you read any Emerson?"

"A long time ago."

"To paraphrase him, looking for the use in something pushes aside the rose in favor of the cabbage."

"So you were wandering aimlessly all that time and you have nothing to show for it?" Her impatience grew. What she wanted to hear was that it was all behind him now. That she, sitting right there in front of him, was his focus, what mattered to him, rather than an old dead mentor. The moonlight seemed to her to reflect off his skin and the wind to brush over his body, as credible as finding a rose growing amongst cabbages. And she felt guilty, her desire that she be the most important thing in his mind.

"I don't know what I have to show, really. As time went on, I missed you more and more. I could've used someone to talk to."

"I guess you lost my phone number?" Her eyes became wide with challenge. A breeze ruffled her hair. Her guilt became anger and she wished he'd not brought her the second drink. He bowed his head slightly and held up his hand, a shield to deflect her sarcasm.

"No. I can't explain it, really. Maybe I was afraid to call, that you would think I was crazy, doing what I was doing. The grief from Raymond's death hit me hard, I guess. After France, I spent months wandering around the places described in the journal. After a year, I was desperate. Too desperate to call you, or at least it seemed that way. I suppose that's a dumb excuse. Eventually, it dawned on me. I had to find a simple place, a place with no history—the ranch wouldn't work—where I could sit back and wait to heal. A place like Walden Pond, maybe. So I bought this place, where I could live in obscurity, loaf, you could call it, until I put the pieces together. Have you read *The Razor's Edge?*"

Her anger reached a boil now, so dumb an excuse she'd never heard before. An email would've been sufficient: *I'm following an around-the-world path in my mentor's journal; will call when I'm back.* And now justifying his failure to send a tiny email with a lecture about transcendentalists? Somerset Maugham? And putting pieces together? What pieces? He'd done her wrong, and she wouldn't fall for it again. If a relationship with him required her to be gullible, she wanted none of it.

"So you've been doing a puzzle for two years? Is that what you're saying? And now you have it spread out on the coffee table, next to a teacup and a coffee spoon, and you decide to call me to come look at it?"

She looked at the ocean, for mermaids riding on the waves, singing. Her harsh words echoed in her ears, defusing some of her anger, happy with herself that she'd shown him that he hadn't cornered the market on literary allusion. Still, the resentment for what he'd done smoldered in her. She wanted to cut him to the quick. Could all their years of friendship and the night in that Austin hotel room be so easily scuttled? Logic gained no foothold with her. And, as absurd as it was, thoughts of lovemaking suddenly rose up in her. Why not? It would be only sexual, an angry pleasure, a way to sweep his puzzle off the table, to bring this moment to a crisis.

"Not quite," he said. "Knowledge, which is what I gained, can have an unpredictable impact on you after you take it in. And, only time makes it clear what that is."

"Well good for you, Jay! But I didn't come out here to do a puzzle with you. In fact, I didn't fly out here to go to Mexico with you. You've tricked me on all accounts."

He stood up and held out his hand, but she refused to take it. Wildly fluctuating emotions kept a grip on her. She'd not wanted a lecture, only a reason why he hadn't called, a reassurance that he still felt for her as he had in Austin. After a minute, she said, "I think it's all very inconsiderate of you. I fly all the way out here, get tricked into going to Mexico, and you can't even give me a good reason why you didn't contact me for two years. Solving a puzzle doesn't do it."

"Okay. I can see we've been sidetracked again, and I've explained myself enough for one day, I guess. I thought about you a lot over the last two years and your being here now is, well, it's what I've wanted for a long time. How about we leave it at that for now? It's been a long day for you. I'll try again tomorrow to explain myself, not just leave it with an apology."

Her fists pushed into her hips, she stood up, anger boiling, her eyes about to overflow with tears, but seeing no alternative than to go into the house. She pushed back her shoulders, resolved that he wouldn't make her cry, defiance pumping through her veins, and finally, slapping her hand into his, walked determinedly with him toward the house. Her emotions were sometimes this way, volatile, and then seconds later, calm. She didn't like her loss of control.

"I haven't seen the bedrooms yet," she announced, when they were inside. It sounded like a complete about-face. She didn't care. Her motivation was to use sex as a scouring powder. She wouldn't let herself be dissuaded, nor permit any affection to arise on account of his half-assed apology.

"No you haven't. We can do so now, if you want." His voice was hesitant.

When they'd made love in Austin, he'd been tentative, which had surprised her because he was so decisive in his lawyering. And her experience over the years was that men were generally frenetic when they engaged in sex, as if making love was an exercise of how fast one could put together a puzzle. Sure, the man would make gratuitous sounds after the last piece was in, but she would lay on her back, look at the ceiling, and imagine herself returning all the pieces to the box, which she would put back in the closet the next morning. In Austin, she'd taken off her clothes slowly, thinking he might back out. He'd looked into her eyes for a long time, as if he'd been assuring her, and himself, that they could stop anytime she wanted.

"Now would be *perfect*," she said.

They went upstairs. The bedroom was above the great room and kitchen, facing the ocean. His slow talking was done, she hoped. Action would be good. Moonlight whirled through a waving palm tree outside the bedroom window onto the ceiling, like she was on a merry-go-round. Her blouse pulled over her head, the bra unhooked, her skirt unzipped, she reclined onto the bed. He slid his lips between her breasts. She shivered. He moved down. She saw the palm tree behind his head. After he returned above her, they moved together in rhythmic undulations, like ocean swells, rising and receding. Blood pulsed through her heart. She heard thousands of small, round pebbles rolling down the shoreline's incline, chasing the retreating water. Their tempo increased. Would she be fast enough for their pleasure to be simultaneous? She didn't want him to go first. But a big wave roared and they arched their backs at the same time, and she stretched out her hands to his shoulders. Was it possible to hold him up, his body made of sculptured marble? Slowly lowering him down to her chest, she sighed. Her anger was gone.

They remained entwined for a long time before he gently moved off her and onto his back next to her. She hoped he would fall asleep quickly. The men she'd known had always done so, a relief, she thought, the sex only for her own pleasure, savoring its aftermath best done by her alone. She looked up at the ceiling, enjoying the softness of the bed, the air, the wind, the light, the sound of the rocks displaced by the receding waves. Once he was asleep, she would go out to the blue bench on the balcony to see if the pelicans were still on the jetty, a line of moonlit statues. But Jay didn't sleep. He rolled onto his elbow and looked into her eyes.

"I am very sorry," he said in a voice so soft she could hardly hear him over the sound of the waves below. "Not calling you is the biggest mistake of my life."

And for the first time that day, a response did not leap into her head.

10.

THE TWENTY-EIGHTH OF OCTOBER, 2017, Millbrook, New York, late in the evening, a waxing moon cast dark shadows on the driveway. Brashner stood quietly on the front porch, the dinner party guests departing. The setting made it easy for him to overhear a conversation between Mary Sanchez and Erin Sesame, who were waiting in a line to hand over their claim check to the parking valet. They hadn't noticed him standing nearby.

"Applying is so completely daunting," Mary Sanchez said, the conversation about her daughter applying to a New York City private school. "It's only October, and everyone I talk to already has the process well down the road." She was a petite woman, no makeup, amber eyes, her dark hair pulled back above her ears, a broad white face with many freckles. He didn't care for her, had barely spoken to her during the evening. Similar to his wife, the way she held herself made her appear severe and unattractive. He couldn't imagine fucking her, which also put him off. Why waste time?

"But you've been here only a month, dear," Erin Sesame said. She was a tall, lithe woman. The manner in which she presented herself, her clothes tailored, her hair arranged neatly, made her alluring, which added to Brashner's resentment of her husband. Erin Sesame would be more attractive to prospective clients than his own wife.

The women continued their conversation, Mary Sanchez saying she wished someone could put in a good word at Dalton, and

Erin Sesame responding that a good word might do more harm than good, Dalton's process being as fair as it was, no favors given for anyone. *That's complete rubbish*, Brashner wanted to say, his assessment of Erin Sesame waning, it being stupid of her to think that admissions weren't influenced by money and connections.

Ruben Sanchez appeared, a small man of slight build wearing an off-the-rack suit and a necktie with a grease spot just below the knot. "Mr. Brashner, I must apologize for leaving the dinner table as I did earlier, but the call was from my boss about a meeting held this morning by your partner in Houston regarding the sale of our portfolio company. I didn't feel like I could ignore it. Are you up to date on that transaction?"

"No," Brashner said, looking around for Sesame, not seeing him, and then hoping that Sanchez might speak freely.

"We've been working on the sale for a few months now. The buyer is proving to be difficult. I had to take the call."

"Young man, I certainly understand," Brashner said. "Duty often calls at inconvenient times. I hope it wasn't bad news."

"Not exactly. The issue between us wasn't resolved. Mr. Sutter hopes to learn more soon."

"Must be a difficult issue," Brashner said, playing it like an offhanded remark, Sesame still not in sight.

"The buyer wants a value guaranty."

"Will Baines is a good lawyer. He can surely handle that."

"He and Mr. Sutter are pretty adamant that we don't give one, that it's not done in deals like this."

Brashner shrugged, wanting to appear uninterested, yet hoping for more. "Of course, good deals are often built on compromise."

"Yes sir."

"I'm sure Will Baines is doing his best," Brashner said, faint praise the best criticism, particularly since he saw Sesame walking toward them.

"Lots of nice artwork in the entry," Sesame said, then moving away to look at another wall, having noticed his wife deep in conversation with Mary Sanchez.

"Of course," Sanchez said.

"By the way, Ruben, did I hear that your daughter was applying to Dalton?" Brashner asked.

"Yes, sir."

"I'm good friends with one of the board members over there. Why don't I give her a call next week and see if I can help?"

"That would be so kind of you, Mr. Brashner. That could really help us."

"Call me Patrick, please. But I can't promise anything. I'll call you this week to tell you what she says, and we can maybe have lunch."

A tit for a tat, Brashner thought, after the Sesames and the Sanchezes departed, sure Ruben would soon tell him more about the deal. He poured himself a cognac and went down to the pool, the clatter of night insects rising and falling, as if swept across the space by a small breeze, not as bothersome as it had been earlier. On a lounge chair, his eyes closed, his expectations soared that Sanchez would be a good mole. Although, what good the information would do him wasn't apparent. Then he was startled to find his wife standing over him.

"Are you dozing or thinking?" she asked.

"Those are not mutually exclusive, my dear."

"I've done all the thinking I can stand for the day," she said. "I'm going to bed."

"Okay. If you must."

He was rankled by her intrusion, but he resisted saying what he thought. Challenging her, even on mundane things, carried too much risk. Once she was piqued, there wasn't an idiosyncrasy of his that went unmentioned.

11.

TWO DAYS LATER, THE THIRTIETH of October, 2017, Millbrook, New York, the sun was almost in the midst of its morning climb, and the shadows from the spruce trees along the perimeter of the lawn were becoming shorter. Patches of fog had mottled the hills beyond the property several hours earlier when Patrick Brashner had sat brooding at the table in front of the large window that faced southeast out of the mansion's library. The night before, he'd not slept well, his mind racing through scenarios about the Global Trading deal. He needed the deal to close so he could have his payday. Without it, he wouldn't be able to pay the short-term loans incurred to finance the recent renovations to the mansion. All of his earnings from the law firm went to pay for his lavish lifestyle, the club dues, the mortgage and maintenance charges for his large Fifth Avenue apartment in the city, and the vacations to Europe and the Caribbean. It made him angry that Ben Lufkin, chair of Branoble Partners in Denver, had linked his payout to Global Trading's expenditure of the proceeds from its sale of its marine terminals. The proceeds had to be redeployed before cash in the affiliated entities was distributed. That hadn't been a condition two years ago when he'd made his deal. He banged his fist on the table and picked up his phone, intending to send an email to Lufkin. He'd not noticed his wife standing in the doorway, watching him.

"Patrick, it's a beautiful day. Why are you sitting inside?" she called out. "Whatever is so important?"

"The firm's offices are open today," he said. Her interruption irritated him. She had no appreciation of how hard he worked. Every day was a weekend for her, and here he was in Millbrook today so she could get one extra day of riding her horses. The stables had cost a fortune.

"Oh, I'm sure, but is anyone in them except for the associates? My friends tell me their husbands frequently take Monday off when the weather is nice. During the winter, you can be there every Monday."

"We're very busy right now. Business doesn't stop for the weather."

"Of course it doesn't. But I'm sure you can attend to it just as well out by the pool. You have all those high-tech connections and your phone."

"Aren't you going riding again soon? I'm hoping we can head back to the city by mid-afternoon. So we can avoid the rush hour." It was no business of hers whether he sat by the pool or in the house. And he liked to make his calls inside, where it was quiet and he could tell the people he called that he was in his office. As it was, she'd run around that morning and opened all the windows. To let the fresh autumn air into the house, she'd said.

"I'm meeting Pamela at the stables now. Then we can have a late lunch and head back," she said, then walked away, the heels of her riding boots clicking on the tile floor and the fabric of her jodhpurs swishing between her thighs, reminding Brashner of the sound made by the street-cleaning vehicles in the city.

He looked at his watch. It was 7 a.m. in Denver and unlikely that Lufkin would be in his office. He decided to call to leave a voicemail and follow it with an email that he needed to speak to him, urgently.

"Good morning, Patrick," Lufkin answered, surprising Brashner. How did Lufkin know who was calling?

"Ben, you're in the office early. I expected to leave a message."

"Most of our portfolio companies are located in distant time zones, Patrick. Global Trading is headquartered in Europe, as you know, so I'm often required to be here at unusual hours."

"Yes, of course. And it was Global Trading that I was calling about."

"That's not a hard guess. Is there an update on the lawsuit?"

"No. I wanted to inquire about the ERIS deal. Where does that stand?"

There was a short pause. "I can't help you there, Patrick. The company is handling that. I leave legal matters to them. Have you heard of a problem?

"I've just heard that the negotiations have stalled over a silly issue."

"Patrick, I really don't get involved in those things. I know we have excellent legal counsel in Houston. The company has worked with her before and thinks highly of her. I'm happy to ask my associate to find her phone number and send it to you."

"Thanks. That would be helpful. But I am also curious about your plans to make a distribution to your other investors." Brashner wondered whether Lufkin knew that Stewart Baines was representing ERIS. He didn't want to ask, for fear that Lufkin would not give him the information about Global Trading's counsel or, worse, alert someone at the company about his inquiry.

"We've talked about this before, Patrick. I'm going to do what's right for all the investors, including you."

"I know. But it was a debacle two years ago, and I need some liquidity on my investments now."

Another moment of silence. Brashner had never heard Lufkin raise his voice, but he'd heard from one of the other investors, the one in France, that he could be volatile. It was probably imprudent to push too much.

"Patrick, you were retained to represent the defendants in the lawsuit and SEC investigation. My advice is that you concentrate on that matter before you worry about liquidity."

"Of course. And that is going well. I'm sure we'll win." Brashner had to hold down his anger. Lufkin wasn't even a party to the lawsuit because his ownership was hidden by multiple layers of intermediary companies. And he was so rich already that a loss wouldn't matter.

"That's good to hear, Patrick. Please keep me up to date on that," Lufkin said, and abruptly hung up. He'd done the same on all of his phone conversations with Brashner. And Brashner didn't like it. It was something he did to his own firm's partners and associates.

12.

THAT SAME DAY, THE THIRTIETH of October, 2017, Houston, Texas, Will Baines drove to work, taking Allen Parkway, which had too many curves for the SUVs to build up lethal velocity. The sight of a young couple walking a golden retriever puppy along Buffalo Bayou tugged his heartstrings. His dog at home, Mason, didn't need a companion, according to his wife. Just more attention from them. The opposite was true, as it happened. Mason now slept between them, a deterrent to spousal amorousness. The dog needed his own friend.

That morning, his wife had departed for Boston. Her mother was ill and he'd stayed home until his wife left for the airport. She'd been going to Boston regularly over the last six months to care for her mother, leaving him alone in the house with Mason after his daughters had gone to college. He'd been understanding at first, but he now wondered whether so many trips were really necessary. Her absence no longer made his heart grow fonder. It only made him lonely and horny.

It was after ten when he entered the tunnel from the garage to his office building. Downtown Houston was crisscrossed with underground passages that were built out with shops. Being late, he didn't have his shoes shined but bought a cappuccino because the barista at the fancy coffee shop always remembered his name.

At his desk not ten minutes and his phone rang, *Patrick Brashner* on the display. Will knew the man wanted to talk about the ERIS deal. The Chinese wall was meant to prohibit that. Will let the phone ring into voicemail, a handy way to deal with Brashner.

The coffee made his chest warm. An alluring image of Belinda from Saturday came into his mind. It had haunted him all weekend. Bending his head forward, stretching the back of his neck, he turned his face from side to side over his desk. It was a ludicrous circumstance, feeling desire for her. A neat pile of papers was on his desk, the ERIS draft agreement on top.

The phone rang again, but he didn't look this time, sensing it was Brashner. As before, he ignored the call, but now the button on the phone flashed after the ringing stopped. His assistant appeared in the doorway.

"I'm sorry to disturb you," she said.

"No problem. You never disturb me."

"It's Mr. Brashner. He's holding. He said he has to speak to you."

"Tell him I can't speak right now. I'll call him back shortly."

"He told me he can't be reached."

"But I saw on the display earlier, the first time he called, his name and office number. Offer him voicemail."

"Yes, but he calls into his office and then has his assistant forward the call so it will appear he's in the office."

"Really? How do you know that?"

"His assistant told me. He's hardly ever in his office. And he has a night assistant so he can do the same after hours."

"Good grief! Tell him I wasn't in my office when you went to look."

"He told me he wouldn't accept that excuse. 'Don't come back on and tell me he isn't in his office,' he said. 'Go find him.'"

She was clearly afraid to get back on the line with Brashner. "Okay. We'll let him hold a minute while you're looking for me.

Then I'll pick up. How about I buy you a latte from downstairs? Stay away from your desk for a few minutes."

"Perfect," she said, exhaled loudly, and left.

He looked at the blinking phone for a few minutes, remembering the short man, always leaning toward him, a pathetic menace in his eyes. Then he picked up the handset. "Good morning, Patrick. How's vacation?" he asked, feigning loss of breath, having run back to his desk, his assistant finding him at whatever imaginary location.

"I'm not on vacation. I'm in my office. Did someone say I was on vacation?"

"No. But I heard that the leaves are peaking. I thought New Yorkers went on the last weekend of October to look at foliage or make that last visit to the beach before winter."

"I'm too busy for that."

"Yes, it is busy, isn't it? The whole firm is busy. It's going to be a good year."

"We stay busy by keeping our clients happy. I'm calling about my good client, Global Trading."

Birdsong came across the line. Will sighed. Birds perched on a Chinese wall.

"Okay. Not sure how I can help. I'm not a trial lawyer," he said.

"It's not about litigation. It's about that damn transaction for ERIS."

"I may not be remembering correctly, Patrick, but I believe that transaction is subject to a Chinese wall between you and me. I don't think I can discuss this with you. Aren't you representing Global Trading in another matter?"

"I'm not asking you to tell me what ERIS is doing, damn it. I'm calling to tell you that I've heard that the strident positions you are taking on title issues are jeopardizing the transaction."

"Who told you that?"

"That's not any of your business."

Arrogant disregard of an ethical obligation, all in Brashner's voice. It made Will defiant. "And the transaction is none of your business, either," he said.

"You are out of line, young man. I have many more years of experience than you on delicate issues like this. I am very busy and I have better things to do than entreat you to counsel my clients properly."

Imperious now, the pitch of Brashner's voice shot through an octave, and Will pictured the man's eyes flashing and nostrils widening. Nothing for him to do but be silent. The birds were still singing in the background.

"Listen to me carefully, William. Heed my advice if you do not want to do yourself a disservice. I have a long and excellent memory. This transaction is in trouble."

Should he laugh at that threat or just put the phone back on its hook? Will wanted to discount the man's self-righteousness and say nothing. But tolerance here was tantamount to indifference. Was it not? The right thing to do was challenge Brashner's behavior.

"Mr. Brashner. Thank you for sharing the information you've obtained about the transaction. I shall give it all appropriate consideration, and I will certainly keep in mind that the difficult issues faced by the parties are putting the deal in a precarious position."

"What does that mean? What do you propose to do?"

"Nothing, actually."

"Nothing?"

"I'm sorry, Mr. Brashner, but on account of our ethical obligations regarding this matter, I'm uncomfortable discussing these issues with you any further. I apologize again. We can get our ethics partner on the line and raise the question with him, if you want."

"I don't need anyone to make any ethical interpretations for me. And you will regret challenging me. I'll see to that."

A sharp click came next and the birdsong was gone. Had he hurled the phone at a bird? Will took his coat and went into the hall. His assistant smiled as he walked by.

"Mr. Baines," she said. "Don't forget your appointment."

"I certainly won't."

Will drove to his psychiatrist's office, which was in a small building at the end of a quiet street in the Houston Museum District. It was his habit to arrive early and sit in his car in the small parking area, collecting his thoughts. What would they talk about today? The doctor never initiated the conversation, that being left to Will, even if it meant sitting painfully quiet for a period of time.

Today Will knew what he needed to talk about, and he was marshaling the courage to raise the topic. Simply, he was incredibly horny, and had been for several months. His daughters had gone to college, and although their absence from the house made for more amorous opportunities, his wife, when she wasn't visiting her mother, had basically shut down all coital interaction, muttering a perfunctory *goodnight* every night while turning on her side, her back to him. It was painful, and he was near panic that she no longer cared for him and their sex life was over. Perhaps she'd never liked it, had engaged in it only as a kind of duty? And now with their daughters gone and her mother sick, he guessed that his wife no longer felt an obligation to make love to him. Why this was so, he didn't know.

Sunlight coming through the trees rippled across the windshield as their leaves moved in the breeze. He put his head back and closed his eyes, watching light and shadows make a pattern on the backs of his eyelids. How would he start this conversation? Then, images of Lyn's breasts moving under her blouse and her long legs flashing beneath her skirt. And images of Eleanor.

It'd been impossible not to look at her after the others had left on Saturday, and not to suspect that she wasn't wearing a bra beneath her sweater. He thought how, if they had sex, she would stretch her back up beneath him, moan, and beat her heels in the small of his back. He felt guilty picturing these things. But something needs to happen if my wife continues to shun me, he thought. And that, he decided, was how he would start the session with his doctor.

13.

THAT SAME DAY, THE THIRTIETH of October, 2017, Los Pelicanos, Baja California, although much later than she usually slept, Lyn didn't spring out of bed, as was her custom. In Houston it was noon. She'd never before been in bed at noon, even when she was sick.

An attractive view of the ocean caused her to prop herself up against the headboard, holding the sheet across her breasts and feeling exotic for having slept naked. There was a warm spot next to her, where Jay had been a minute before. Her hand slid over it. How nice it would be if everything around her could stay in place for a while, the whole day, even. He came out of the bathroom, noisy, wearing a T-shirt and pajama bottoms.

"We'll go out for lunch later. But I've got to have coffee to get me conscious enough to even start the car. I don't deliver, so come down when you're ready," he said, as he left the room.

A group of pelicans flew in formation a few feet above a wave that was about to crest. They were lined up, one behind the other, and none of them moved its wings for a long time, until the leader flapped briefly in order to maintain altitude and the rest followed. Did they have a destination? Were they looking for a school of fish? Or were they skimming the waves just because they could?

Just because they could? For her, everything had a purpose. The law, eternally purposeful, was her life, after all. Why do anything without a client? Or billable hours? All cynical thoughts, she had to admit. But she couldn't help them.

A warm breeze blew through the open window. It slid around her, pushing back the hair over her ears and tickling the skin on her arms. Was this what the pelicans were feeling? She threw off the sheet covering her, stood up in front of the window, quite naked, and stretched out her arms, wanting the pelicans to see her, even as far away as they were. They flew on. Still, she felt so free.

It didn't last long. A wariness came over her. This always occurred when she was away from the office a few days, an inexplicable compulsion, demanding a return to her familiar routines, whether or not she was having a good time.

On the bedside table was her phone. And now another compulsion. She dialed Will's mobile number, thinking he might dodge her call to his office phone. Then she turned back to the window, still naked.

"Will Baines," he answered.

"Do you miss me yet?" she sang. "It's Lyn." She pushed her chest out and tilted her head back.

"Oh, hi. There's nothing to report, actually," he said.

"So you don't miss me?"

"Uh, I believe we agreed that I wouldn't pursue anything until you returned."

"Oh, right," she said. "So have you?"

"Have I what?'

"Done anything about our deal, of course?"

"No. Nothing has happened. It's only Monday."

"You're right. But I wanted to make sure you weren't worrying about it. Are you?"

"No. I'm fine. I don't think ERIS will quit yet."

"Good. But I hope they don't want to do anything for a couple more days. I'm in a house right on the Pacific Ocean."

"Sounds nice. I'm sitting in my car. Just finished an appointment."

"I've been sitting on the beach without a care in the world. You would like that, I'm sure." She wasn't actually sure, but exaggeration was allowed at times like this.

"Maybe after the deal is closed," he said.

"Oh, Will, there's always another deal after this one closes. You know that. In any case, unless something happens sooner, I'll be back on Thursday. But don't feel you can't call me if something comes up. I will tear myself away from this paradise for you." Had she really planned to stay until Thursday? It felt like a long time, until Thursday, now that she'd said it. He sounded down in the dumps about something. But she wouldn't ask. It might ruin the rest of her day.

"Thanks," he said. "I appreciate it."

"De nada, amigo. Adios," she said, and hung up.

Jay's two-year absence still annoyed her, not quite washed away by her surroundings. The day before, she'd stood for twenty minutes under an outdoor shower on the inside patio, made private by a bougainvillea, surrounded by blooms and a sky becoming pink as the sun moved toward the horizon. And there were no bugs. Where were the mosquitos?

The pelicans came flying back. She covered her breasts with her arms, suddenly bashful. But she'd not felt this good for a long time. Humming a tune, she put on her clothes and went downstairs. After some coffee, she would suggest an excursion to several places she'd read about in a travel magazine on the flight from Houston.

14.

THE NEXT DAY, THE THIRTY-FIRST of October, 2017, Los Pelicanos, Baja California, bright sunshine, not a cloud in the sky. A few surfers were sitting on their boards on the break that was beyond the long straight stretch of the malecón above the beach. A pod of dolphins, unfazed by the surfers in wetsuits, lazily swam in a line about ten yards further out, their beaks slightly breaking the water's surface, their dorsal fins moving higher into the air, and finally their flukes springing up, leaving a trail of water droplets. Jay and Lyn had coffee on the patio. Lyn reclined in a lounge chair, her eyes shaded by a straw hat. Jay read a book, a collection of essays written by David Foster Wallace. He occasionally chuckled at a passage, a muted version of a nearby squawking seagull. She couldn't focus on her book, open on her lap while she looked into the distance. The opportunity to relax was perfect, but inclinations sprang up inside her—time sheets for last week, an appointment with the dental hygienist. The gulls flapping overhead called her to action. How would she ever retire? It was impossible.

What she needed to do was call the VP at her client, already a day later than she'd said she would. But she couldn't dial the number, the memory of Gerald so dispiriting. What she wanted to say about him would be unprofessional. So she sent an email. *Out of the country for a couple of days. Saturday meeting didn't resolve the issue. Call Gerald.* That covered it, at least until she got back to the office. And what had Will Baines been doing on

Saturday, looking at her legs the way he was, a grimace of sad lust on his face? Maybe she'd imagined it. It was a bit absurd. He didn't have the spontaneity nor, to be frank, the backbone to pull it off. It was the opposite, he the one more likely to be seduced by her. An entertaining thought. She smiled.

"Someone send you a joke?" Jay asked.

She was still looking at her phone and hadn't noticed him looking at her. "The office doesn't know where I am or whom I'm with. It would cause a stir, I'm sure."

"So let's post it on Facebook," he said, reaching for his phone.

"No way!"

"Why not? It will confirm what everyone has suspected for a decade."

"It wasn't true back then. We were very proper."

"So what?"

"Easy for you to say that. I still work there, remember."

"Fine. I'll keep it secret," he said.

"And I doubt you even have a Facebook account."

"Can I get a picture just for me?"

"No! Quit."

She couldn't think why, but it disappointed her that he wasn't more insistent. Why not tell the world they were together in Mexico? Was something real if it was secret? If there was no record of it? And it worried her. If Jay thought it was only temporary, there was no reason to tell anyone anything.

"I suppose we could tell a few friends," she said.

"I don't know. I don't have as many friends as I used to. I did tell Rosie at the ranch I was here, in case there was any business that needed taking care of. I could tell her that you're with me this week."

"I don't know Rosie. And my friends wouldn't believe it if I told them." She'd not met Rosie, only remembered she took care of things at the ranch. And why would he tell her? What friends Lyn meant, she wasn't sure. All acquaintances, that's what they were. Not really friends. Keeping up a conversation with them, she knew how to do, being witty, laughing at jokes, remarking on current events, even sports news. But personal thoughts, secrets, were not something she shared much. Not at all, actually. She told her sister tidbits now and then. But her sister had her own problems. Lyn struggled when she had to listen to problems that were impossible to solve, meaning those that weren't her own. Her own inner life she kept in control by keeping it locked up.

"Okay, but a picture would be better than a thousand words," he said, holding up his phone.

She waved her hand at him. "Quit!"

"Whatever. This is too weighty a problem for me to solve on an empty stomach," he said. "How about we head for lunch."

"Good. Can we drive down to Ensenada? It looked interesting in a travel magazine I looked at."

"Okay. It's not as great as they make it out to be. But it's not too far, and afterward we can head into the Valle de Guadalupe for some wine and a late lunch."

"That sounds nice."

"Maybe it's a long way to go for lunch, but the view of the coastline from the road on the way down there is good."

"It's a good plan. Eat and drink our way across Baja?"

"We'll be back up here in time to burn off some calories before dinner."

"Oh, I bet you say that to all the girls."

"I didn't mean that," he said. "I was thinking we would do several laps on the malecón when we get back. Something like riding a horse on the ranch at sundown."

"That sounds nice also, and I hope you mean that there are no other girls." Was she jealous? What a strange feeling. She'd not been jealous a minute in her life.

"That would be a good deduction on your part."

〜

They drove south on the Carretera de Cuota, passed one gated community after another, an enormous beach at Playa La Mision, and then a golf course, all refuges for expats, mostly American. After that, the residences stopped. It was the point at which the border cities, Tijuana and San Diego, were too distant, the drive almost two hours before the border wait, making easy access to the modern variety of groceries too difficult. The landscape became rocky and there were towering hills. The road climbed through several curves, broad views of the ocean surprising her occasionally.

"You can't see it from here, but just over that ridge is the Energia Costa Azul LNG receiving terminal. It supplies natural gas to an electric-generation plant in Rosarito. Or, at least, that was the plan when they built it."

"I remember that deal. It was a Sempra project. Right?"

"It was."

"I've always wanted to see an LNG terminal, not just the boring project documents." She resented that she hadn't traveled to see the projects she worked on. One had been in Bilbao, Spain, a couple of years earlier. Jay had done a great deal of foreign travel during his career, while she'd stayed at home and pushed papers. It'd had made her angry when she'd heard that he'd been in Bilbao at the time of the closing ceremony, and she'd not been invited. And he'd been several years retired then. "I wasn't invited to the Bilbao ceremony," she said.

"I wasn't there either, if that's what you're asking."

"Okay. Maybe it was just a rumor I heard."

"I was in Bilbao, but not for the ceremony. Raymond and I were in Spain on a birdwatching trip. Most of the time we were up along the coast of the Bay of Biscay, below Normandy, and after that we went to San Sebastian. We went down to Bilbao for a couple of nights, and I ran across some of your clients in the hotel. They are probably the source of your rumor."

"That's right. I didn't ask them for any details because I didn't want them to know I was pissed I hadn't been invited. Didn't Raymond die around that time?"

"A few weeks later. But I did call you during that trip to invite you to the ranch, in case you forgot."

"Only to cancel later. Maybe I'll look at a calendar. But it will just make me angry again, so maybe I won't. And, now it occurs to me, it proves you knew how to make phone calls from foreign countries."

"I'm sorry. I can't say it enough."

"Oh, forget it." She didn't want to get bogged down with her hurt feelings. Why they wouldn't go away, she wasn't sure. It might take a thousand apologies. And now, she didn't want to be angry. They were a thousand feet above the Pacific, which stretched out to the horizon in a giant arc, the road, slicing through a bluff of red sandstone, precariously close to the edge of a cliff. "How in the world did they construct this road?" she asked.

"It was a big project. And they've had problems. The road collapsed at one point and had to be closed for months. That's why you see all the new excavation over there."

"How did people get to Ensenada after the road collapsed?"

"The old road goes through the Guadalupe Valley. We'll take it going back. Down below us now, where you see those circles on the water, they raise tuna that is exported to Japan."

It seemed stupid. Why not raise them in Japan, where there was plenty of ocean? She kept the question to herself.

"Did you take pictures in Bilbao?" she asked.

"I sure did," he said, chuckling. "And I can show them to you to verify that I was really there to watch birds."

"I'm not conducting a deposition here. I like looking at pictures."

"Sorry. I was joking. Really."

"It's difficult for me to picture a man as old as Raymond—you said ninety, right?—hiking around Spain with binoculars."

Jay laughed. "He wasn't a doddering old fool, Lyn. He was quite vigorous for his age."

"Sorry." It was hard not to ask questions. So many things in life were curious. Talking about Raymond was probably hard for Jay. He should get over that. "Did Raymond's wife go to Bilbao also?"

"Oh, no. She didn't want to leave her bakery, and I think she sometimes liked a break from Raymond. They were a different sort of couple."

"I'd like to hear more about them. But let's wait for later, when we're face to face, with glasses of wine in our hands."

"Perfecto! And then you can look into my eyes to see if I'm telling the truth," he said, and laughed.

He was being a bit defensive about the birdwatching trip, she thought.

—

They stopped briefly on the main street in Ensenada, where they were assaulted by hawkers and squashed by tourists from a cruise ship. The shops were run-down, some even seedy, and most of the local people walking around had vacant looks in their eyes.

On Highway 3 next, they drove into the Valle de Guadalupe, dusty roads, an arid environment, yet with many vineyards and fruit trees. If there was a river, she couldn't spot it, only dry gullies, where she imagined water sometimes rushed. At a cava on a hillside overlooking vines and lemon trees, they tasted a nebbiolo and a zinfandel. The valley was like a scene from the old world, none of the finery one saw in the Napa Valley. The wineries had red Spanish tile roofs, some in disrepair. Vineyards weren't planted in square blocks. They seemed to flow together, haphazardly. The vintner was an American woman. They asked her to lunch, where she told them about her oenological studies and how she'd designed the label on her wines, *VinTango*.

How to describe this place, this tapestry of views and sounds and tastes, an oasis carved between boulder-strewn, cactus-laden mountains? It was both rural and elegant, no tacos for lunch at Finca Altozano; instead, Pulpo Del Pacifico a las Brasas and Col de Bruselas Fritas. A memory of a trip to Marfa, Texas, came to Lyn, a place that was rustic Texas but with surprises, like a dinner at Cochineal, pink tables on the patio, and a menu with lobster tail, pomegranate sauce, and Beef Wellington with seared foie gras. She sighed to herself. Marfa had been a long time ago, and she'd spent a good part of that trip calling her office from a pay phone.

~

Back at Los Pelicanos, late afternoon, the wind was easterly off the desert, warm and strong, making the leaves of the palm trees above them rattle and snap, reminding Lyn of the sound from a baseball card clipped next to the spokes on the wheel of her bicycle when she was a girl. How she'd loved to ride fast, that whirling just below her, a witness to her speed. Jay had fallen asleep on a patio lounge. Lyn was energized. Taking a nap was pouring opportunity down the drain. The wind attacked the waves, transforming the tops of their breaking ridges into vertical white plumes of sea spray. The sight filled her muscles with energy. She had to move, if only to pretend she was riding her bike again. So she slipped away and walked toward the late-afternoon sun, the wind at her back.

At the far end of the malecón, a flock of pelicans had taken up residence at the top of a bluff. She sat on a bench and watched them. Several would swoop up the face of the bluff, and as they were about to alight, a few would take wing to make a space for them.

Her phone vibrated, its screen showing a 212 number. New York City? Rolling her eyes, she declined the call, turned sideways to stretch out her legs, leaned back, closed her eyes, and pointed her face at the sun. The phone vibrated again. This time it was her associate.

"Hey there. Everything okay?"

"It was. Then I got a call from some guy who demanded that I conference you in. I refused and he got really pissed. He said you weren't answering his calls. I don't know why he thought you'd answer a call from me."

"Well, I didn't answer his call and I did answer yours. So maybe he had the right idea."

"Be that as it may, I wouldn't call him back. He's a jerk."

"Did he tell you his name?"

"Patrick Brashner. He was shouting. I can send you the number he gave me. He wouldn't tell me what he wanted. And he was very officious. His assistant had placed the call. He told me you being in Mexico was no excuse."

"He said I was in Mexico?"

"I told him I didn't know where you were. And then a few minutes later, a guy from Branoble called to say he'd given Brashner your number and told him you were on vacation."

"Okay. And no news from the Global Trading guys?" she asked. How did Branoble know where she was? She'd told no one.

"Not a peep."

"Good. Let's hope it stays quiet. I'm back Thursday."

"Está bien," he said, chuckling. "I'll call you if something happens."

The pelicans were still playing musical chairs. She made her way slowly down the rocky beach to its swash zone and walked into the numbingly cold water until her ankles were covered. A wave came in, and the water rose to her knees. As it retreated, her phone buzzed again. She suspected it was the Brashner man and she felt contentious, more from his knowing where she was than anything else. Stumbling back toward the water line, she pulled the vibrating nuisance from her pocket.

"Hola. Quién es este?" she asked.

Jay would've cringed at her rough South Texas Spanish. How had he become fluent? He'd spoken like a native Mexican when he'd chatted with an HOA guard on the malecón. And then in the valley today he'd seemed to know the local jargon when he spoke with the waiters at the restaurant. It puzzled her. He'd grown up on a ranch, not in an embassy. Had he been here long enough to become so proficient? She didn't really know a lot about him, she thought. She'd returned to the bench now.

"Hello," she said, there having been no response from the caller.

"I'm sorry, but I didn't understand you," a woman said. "I'm trying to reach Belinda Larkin."

"You've reached her. She's in Mexico. That's why you don't understand her."

"I'm calling for Mr. Brashner," the woman said, her voice sounding meek. "He's been trying to reach you all day."

"So, who's he? Never heard of him."

"He wants to speak to you."

"Fine. Just put him on the line."

It made Lyn feel bad, being rude to the man's assistant. She wanted to throw her phone and the man into the ocean, imagining how he would flail his arms and legs in order not to drown. The sun had moved toward the horizon. Grey Goose soon. Straight up. No en las rocas.

"Ms. Larkin," Brashner said. "Thank you for taking my call."

His voice was urbane and slick, sticking to his words like wax on a gaudy piece of furniture. It put her off. Men who spoke like that, particularly men who had someone dial the phone for them, were pompous.

"I'm sorry, but do I know you?"

"My name is Patrick Brashner."

"I got that part from your assistant. What do you want?"

"I'm sorry if I've disturbed you on vacation."

Lyn looked at her watch. It was eight o'clock in New York. No doubt he was sitting in a big leather chair wearing his smoking jacket. The flock of musical-chair pelicans evacuated their perches and, not even bothering to line up, made a hasty retreat up the coast in the direction of Jay's house. A good idea.

"I'm back in my office on Friday," she said. "Call me then."

"I'm afraid this cannot wait until Friday."

"There's nothing in the world you could be calling about that can't wait a couple of days."

"It's about the Global Trading transaction, which needs your immediate attention."

She paused. A wave broke nearby. "Sir, I don't discuss transactions with people I don't know. That includes you! You are welcome to contact the press department at Global Trading. Please don't call me again."

He was too arrogant to be a reporter, and she meant the insinuation he was to be an insult. But it didn't matter. Nothing mattered, except following the pelicans.

"You do know me. I'm a partner in New York at Stewart Baines," he said.

He could've started with that explanation. Too late now. Too bad for him.

"Well, I've never heard of you! You aren't on the working-group list. If you are who you say you are, call Will Baines. He's the partner in charge at your firm."

"Excuse me, Ms. Larkin, but I am the partner in charge, and Mr. Baines works for me."

She paused a moment. "I'm sorry. What was your name again?"

"Pat Brashner."

"Okay Mr. Brashner. I'm sorry to repeat myself, but I've never heard of you. And I am out of the country, as you evidently know, with no easy way to confirm you are who you say you are. So it would be imprudent for me to speak to you about whatever it is you want to speak about. And as you are, as you say, a partner at a firm as reputable as Stewart Baines, I'm sure you can understand why it would be entirely inappropriate for me to speak to you under these circumstances. If I may be so presumptuous as to suggest a way to handle this matter, you should call Will Baines, and the two of you can call me together if the matter is as urgent as you say. Hopefully, that can wait until Friday."

"It is a big mistake not to talk to me," Brashner said. "It is a disservice to our mutual client, Global Trading."

Had she misheard? That was her client. She was suddenly tired and felt old, too old to pay deference to a hotshot New York partner who thought a Houston woman was beneath him. "You must be confused, sir." It was all she could think to say.

"What?"

"If you are a Stewart Baines partner, your client is ERIS."

"In this transaction, yes. But I represent Global Trading on many other matters."

"Funny that I've never heard of you, then. Did the general counsel at Global Trading ask you to call me?"

"No, not directly. He expects me to look after their best interest in general."

"And I suspect the same is true for ERIS? Are you looking after their best interest?"

"Yes. Of course."

"And did Will Baines ask you to call me? Does he know you're calling me?"

"No. He works for me. I don't need his permission."

"So, you've taken it upon yourself to protect the interests of both parties in the transaction. Your client and mine? And to leave Will Baines out?" She wouldn't be bullied by him.

"Ms. Larkin, your queries are unwarranted and ill-advised. My call is only to offer friendly advice that the transaction will soon collapse unless both parties are open to compromise on the agreement, and I'm sure I can help, on account of my good relationships with both clients."

"Ah, I see. But don't you think you might have a conflict of interest in this matter? I'm not accustomed to a lawyer representing both parties in a transaction. Is that something you do in New York?" She knew she was poking a snake in a corner. But she'd had lots of experience with snakes.

"I don't appreciate your attitude, Ms. Larkin. There will be consequences for you if this transaction falls apart."

"Was that a threat?"

"I was only speaking plainly."

"Okay. Can you tell me then, plainly, what consequences you refer to? I would like to be properly threatened, if that's what you intend."

"You are gravely mistaken in your presumption that my calling you is improper. There will be consequences for such a mistake. It's as simple as that. And I am very experienced in matters such as this one."

Saying more would be a waste of time. The man was horrid. The sun was going down. She made her voice sweet with her best Texas accent, honey about to drip from a spoon. "You're so right, Patty. I'm just a Texas lawyer, and my knowledge of the ethical rules of the NY Bar is undoubtedly incomplete. But I'll be sure to give them a look when I get home and then call my client, who is apparently also your client. Now, y'all have a nice evening. Adios." She hung up before he could respond.

Strolling up the malecón, inhaling the present, the air fresh, her senses sharp, the energy she felt when she'd left Jay sleeping on the patio was renewed. True, she was two-timing the law, and with a man who'd treated her badly two years before. But Jay wasn't like Brashner. She thought about that. Retirement could leave the Brashners of the world behind and make a relationship with Jay real, more than just an affair. She passed a tidal pool carved out of a sandstone outcrop above the low-tide line. What was below the shining puddles that reflected the dimming sky? It was all so curious. There would be more time after she retired to discover these things. She could spit out Brashner, all the men like him, and all the other butt-ends of her career days, as if they were cherry pits.

15.

THE FIRST OF NOVEMBER, 2017, New York City, late morning, forty-four stories above the ground, the rush of Sixth Avenue traffic was audible in the offices of Stewart Baines. Brashner brooded at his desk. The Larkin woman had been impertinent to challenge him the day before. He looked at her picture on her firm's website. She was pretty, in a provocative way. He undressed her in his imagination. She'd insulted him. He was still angry, which made him want to fuck her even more.

Patrick Brashner was born in Queens, but his family moved to a brownstone on West Ninety-First Street when his father, a successful dressmaker for affluent women on the Upper East Side, opened a store on Madison Avenue. His three older sisters entertained themselves by making him wear dresses until he was old enough to go to school, where they'd continued to drag him around like he was a doll. The boys called him *Patricia*, sometimes *Patty*, like what the Larkin woman had called him. It wasn't the nickname for an Irish boy, he was sure. As he got older, he tried to alter his appearance to look tough. The problem was that he was five foot five and slight of build. So his posturing at that time hadn't worked out. But once he became a law partner, he made good his threats.

"Mr. Brashner," his assistant called from the doorway. "Mr. Silvers asked me to remind you that there's a partners' meeting today at noon."

He glowered at her, his secretary, not an assistant at all to his mind, whatever was the firm's practice. She was a woman. All he wanted her to do was get his coffee and make his phone calls.

"Those meetings are a waste of time," he snapped.

"Yes sir. I'm sorry," she said, and began to leave the doorway.

"Wait. Did Mr. Sutter return my call?"

"No sir."

"How about Mr. Sanchez?"

"No sir."

"Try them again. And close the door behind you."

His face was reflected in the monitor screen, eyes dark with menace. He needed the Global Trading deal to close. Will Baines, the Larkin woman, and Wallace Sesame were in the way, all playing by the silly rules. He hated not getting what he wanted when he wanted it.

He reached into his desk drawer and pulled out a hard plastic cube, embedded in which was a pair of brass bull's balls, given to him by a client after he'd bullied the woman lawyer representing the other party in a litigation into agreeing to a favorable settlement. It made him feel better to stroke the cube and remember his victory. It used to sit on the top of his desk, but a woman associate had complained to the managing partner that the cube was offensive.

Chinese wall or not, he planned to whisper to the Global Trading chairman's nephew that his counsel wasn't doing an adequate job. She should give up their silly demand for a guaranty. But the man would probably be spooked by his allegation about a woman. That she was a woman gave her an unfair advantage. It made him angry again. He, not she, should be representing Global Trading. The deal would be closed by now. But he doubted the Global Trading executives would listen to him, not able to see anything past her tits.

What to do? He thought he should read the provisions in dispute, and he'd sent a message to an associate in the corporate department who could get him a copy of the draft agreement. Then he might go to Houston and confront Will Baines in the presence of Ed Reid, the firm's managing partner, who was resident in the Houston office. He would make clear that failure by Will Baines to compromise the issues was imprudently endangering the deal. Something in the draft to prove his point, he was sure.

Then, a knock on his door. "What!" he shouted.

A young woman entered and walked reluctantly a few feet into the office, shoulder-length red hair, sharp professional features, and a bright complexion. Brashner was often attracted to red hair. But he wasn't in the mood to speak to her, and he looked back at his desk to appear busy.

"Who are you?" he demanded. "What do you want?"

"My name is Maura Gillis," she said. "I'm an associate in the corporate section. You sent for Paul Haden, but he is out of the office at a meeting, and the partner we both work for asked me to see if I could help you in his absence."

About to tell her to leave, Brashner looked up and noticed that, despite their considerable size, her breasts stuck straight out from her chest in a defiance of gravity. "Oh, yes. You're very nice to volunteer," he said. "Sit down, won't you?"

"Thank you."

"Maura, there's a corporate transaction in progress that I've been asked to help with. I need a copy of the latest draft of the agreement so I can review it for litigation weaknesses. I would like you to retrieve a copy for me." A vision came to him of her undressed, leaning back on her elbows and raising her legs over her, beckoning him to move toward her. But her face showed puzzlement, not willingness.

"It would be easy to get it off the server," she said, and looked at his computer. "I assume you have the client and matter numbers. Then you'd have it in a second. I could show you how."

Ordinarily, the thought of her bending in front of his computer monitor would entice him. But he didn't want his credentials associated with retrieving the draft agreement, which would be the case if done from his computer.

"I doubt you could, Maura. I'm old school. I can barely figure out how to get my email. And I have no idea about client matter numbers. I thought perhaps you could just look it up at your desk and print out a copy of the draft for me."

"Hmmm. Who is the partner on the matter?"

"Will Baines."

"So, it's in Houston?"

"Yes. But it's a New York client." Irritated at this associate, big tits or not, interrogating him and looking skeptical, he thought to tell her he didn't need her help after all.

"Okay," she said. "I know the associate in Houston who works a lot with Mr. Baines. I'll call him to get a copy in a jiffy. I won't even need to search the client matters."

"Yes, but I'm not in that much of a hurry. And I would rather that Mr. Baines not think that I'm looking over his shoulder."

"Oh. I thought you'd been asked to look at the document."

"Yes. Yes. I have. But it was the client's general counsel who asked me, not Mr. Baines. I've done a lot of work with the general counsel in the past, and he hasn't worked with Mr. Baines before. So, I'm just doing some handholding."

She'd sat back in her chair, while he was speaking. And now she tilted her head a tiny bit to the side while she looked at him, like she didn't believe him. But she didn't need to believe him, as far as he was concerned. She only needed to do what he asked. He stood up abruptly and put his fists on his hips. She got up and backed away toward the door.

"I understand. No problem at all," she said.

"Very good. Much appreciated, Maura," he said.

"Oh, I do need the name of the client."

"Of course. It's ERIS. And the other party is Global Oil Trading."

The door clicked closed and he was sweating a little. Maura was a nice name. He looked her up on his computer and studied her picture for a while.

16.

THE FIRST OF NOVEMBER, 2017, the Pretty Horses Ranch in the hills of Cantamar, Baja California, Jay rode a horse on a hilly trail. The warm winds of the day before had abated, and there was a slight westerly breeze. A few clouds wandered in the distance, their shadows dotting the ocean, hiding the sun's reflection off the waves. He'd dropped Lyn at the Black Cross Winery nearby to talk to the proprietor, Robyn, before lunch. Lyn wasn't much of a rider, she was happy to stay behind, and Jay needed some time alone, having been in her company for several days. He did his best thinking when he was on a horse.

Pretty Horses wasn't the same as the Jackson Ranch, but nothing was. The trail Jay liked best worked its way down a hillside across a few arroyos. Near the end there was a small rise from which he had a peaceful view of the Pacific. In the late spring, when he'd first arrived, this hillside had been covered with wild arugula. But the weather had been very dry at the end of the summer, and the grasses were all brown and dusty looking. In a way, that made the ocean more attractive. Still, nothing could better the sweeping waves of bluebonnets in his favorite Jackson Ranch meadow.

The mare he rode was docile. He barely held the reins and guided her with light nudges on her sides with his knees. Patsy could read his mind at times like this, knowing when he wanted to stop and think. He pulled the reins to stop a moment. This mare was patient and she stood quietly on the rise and looked out at the ocean with him. He took off his hat to let the sweat on the top of his head dry. It barely took a second.

Jay gave the mare a nudge and she turned back toward Pretty Horses. The sun was behind a cloud; the breeze from the ocean was cool. They'd go back to Los Pelicanos after lunch, and he planned to take a nap. Lyn wasn't much at napping. She'd go out to watch the pelicans fish and probably chat up some residents strolling the malecón. He expected she would be happy to head back to Houston tomorrow. Not much excitement here once the novelty wore off, and she could wear things out faster than anyone he knew. Retirement wasn't going to be easy for her.

~

That evening, Ollie's Pizza Restaurant, close to Los Pelicanos, was packed, people waiting outside, the sound of diners laughing, energy at the entrance door. Inside, walls made from old brick, the tables stainless steel, a personable atmosphere, different from the trendy places in Houston, and a long wood bar overlooking an open kitchen with a bricked wood-fired oven at one end. A woman selling blankets and baskets moved around the room, and several men in costume with guitars serenaded a couple at a table in the corner. Jay had a table reserved, knowing the owner. On their way to be seated, they passed a lone American man—Lyn had seen him shuffling down the malecón the day before—at the bar, wearing khaki trousers and a faded blue dress shirt, leaning sleepily over a glass of red wine. At the other end of the bar were two men eating a pizza, looking out of place in old T-shirts and dirty shorts. One of them had a piece of pepperoni stuck to his shirt, up near his chest.

A chef with a long stick slid a pizza into the brick oven. Another man washed dishes at a metal sink. Several people stopped to talk to Jay and be introduced to Lyn. The owner,

Richard, soon came to the table as well, a New Yorker with white hair and rectangular glasses, an amused smile on his face. He looked directly at her when he shook her hand, his eyes showing interest and hesitancy, eyes that took in dozens of faces every evening.

"Who would have thought to open a restaurant like this in Mexico?" she asked. "Baja is the land of fish tacos. No?"

"It wasn't planned," he said. "I moved here to retire. But I got bored after a year and decided to open a pizza joint."

"Come on. It's not just a pizza joint. Were you a restaurateur in New York?"

"I didn't know the first thing about running a restaurant or making pizza. I thought running a pizza joint would be fun. And I got lucky."

"Richard was an actuary in his earlier life," Jay said. "That probably explains it."

"Right. I know just when the pepperoni will expire," Richard said.

His deadpan expression made Lyn laugh. A handsome waiter wearing a trilby with a colorful band refilled their wine glasses. The waitstaff were neatly dressed.

"Your staff is very good," she said.

At a nearby table, several young men drank beer, laughing too loud, one with a donkey's bray. At another table, a little girl peered at her, the eyes barely above her plate. Lyn smiled, but the girl turned away after a guffaw from the other table.

"I'm happy I live in Mexico," Richard said. "Those types go back to the US after the weekend. And they don't come here very often. We're not their kind of scene."

"So why isn't your name Ollie?" Lyn asked. "Or why isn't the place called Ricardo's?"

"Ollie was my dog, recently deceased."

"Ollie was more popular than the bartender," Jay said.

"And the owner," Richard said.

"So sorry," Lyn said.

"That little girl over there. Her parents own a place at Los Pelicanos. They're here about once a month. She used to sit next to Ollie and talk to him."

"I bet she misses him."

"I do too. So there's a puppy to take Ollie's place."

"Where is he?"

"Not old enough to hang out at the bar just yet."

"And what's his name?"

"Ollie Dos, of course."

Lyn sighed and looked back at the little girl, who was ignoring her now. Life was simple in Baja. But she couldn't live here. How long would Jay stay? She studied his face for a minute while he listened to Richard's idea about a gelato place next door.

The ugly Americans left, in their wake a comforting din of activity around her, like a warm bath, soft heat pushing stress aside. Relaxation never lasted long for her. She would step out of the bath when the water cooled, and her body would rev up, like she'd stepped on the gas pedal. It was hard for her to disguise her surplus energy, never sitting still, tapping her fingers on a knee beneath the table, twisting her ankles, stretching her toes. Her curiosity was much the same, a frenzied mental acuity. Traditional life didn't appeal to her, a home and a husband and children on a street in West University. Her sister's life. Lyn pitied her, the soccer mom existence. She was a woman with dark moods and horrible prospects: the children would leave home, the dog would die, and her husband would do one or the other.

The flight to Houston was the next day. Lyn would leave behind the pelicans and Jay. Ollie's was a good send-off. She'd had her fill of romance, if that was what it was. Here the commotion and the crowd distracted her.

Her phone buzzed, vibrating up her legs from the bag at her feet. A text from her associate. *Gerald Kent wants to meet on Friday to talk about title diligence. I have a conference room. About time. Right?* She replied. *Good news. Alert Will Baines.* Another text came very quickly. *That man Brashner called again. Wants a copy of the draft.* A request for a duel? *Ignore him*, she typed.

"We were boring you," Jay said. He put his hand on top of hers. She'd not noticed that Richard had left. "He went to talk to other customers. It was nothing you did."

"I'm so sorry. I was thinking about a text I just received from my office."

"Ah, getting ready to go back, are you? You must have a deal gearing up."

"It's only silly things." She'd not told Jay about the deal, nor of Brashner's phone call. No need. It was work gossip. "It can wait for me in Houston."

⌒

Back at Los Pelicanos, the waves emboldened by the darkness, crashing against the malecón's seawall, bursting seawater hard to dodge. At a high point, they sat on a bench, protected from the ocean's commotion.

"I suppose I should tell you some more about Raymond," Jay said.

"Yes. I suppose you could do that," Lyn said. "But we can skip it if you want."

"Okay. You'll most likely think it boring anyway." He'd worked out in his head how much he could tell her, and he thought he may have just been given a pass. But she turned to him suddenly, the intensity in her eyes making him lean back, like he'd been pushed by an invisible hand. It confused him, how she so easily abandoned ambivalence.

"I promise you I will not be bored," she said.

His nerves made him laugh. "Fine. Raymond was a child prodigy. His parents were diplomats and they lived in various European countries when he was growing up between the two world wars. They sent him back to college in Saint Paul before the Second World War. Raymond graduated when he was eighteen, two years after the Japanese bombed Pearl Harbor. And then he was recruited by the Office of Strategic Services, which was an intelligence organization Roosevelt formed at the beginning of the war. After a mission in Yugoslavia, he trained as a frogman in Hawaii and went to the Pacific to help clear pathways to the beach for amphibious landings as the navy moved through the Japanese-controlled islands. From there, he was secretly dispatched by submarine to French Indochina in the beginning of 1945, where he lived with villagers as a Red Cross worker. He actually met a young Ho Chi Minh during that time."

"That's incredible."

"It is. But the OSS forgot about him until the end of the war, when the French began to demand that Indochina be handed over to them after the Japanese surrender. The French didn't want any Americans there, and Truman caved to de Gaulle's pressure. Truman also disbanded the OSS but was soon persuaded to form a new intelligence group, which became the CIA. Raymond was one of its first agents."

"So how did you meet Raymond? That was so long ago."

"Through my college roommate."

"Okay. How did Raymond know your roommate?"

"Raymond rescued him in 1953 in Vietnam."

"What?"

"Raymond was friends from OSS days with his parents, who became missionaries after the war and went to Vietnam. Mercenaries murdered the parents, but my roommate was hidden by villagers. Afterward, Raymond snuck into the country and retrieved him."

"Snuck?"

"The French had reestablished their colony after the war, and they didn't want the CIA there. That's a history lesson we can probably skip."

"Okay. But his parents were murdered?"

"Yeah. But he was really young when it happened. Raymond visited him regularly. By then, he'd joined the State Department. Raymond spoke more than five languages, including Vietnamese. And he was well connected. He helped my roommate and me get into the navy reserves officer training program, and then into law school. After graduation we were supposed to go into JAG, but Raymond arranged for us to do the rest of our service at the CIA." What Jay couldn't tell Lyn was that Raymond's State Department position had actually been a cover, not uncommon during Cold War times. There were holes in this part of his story, but he was sure he could avoid them, like he did when galloping Patsy through a pasture.

"What? You worked for the CIA? Were you a spy?"

Jay laughed. "I worked in the Office of the General Counsel. If I was undercover, it was that I was covered up by books in the library."

"Still, your resume doesn't say anything about the CIA."

"I was still in the navy during that time. After I finished my two years, I was hired by the State Department and worked with Raymond in a department called Embassy Operations. We were a diplomat transition team. When there was a change at an embassy of an ambassador or other high-level diplomats, we interviewed the outgoing people and briefed the new people. It was more complicated than it sounds. Often the new guys didn't have a clue about the customs and the issues in the country they were going to. Raymond was brilliant at understanding cultures. It was a great job. I went to a lot of countries."

"This is why W&K hired you for the international energy practice."

"Yeah, I guess I knew my way around the world a bit."

"But wasn't it hard to leave Raymond to go to W&K?"

"Not so much, because Raymond was on his way out. After I joined W&K, he was forced to retire by State Department rules. Then he and his wife moved to the Hudson Valley and he took up birdwatching."

"So he went from jetting around the world with diplomats to birdwatching. That must've been depressing. It would be for me, anyway."

"He adapted. And he adored Megan, his wife. He loved spending time with her. She opened the bakery I mentioned." He wanted to explain how birdwatching was much the same as spying, but he couldn't.

"Right. What's happened to the bakery?"

"I've leased it to a woman in town. I'm the Hatchers' executor. Did I tell you that?"

"No. It must be hard, all the reminders."

"I'm hoping it won't be bad, now that time has passed. But I need to go up there soon and deal with things."

Lyn was quiet for a time and looked out at the waves. A dark ocean, out beyond the malecón lights. Jay felt as if he was swimming there, struggling through swells of lies. It was a bad feeling. The problem with lies was that more of them are needed to cover up the first ones, and before you knew it, maintenance of the subterfuge became a huge burden. He heard shouts from further down the malecón, maybe renters drinking beer in the jacuzzi. It was the flaw of his otherwise nice community, that short-term rentals were permitted.

"It's still going to be hard," she said. "It was such a freak thing, you know."

"You're right. If they'd just died in their sleep, I would've felt bad, of course, but it would've have been easier to accept."

"I understand. I'm so sorry," she said, and grasped his hands. "I can't imagine."

"As stupid as it sounds, I wanted it to be murder, and I wanted someone to pay for it. That sounds bad, I know." The spy knows that good lies have truth in them, but he was on thin ice.

"It isn't bad, Jay. It was a huge tragedy. We all think such things when that happens."

"I guess that's right. But I simply couldn't carry on as normal. It was impossible at the time to be the executor, you know, catalog their belongings and pack them in boxes. My father used to tell me when I was frustrated to go ride my horse to the meadows and stay out there until I felt better. But I didn't have my horse, so I put the executor stuff off and left the country, as you know."

"Yes, I know."

"And it sounds dumb now, like I said. I should have just gone back to the ranch."

"You did what you thought best. And I'm sorry for not giving you the benefit of the doubt. I've been pissed at you for two years. That's unfair."

"No, I should have called you while I was away. I didn't. I couldn't talk to anyone. I wasn't fit to talk to anyone. I'm a little surprised I'm even talking about it now. I guess I've never been good at talking about my feelings."

"None of that matters now," she said. "And I'm not very good at it, either."

"Then that makes two of us."

A few minutes later, Los Pelicanos, at the swimming pool, the air clear now that the haze between them had departed, the slate wiped clean, an undertaking to talk about themselves. It was risky, she not having done such a thing before, always guarding her feelings and thoughts, a part of the armor she wore to prove that she was as good at her job as any man. That had worked fine in her professional life, but she knew it would be a hindrance for a relationship with him. Near the pool's edge, she yanked his hand and wrapped her arms around him. The reflections of the pool's lights rippled on the water, as if inviting her to dive into the pool, fully clothed, her loafers still on her feet, and pull him in with her.

They walked on around a bend. The sound of squealing drunk girls greeted them. A game of cornhole in progress, beer cans and tequila bottles on a ping-pong table, towels and bathing suits hung on chairs. When a bean bag hit the target, the thrower pushed out his chest, shouted an obscenity, chugged a beer, and then flattened the empty can against his forehead. The girls bounced on their toes.

A large man, a tattoo on the side of his neck, sleeveless T-shirt, standing close to the malecón, smirked at their approach. She tugged Jay's hand to keep them walking. But a security guard walked up beside them and Jay stopped.

"You people got a problem?" the smirking man asked them.

"We were just walking by," she said quickly, tugging again at Jay's hand.

"Señor," the security guard said. "People live nearby. You are too loud. There are rules."

"Rules!" The man turned to his companions. "Didya hear that? They got rules here in Mexico." After a chorus of expletives, the man turned back. "We don't care about no fucking rules. What you going to do about it?"

"You will be fined."

"Good luck with that." He stared at the guard a moment and then leaned forward to point his finger at Jay. "Hey, man, what you looking at? This is none of your fucking business."

Jay ignored her continued tugging at his hand. "It's a right nice evening," he said, in a pleasant voice.

His cowboy charm wasn't going to work on a bully, she thought. The man didn't back down. "So you and your girlfriend should go and enjoy the nice evening and stop standing around gawking at us."

"Don't think that's gonna happen, friend," Jay said, slowly.

"I'm warning you, dude," the man said, and stepped onto the malecón within a few inches of Jay.

"Are you?" Jay smiled. The man pushed Jay's chest. It had no effect, like he'd just pushed a rock wall. Jay's face hardened. Lyn was sure the man was going to hit Jay. She looked at the security guard. Did he have a gun? A can of mace? No, only a two-way radio, putting out static and garbled Spanish. A siren sounded in the distance.

"Hey Joe, let's chill," one of the girls said.

"Señor," the guard said. "We have called the policía."

A last look at Jay, the man backed away. His friends became sober. They straightened their clothes and walked casually back to their house, as if a choreographed dance had just ended. Would they bow from their doorway? Police cars came through the gates and drove down the hill, several police officers coming out of them when they stopped, wearing camouflage and carrying large rifles.

"Thanks for your help, señor," the security guard said to Jay.

"De nada," Jay said. "Just a bunch of college kids. Sorry they were rude to you."

Walking away, she felt as if a sudden gust of wind had stopped, the disturbance fleeing out over the ocean. She'd never had to stand up physically to an aggressor. It had always been a man, coming on to her a little too strongly, and then her joking refusal and her walking away a good enough response. Jay's reaction to the man was foreign to her. It was a side of him she'd not seen before.

⌒

Los Pelicanos, another hundred yards, another bench, this one at the edge of a curve, in front of a big house, along a stretch of shoreline with smooth rocks, baseball size, polished by the ocean. Lyn folded her arms across her chest when she sat down. It wasn't cold. He knew he should've kept walking earlier, when she'd tugged his hand, but it was instinctual, he was doing it before he knew it. A reminder, perhaps, that his old days were still with him.

"What the hell, Jay. What were you thinking?"

"It was nothing, really. That guy was out of line."

"Nothing? He was going to punch you. I was sure he was. He was bigger than you."

"He wasn't going to hit me."

"How do you know that? And what was I supposed to do with a man with a broken nose and no front teeth? Do they even have dentists in Mexico?"

"You're exaggerating now. You know what we call guys like him back on the ranch?"

"No. And I'm not sure I care."

"All hat and no cattle."

"I still think you were being foolish." But she'd smiled at his expression.

"Okay. The excitement is over, in any case," he said. "Let's sit awhile and enjoy this place."

The shoreline in front of them looked like an odd beach, no sand, only round rocks angled from waterline to berm, coastal badlands. The waves pushed the rocks up the incline. Their retreat with the withdrawing water made a blurry clamor, until the next wave roared. It was a muscle cramp: sharp pain, then relief. Or an argument: confrontation, then accommodation. Jay thought of a barrel racer making her turn.

"Those guys sobered up fast," she said. "Didn't you think? I guess they didn't want to get arrested."

"I'm not sure they were actually drunk," he said.

"Why do you say that?"

"That man was sitting in the bar at Ollies, but drinking a coke, not a beer."

"What! You noticed that?"

"Couldn't miss it. He was gawking at you. I'm sure he thought you were hot. If he got too horny, I was going to have to defend your honor."

"Quit!"

Lyn leaned forward and put her elbows on her knees. Jay wanted to go back to the house, but he sensed she wanted to stay. The moonlit malecón was pretty. In the distance were the sandstone cliffs where the pelicans sometimes hung out. This spot was more like his ranch than the white sand beach below his house. Maybe she would go back to Houston and decide he was too much trouble. He suspected Baja wasn't her kind of place. It might help to tell her he planned to go back to the ranch soon, but he wasn't ready yet.

"I suppose it could've been a distraction," he said. "Maybe we should go back to the house and make sure someone isn't there going through our stuff." Something wasn't right, he wanted to say.

"What! Stealing my bathing suits?"

"Our stash of Grey Goose, more likely."

"Then we should get back there pronto!"

They headed back. The house where the commotion happened was dark. "Are you sure you didn't know that guy? He wasn't some old boyfriend stalking you?"

"Quit. That's not even funny. Every man I've gone out with was way too dull to live in Mexico. Except you, of course."

He stopped her at the door, took her hand and faced her. The ocean's expanse was behind him. He didn't want her to leave the next day.

"I'm sad you're leaving tomorrow," he said.

She looked away. The moon shone, the breeze rustled the palm leaves, the waves sang a harmony. He walked around her and breathed in deeply, promising himself he would remember her fragrance, mixed with the ocean smell. From behind, he put his arms around her, and over her shoulder the ocean's surface winked at him. It would be nice, he thought, to stand like this forever. But she pulled away and turned to the door.

"Come on, padner," she said. "I hope you haven't tired yourself out with all that roughhousing. We've got time left before my flight home."

17.

THE NEXT DAY, THE SECOND of November, San Diego, California, in the airport parking lot early Thursday morning, a marine layer from the harbor enveloped them, scented with car exhaust and fumes from jet engines, which whined intermittently from the other side of the airport terminal. They'd been quiet during the drive from Los Pelicanos, except for bursts of casual conversation, which punctuated an atmosphere of wariness born of fear that a departing remark might bring on the collapse of their nascent romance. She held Jay's arm on the walk into the terminal building, her carryon held with his other hand. Then a hug and a thank you before she moved through the security checkpoint. Her blue jeans blended into a mass of other jeaned travelers, and he saw one last flash of her red sweater before she disappeared down the concourse, not looking back once.

Jay turned toward the exit. Lyn's visit had brought him a spark of optimism that the burden of being a spy, reborn after Raymond's murder, might finally be offloaded.

A woman blocked his path, a smile on her lips, a sparkle in her eyes, and her hands on her hips, looking like she was ready to tackle him if need be.

"Hello, cowboy," she said.

"Hello, Anna."

"I knew it was you, despite your disguise. Are those flip-flops?"

"Yeah," he said, looking down and holding up one foot for a moment. "I suppose they are."

"They've got a really nice restaurant at the Sheraton marina across the street. How about breakfast?"

"I could do that."

"Good. You can give me a ride. I took their shuttle over here."

They didn't speak until they sat at a table in a corner. It was a spy thing. Don't talk when you can't see your adversary's eyes. It wasn't a coincidence. She had a purpose. He looked at the menu longer than he needed.

"So the cowboy cometh," she said. "You've been traveling for two years since France."

"Yeah, I just got started and it was hard to stop, if you know what I mean."

"Not sure I do. I'm just a homebody."

"Right."

"And now you're hanging out in Baja. Ranching has lost its attraction? You've forgotten your old friends? Except for that pretty woman who just left for Houston, of course."

"You're very well informed. I was going to send you a post-card. But hadn't got around to it."

"I was becoming impatient. And missing you. Maybe a little."

"Since you know my whereabouts, you must also have my phone number."

"It's not the same."

"Your grandmother is well, I hope?"

"Still kicking. Look, I came to see you at the request of your old friend Ben Lufkin. You do remember him?"

"You mean your boss. I've been trying to forget him."

"Not so much my boss as he once was. I'm working for one of his portfolio companies now. He asked me to remind you that you've still not had your interview about Raymond's estate."

"You had to come in person for that?"

"He insisted that I do that. You fell off the face of the earth after France, until you showed up in Baja and bought a house. He didn't want to miss the opportunity. You know, a personal visit always makes a better impression. The people in Washington really like to get their files closed."

"Not sure I'm ready to go to Denver yet," Jay said. He'd never been as close to Lufkin as he'd been with Raymond. Lufkin was younger than he, and he could be haughty and officious, more even than what was necessary for his cover of being a private equity mogul.

"Oh, it won't be in Denver. It will be an overt government employee. GAO or something like that. All official. But it can't be in Baja or at the ranch. You're only the Hatcher executor. They'll have to go to Raymond's farmhouse to meet you. That's what I've been told."

"I have to go to New York soon to work on Raymond's estate. An Agency man was there before I went to France. I had no patience at the time."

"So I heard. I'll tell Lufkin you'll make yourself available. By the way, you didn't mention that I'm a beneficiary in Raymond's will."

"You are very well informed. I didn't tell you in France because I hadn't yet gone over the papers. In fact, I didn't look at them until I got to Baja. How do you know what's in the will, anyway?"

"Oh, it's in the Agency file now. When Lufkin gave me the assignment to keep an eye on you, I was given access to most of the Agency records about Raymond. You did file documents in the probate court."

"I don't believe they make those public."

"They don't," she said, and raised an eyebrow.

"So Lufkin knows now that you're Raymond's grand-daughter?"

"I don't know how he would. It's not stated in the will or any of the Agency records on Hatcher. And I certainly didn't tell him."

"Still. How hard would it be to find out?"

"Very hard, actually. The nuns didn't put the father's name on my mother's birth record. And Vera didn't tell anyone who she'd had the affair with. She only said he was 'a Hungarian comrade.' I'm not sure she even told my mother."

"Okay." Did this bother her? He wasn't sure why it would. She was a woman who held her cards close to her chest, even more so than Lyn. Looking at her face, he was sure she was planning something, a scheme he couldn't imagine if he tried.

"Raymond certainly kept it to himself."

"I guess it doesn't matter, anyway."

"I don't think Lufkin has even looked at the Agency records about Raymond's past. There's a report about Raymond and my grandmother working undercover in Budapest in 1957. Maybe that's why the Agency wants to interview you—to be sure there is nothing in Raymond's papers about Budapest. The Agency's record about that mission has *Classified—Need to Know* appended to it, so I couldn't access it. Regardless, none of this should be of any interest to Lufkin. It's long before his time."

"I certainly won't tell him." The Agency operation in Budapest was described in some detail in one part of Raymond's journal, and its disclosure would prove embarrassing to the Agency, even after so many years, somewhat like the Bay of Pigs revelations had been. Did Anna know about the Agency involvement in the Hungarian uprising? Or Raymond's assassination target in Hungary? Or the connection with Suez? They were dancing around that mission's details, but he didn't know why. And he was still a little wary about why Anna had come in person. So he didn't mention the journal. This little slice of historical intrigue made him weary.

"Thank you. Am I going to be a rich heiress?"

"I haven't done an accounting, or even had the property appraised. You probably shouldn't change your lifestyle just yet."

She laughed. "Damn. Working for a living is tough. Maybe I could take over the bakery."

"Tell me about Lufkin's company you're working for. Where is it?"

"Dallas. So I'm not even in Denver with Lufkin. It appears I'm a casualty of equal rights. I'm a big-shot executive at the company, which is in Chapter 11."

"You're a bit young to be a CEO."

"Not quite yet! I'm the CFO. I see Lufkin at board meetings."

"Did you tell him about our tour of the French vineyards?"

"Oh, yes. I gave him the important details, how we bumped into Parnell and all. He wasn't interested. Hasn't mentioned it since. He asked me a couple of times whether I'd heard from you. But of course I hadn't. Not even a postcard."

"How about my old law partners in New York. Any of them doing any work for Branoble?"

"No. If you want gossip, I did hear about Parnell. He was arrested after his uncle was found. The police thought Parnell had killed him to get his inheritance early. But the death was eventually ruled a suicide. I'm sure the Sûreté intervened. Too much dirt on Piquart would probably come out at the trial."

"I'm sure you remember that Parnell wasn't one of my favorite partners." Jay remembered Anna in her nightgown, telling Parnell he was a naughty boy and then embracing him and the shotgun from behind, her finger on top of his on the trigger, Piquart's brains suddenly splattered on the bedroom wall. It was humorously horrific.

"But one of your favorite law partners in the W&K Houston office is now representing a Branoble company, Global Oil

Trading. You remember that company? Weren't you and Raymond at the closing ceremony in Bilbao?"

"As I told you in France, we were on a birdwatching trip up the coast, near San Sebastian. What Houston partner?"

Anna smiled. "Lyn Larkin, of course. Come on, Jay. I just watched you watch her go back to Houston. Global Trading is buying an oil and gas company. I'm surprised she didn't mention it to you. Or is she so proper that she keeps her client confidences during pillow talk?"

He tried not to react. "Lyn would never mention the parties in an active matter. And how do you know all this?"

"Lufkin's files, mostly. It was all logged by one of his Branoble lackeys. Your entry into Mexico through Mexico City. Your purchase of the house in Baja. Your border crossings into San Diego. Nothing is secret from someone with Agency resources. Until you cross the border into the US, of course!" She laughed, arching her eyebrows, her very presence across the table rebutting her last statement. "In any case, Lufkin told me about the Global Trading deal. It was easy to connect the dots. I remembered that you and she were friends, and the Branoble guy told me she was their counsel. You called her from Mexico on your cell phone. And when I checked the flights from Houston to San Diego on a day you crossed the border, last Saturday to be exact, there she was. I only had to wait for her to book the return flight. That's how I knew where to find you at the airport."

"So I have active surveillance?" He'd assumed that they'd look for him after France, and he'd made a game of it, once using his known credit card at a restaurant in Hong Kong, then waiting in a bar across the street to see how long it took for surveillance guys to show up. Not long at all. A little more than an hour. After that, he kept using cash from his offshore accounts no one knew about and a passport he'd obtained from an old friend in Qatar. And he assumed after a while they would lose interest and drop the human intelligence operation. Too expensive. Then he purposely used his real passport to travel to Mexico City. That would show up on the computers, as would his trips to and from San Diego. All a part of his reentry plan. Give them plenty of opportunity to make contact, which, he supposed, Anna was doing.

"That's my job, alright. What do you expect, disappearing like you did? I'm sure Lufkin is just worried about you."

"What he's worried about is an old horse that escaped from the stable and is coming back to bite him in the ass."

"I don't know about that. Anyway, he's given me the responsibility to keep track of you until you give a formal interview to the Agency. That's convenient, isn't it? The hen is watching the fox!"

Jay liked the look on her face when she laughed. But she was no hen, and he had no interest in returning to the life of a fox. He wanted only to put that life behind him, what he'd tried to do two years before and failed.

"So, get yourself to New York and do the interview," she said. "That's my advice. And then Lufkin and the Agency will lose interest. And I can stop spying on an old cowboy. It's boring."

"You're right. It's a damn nuisance. I should probably go to San Saba this weekend and then New York right after. I haven't yet been to the ranch."

"I know. And I'd like to visit your ranch."

"After I get back from New York. Love to have you."

"Okay, we're done here and I have a plane to catch. Can I tell Lufkin there's nothing else he should worry about?"

She sounded too casual. He looked into her eyes. They reminded him of Raymond. She wasn't telling him something. And for now, he would keep the journal to himself.

"I don't know a thing," he said.

18.

THE SAME DAY, THE SECOND of November, 2017, Houston, gloomy, the air heavy but moving, roiling like water about to boil, the humidity was wedged against a cold front pushing down from the north. Will sat in his office thinking about Eleanor, who'd just left. She was hard to attend to sometimes, she was so beguiling, a goldfinch perched on a branch. Larry Sutter, from ERIS, called.

"Global Trading has come around, I think," Larry said. "They're willing to continue without any guaranty, but they want more time to do property diligence before they sign."

"I suggested that months ago, Larry." Will was sure that Gerald would find other issues to hound him about. And the same was true for Brashner.

"You're right. I would like to tell them they've run out of time. But we think that if we yank this deal right now, we won't get any of the other bidders back at their last price. So we want to keep trying."

"Larry, how about we propose that we close right away with an adjustment provision in the agreement that would let them recover for ownership defects they discover later. We can put a limit on the time and the amount. Then they can do their diligence on their own time."

"That's actually not a bad idea, Will. How soon could you have something to look at?"

"Late this afternoon." He'd actually already started drafting something.

"Let me call them," Larry said, and hung up.

A waste of time maybe, but Will went to work on provisions for his proposal. Maybe he would soon see the last of Gerald and Brashner. Larry's return call came quickly, less than an hour.

"I got very aggressive with them," Larry said. "I wanted him to think this was a compromise for their sake, not ours. So I told him we had to settle this right away, that his lawyers wouldn't get a draft of the provision until they showed up in Houston, and that we'd either sign the agreement quickly or the deal was off. So how about meeting tomorrow?"

"Tomorrow? You're kidding!"

"No. I told him his guys needed to get on a plane right now and they needed to be in your offices tomorrow."

"And he agreed?"

"He didn't think he had a choice. And it turns out that their advisor was already on his way to Houston to interview landmen for the diligence. But I told him we needed an actual Global Trading person with the authority to make decisions. What was their advisor's name?"

"Gerald Kent. Not one of my favorites."

"Then someone will be there to hold his leash. Sanchez and I will fly down tonight. Send me the draft as soon as you can so I can read it on the plane. I have to find Sanchez. He knows nothing about this yet."

"Okay with me. See you tomorrow."

⁓

Working through lunch, Will sent a draft to Larry an hour later, feeling positive after the work, his skepticism gone. He had only to tell his associates and ask his assistant to reserve the conference room before going home to change clothes for a charity benefit that evening. His assistant came through the door.

"Your two o'clock appointment is here. I put her in the conference room next to reception."

He'd forgotten. "Remind me who she is."

"Her name is Anna Stegineo. She is the CFO at a company in Dallas owned by Branoble Partners. She told me Jay Jackson recommended you. She is looking for counsel on corporate matters."

"Right." He remembered Jay Jackson from when he was an associate, years before. It was a deal involving a purchase of an oil-products pipeline. Jay had represented a company owned by Branoble Partners. W&K, Belinda's firm, still did a lot of work for Branoble. But Jay Jackson had retired, Will thought.

"I put coffee and beverages in there. Do you need any food?"

"No. I doubt the meeting will last very long."

Will walked to the conference room. Anna was much younger than he'd expected, very young to be a CFO. Her clothes were somewhat masculine. Dark-blue blazer, white blouse, and black pants. But she wore them as a well-proportioned and athletic woman would. They made small talk for a few minutes. She'd just flown into Houston from San Diego on a private jet and come to his offices straight from Hobby Airport. The plane was waiting there to take her back to Dallas.

"Anna, what can I do for you? I'm surprised you aren't meeting with W&K for your legal work. I think Jay Jackson has retired, but there's a woman there who does work for companies that Branoble owns."

"He has retired, and, yes, Belinda Larkin does work for several companies they own, if that's who you're talking about. I've not met her. But I want to have independent counsel. A law firm that doesn't have any Branoble connections. My CEO is worried that W&K may be influenced by them. Jay, and several others I talked to, spoke very highly of you."

"That's a nice compliment. Do you have a particular matter pending?"

"Not quite yet. We are just coming out of Chapter 11 and there is a deal on the horizon. I want you to start with a review of all of our corporate governance documents and a review of our executive compensation plans by your tax group. I actually brought a disk with all those things loaded on it." She reached into her bag and took out a thumb drive. "By the way, there is a lot of speculation in the press about the bankruptcy and whether Branoble's ownership will change. Don't speak to them if they inquire. They've been hounding me."

"Of course. First, I might have to ask for a conflict-of-interest waiver. I had to get one for a transaction I'm now working on that involves another Branoble affiliate that one of my partners in New York does litigation work for. I don't know if he also does other work for Branoble."

"Who would that be?"

"Patrick Brashner."

"Don't know him. But I'm quite sure Mr. Brashner doesn't do any work for my company or any other Branoble companies except the one you're referring to. You should check your records to confirm that. And we're happy to give your firm a waiver if you want one."

Will suspected Anna knew all about the Global Trading transaction but was being professional and not mentioning it. That impressed him. "Okay. It won't take me long to check and I can then open a file. What's your timing?"

"Next week for the work is fine. But I would like confirmation that Stewart Baines will take us on as soon as possible. Could you get that done by tomorrow? We have a potential transaction that we might need you to look at. It may start quickly, but I can't talk about it yet."

"Definitely. I'll get the process started right away."

She pointed at a photograph on the credenza behind him. It was a picture of Will's wife sitting next to Mason on the couch. "Nice picture."

"Thanks. That's my wife and our dog."

"Beautiful dog. What's his name?"

"Mason."

"He looks smart."

Will laughed. "Thank you."

She stood and held out her hand with her business card. "Great. I'll expect your call about your conflicts check tomorrow then."

Will got the client matter request filed, made sure conference rooms were reserved for ERIS, and then drove home, five o'clock, the traffic slower than he was used to, since he normally didn't leave the office before six. On Kirby, he banged the flat of his hand on the dashboard, his earlier sanguineness drained from him by a driver ahead talking on his cell phone, no attention to how slow he was going, or the line of cars behind him.

Will's wife was the host of that night's benefit, and she was on another one of her trips to visit her ill mother. She'd called him that morning to tell him that she had recruited Belinda to take her place. *She'll be your date*, she'd said. *It will be fun and you won't be alone.* He had no pleasant expectations for the evening. Not one. Mason wasn't sitting at the window in his usual place when Will pulled into the driveway. The house reminded him of a flat black-and-white photograph.

That evening, at the Four Seasons Hotel, Houston, the darkness had started early on account of the heavy clouds. Before he'd left home, Will had watched birds hopping across the pecan tree's branches that hung over his pool. He knew nothing about birds. And Mason was no help. Normally, he would sit on the couch with him, offering comfort by putting his head on Will's lap. Not tonight. The dog had stayed on the floor until Will went upstairs. There he'd watched Will dress in a blazer, dress shirt, no tie, and slacks, looking either skeptical or worried, Will couldn't decide.

In the parking garage across the street from the Four Seasons Hotel, all the men climbing out of their cars were wearing suits with ties, making him anxious that he wasn't. Inside the ballroom, a glass of wine in his hand, his aplomb was restored. Other men were dressed in business casual, and his anonymity, standing on the edge of the crowd, was assured. Then he felt conspicuous standing alone, and he looked for one of his golf buddies. Normally, he would stand next to his wife and pretend to listen to her conversations.

"Hey there, Will," Eleanor said, at his elbow unexpectedly, a dress with a sleeveless top held up with a small collar around her neck and fitted elegantly down her torso and hips, then flaring out for a few inches on the top of her legs. Her smile was so wide that the ends of her mouth blended together with her ear lobes. Light shined off her bare shoulders.

"Hello Eleanor," he said, working hard to keep his eyes on her eyes. Clearly, she'd changed the clothes she'd worn earlier at the office. Her dress offered a lot to see and even more to imagine. She stood toe to toe with him. His skin hot, he slid his feet back.

"Nice party, isn't it?" she asked.

"Really nice," he said, putting his wine glass into both hands like a shield in front of him, her skin so smooth he longed to touch it.

"I love galas. It's too bad your wife is missing it, since she was a co-host and all."

She'd done a remarkably precise job applying her eyeliner, and her skin around her eyes was so natural, not a blemish anywhere. He was too close to her. Beginning to sweat, he backed away another step, abruptly, as if separating from a magnet. "Right. I wish she was here, but her mother is very ill and she had to go to Boston."

"So awful, I'm really sorry to hear that. But I'll be at your table to keep you company." Her voice was seductive and her scrutiny of his face unsettled him. He looked down to break eye contact. Her dress was very short and her legs were as bright as her shoulders.

"That's nice," he said, his legs feeling weak.

"It's so crowded in here. And you look hot, Will. Let's go to the patio," she said, her hand moving to his forearm, the grip feeling hot on his skin.

"Thanks, but I need to stay in here and mingle. You know, being a host and all."

"Sure. Of course. Aren't you glad the weekend is almost here? Have any plans?"

Nick, his other associate, walked up. Will pulled away from Eleanor's grip and clumsily extended a hand to Nick, spilling some wine in the process.

"Mind if I join you guys?" Nick asked.

"Glad you could make it, Nick."

"Glad to be here. Hello Eleanor. Nice to see you."

"Likewise, Nicolas," she said. Her voice sounded like a freezer door opening. The place where she'd grasped his arm now felt very cold.

"So, did Global Trading back down on their demands?" Nick asked. "That's what tomorrow's meeting is about?"

"Not completely. We offered a small compromise, but we also demanded that the agreement be signed before Monday. So they're flying over right now to be here tomorrow and stay as long as it takes."

Eleanor's expression changed. Will had discussed his adjustment mechanism with her but he'd only told Nick about the meeting. There was an awkward silence.

"I haven't made it to the bar yet," Nick said. "Let me get you refills while I'm over there."

"How nice of you," Will said.

"Likewise," Eleanor said, thrusting her glass at Nick as he departed. Her face now was hard, her eyes cold, the seduction in them gone. "So, we have a meeting tomorrow?"

"Yes. I'm very sorry, Eleanor. I should have told you already, but I left the office early."

"No big deal. What time?"

"First thing in the morning. They won't arrive until noon, but we can get organized and then go through my draft of the compromise provision, the one we talked about and I sent you this afternoon. The more eyes on it, the better."

She looked off into the distance, and he wanted to kick himself. Was she thinking he valued Nick more than her? And had she just been a bit forward with him? She'd not done anything like that before. The sweat on his body was cooling. It had been nice, her flirtations, he had to admit. He was lonely, his wife away and Mason being aloof that afternoon. Thoughts of an amorous adventure came to him. Nothing wrong with thoughts like that, his psychiatrist had told him. She smiled, as if she saw the bulge beneath his slacks.

"Fine," she said. "Excuse me a minute. I have to go say hi to someone."

His spirits fell when she walked away. But being horny in public was a damn nuisance. He wished he could go home, maybe get drunk on the couch watching TV.

"Where'd she go?" Nick asked, when he returned.

"She spotted someone, I think."

"She seems a little edgy tonight, not herself."

"Probably my fault. I hadn't told her yet about the meeting tomorrow."

"Oh, sorry I brought it up. I didn't think."

"I may have hurt her feelings."

"She'll get over it. Here she comes."

Eleanor walked toward them. Her dress was made of a shiny silver material that sparkled, fitted to the curves of her body and moving with it when she walked. Will checked to be sure his blazer was buttoned.

"Thanks so much, Nick," she said.

"No problem. By the way, what's our table number? I heard at the bar it was on the back of my name tag, which I neglected to pick up on my way in."

"What?" Will was still hypnotized by her dress.

"It's table two. Will is lost without his wife," Eleanor said.

"Good thing Nora is here," Nick said. "I'll meet you at the table. There's a friend of mine from W&K I want to catch up with."

Will knew he should move away also, make an excuse, go to the men's room, but the recurrence of his erection stopped him. He didn't want to leave, the desire was so pleasurable. The whole thing was ludicrous. Eleanor was only having fun at his expense. He could be grandiose in his imagination, but when it came time to act, he didn't have an ounce of confidence, nor would it be even remotely appropriate.

"Eleanor, how about we go find the table?"

"Let me ask you something, Will. If we were alone together, would you still call me *Eleanor* instead of Nora?"

Yes, of course I would, was what he wanted to say. It was accurate, even if at odds with his desire to jump into bed with her. She moved closer and grabbed his forearm again. The lawyer in him thought to say, *that's a moot question*. How absurd! The right response was *thanks anyway but no*. How to say that without hurting her feelings? He drank off his wine and smiled at her. It was entirely unexpected to be in such a position, where he should say no to what he'd pictured in his dreams. He desperately wanted to say *Yes. I would gladly call you Nora. I'll prove it. Right now!* The next response that jumped into his mind was, *I'll have to give that some thought*. He was sweating again. Like a pig.

⌒

Lyn was chatting with two associates. She'd tried to make eye contact with Will, but he hadn't noticed her because he'd been so busy flirting with the young woman associate, whose name she struggled to remember. The associates were talking about baseball. Astros and Indians.

"Who is that young woman with Will Baines?" she asked, interrupting them.

"Eleanor Sorel," Nick said, as they watched Eleanor grab Will's arm. "She's normally very buttoned up and not usually like that."

Of course. She remembered the young woman now from Will's office. But she'd been wearing a baggy sweater then. Will's wife had made a joke when she'd asked Lyn to go to the benefit with Will. "You'll need to keep your eye on him," she'd said. But Lyn didn't think she'd meant anything like this. Was it what it seemed? Regardless, it was time to intervene, time to rescue her friend's husband. From himself, most likely.

She handed her empty glass to a passing waiter, and in a few seconds she was next to Will. "There you are! I've been looking all over for you. What kind of a guy doesn't find his date right away? Hi Eleanor. I'm Belinda Larkin. We met last Saturday at the Global Trading meeting," she said, putting one hand on Will's shoulder, offering the other to Eleanor.

"Of course," Eleanor said. Game over, Lyn thought. But Eleanor was no longer looking like a seductress. It was hard to tell in the ballroom light, but it appeared that her face was flushed from embarrassment.

"I was worried you were going to stand me up, Will, and I'd be sitting at the table with no one next to me," Lyn said, and a gong sounded. "And you see! It's time to sit down!"

"You're at our table?" Eleanor asked.

"Of course. I'm Will's date."

"I was just going to look for you," Will said. "I should've found you as soon as I got here. Sorry."

"You're too sweet, Will."

The gong more insistent now, the crowd was dispersing, sliding around tables, looking at numbers, like the shore birds at Los Pelicanos, the ones with the long orange bills that walked around the rocks at low tide, looking for crabs. Lyn took Will's arm. Eleanor's dress was pretty, and Lyn was envious. She couldn't bare her shoulders anymore, the skin no longer smooth. Just a few years ago she'd been bold enough to wear a dress like that, but not tonight. That irked her.

"I just heard from Nick that the Global Trading guys are showing up at noon," she said to Eleanor. "Just like Gerald not to let me know their schedule. He'll probably tell me in the morning."

"Sorry," Eleanor said. "He's so rude."

"Not your fault, dear."

Lyn wanted to slap herself, calling Eleanor *dear*, something an old woman would do. So she drew Will closer to her, something an old woman wouldn't do, feeling the heat from his body, and a small trembling. The man whapped the mallet against the gong right next to them, and Will jumped like a cat on hot pavement.

"We should get to the table," Will said.

"I'll meet you there. I need to stop at the ladies first," Eleanor said.

They walked in the opposite direction, toward table two. Will walked stiffly, like a toy soldier.

"So how long has Eleanor been an associate?" Lyn asked.

"Only two years."

"She seemed a little distracted. I hope everything is okay?"

"I told Nick about the meeting but forgot to tell her. I feel bad."

"Associate politics are difficult," Lyn said. She felt a little peevish at dealing with Will's formality and his associate's flirtatiousness, if that was what it was. Her hormone levels were still raised from Mexico. What a thrill to spring up naked in the mornings and go to the porch to look for the pelicans. The memory pushed aside her annoyance, restored her positivity.

"Sorry I didn't get back to you earlier, Will. My plane was very late and the office was crazy. Gerald showed up to interview landmen. I like your proposal to Global Trading, and I think it will get us there. Maybe a few tweaks. I can't tell you Gerald's reaction. He didn't tell me."

"I'm cautiously optimistic," he responded.

"Good. One of us should be. I'm not such a cautious person."

"I doubt that."

"How can you say that? Don't I strike you as footloose and fancy free? I just snuck off to Mexico. That's pretty good for an old woman like me. I'm acting like I'm your age."

"I'm not at all daring, to tell the truth. I'm happiest at home with my dog. And you're not that old, by the way."

"Oh, you're sweet to say that. But I'm so much older than you. And I was like you not long ago. All work. No fun. Things have changed for me. Not for the worse. Not at all. But very different. I'm thinking about doing completely new things. The firm will make me retire soon, and I want to be ready." A bit of hyperbole, she thought. But it was okay. The boy needed to lighten up. That's what he was, a boy kicking a can down the sidewalk because he had no friends.

"That's my biggest fear," Will said. "I wouldn't know what to do with myself if I didn't go to the office."

"Yeah, I remember feeling that way. You should find a really good hobby right now, before retirement is upon you. Take your mind off the office now and then. Think big!"

Lyn wondered how suddenly she'd come to talk about her retirement like this, something that had scared her to death just a few days before. Jay could turn out to be a promising alternative for the office. But was he going to call her? What time was it at Los Pelicanos? She looked at her watch. And then she remembered the story about old Colonel Baines, who'd kept going to the office after he retired. He was found slumped over in a stall in the men's room, with a dirty asshole and clutching the *Wall Street Journal*. It wasn't a story to tell Will. That would be coming on too strong.

"I'd like to believe that," Will said. "But I can't imagine what I might do for a hobby. And thinking big makes me anxious."

"You're already anxious. Could it be worse?" She was pretty good friends with his wife. It was funny, she thought, how women so many years apart in age could be friends. Men not so much. The silent formality. Regardless, she knew that Will's wife wouldn't object if she badgered him a bit.

"Maybe not, but I don't know, trying something new always makes me feel naked. I worry that I will just embarrass myself."

"You can go be a nudist for a while. That might cure your self-consciousness!"

Amused to envision him walking around naked, she studied his reaction. Alarmed, hesitant, worried that she wasn't kidding. He was such a stiff man.

"That's not really me," he said.

"You wear pajamas to bed. Don't you?" she asked.

"Of course I do. What if there was a fire?"

She saw that he was nervous, talking to this old woman about nakedness, she having fun at his expense. "But sleeping nude could be thrilling. Don't you think?" she asked, her voice casual, like they were discussing the weather.

"I suppose."

"And you know, it wouldn't hurt you."

"What wouldn't?"

"Oh. Being naked, of course! Now who's my other seatmate?" she said, looking for the name card at the place next to her.

⌇

Will motioned to a waiter to fill his wine glass, his third. His face was hot from the naked women crowding his imagination, first Eleanor, and now Lyn. He closed his eyes for a moment and, when he opened them, saw that Lyn wasn't naked. She was conservatively dressed in an embroidered blazer over a baby-blue silk blouse. Her conversation with the people on the other side of her was animated. He sat back and looked around the room.

The sound in the ballroom was clamorous. The food service staff dashed in every direction, delivering drinks, then salads, and, finally, preparing for the great rollout of rubber chickens or stiff beef medallions. A swarm of bees making their way through a flower garden. Lyn turned back to him.

"Did you just return to Houston today?" he asked her. "I'm sure the last thing you wanted to do tonight was attend a benefit."

"Not at all. I've been looking forward to it. But I'm still on Baja time. If I wasn't here, I would be sitting at home watching reruns and wondering when I would get tired enough to go to sleep."

"Yeah, you said Mexico a minute ago. But I thought you went to San Diego," he said.

Her eyes widened. "So did I! It was a bait-and-switch by the man I was visiting."

"How's that?"

"He hadn't told me he lived in Baja. It scared me at first. You've probably heard all the stories about cartels murdering people. It's nothing like that, really."

"Well, you're back alive."

"That's for sure."

The woman on her left said something and Lyn turned to her. It annoyed him, going in and out of conversations, losing his train of thought, wondering if he should lean in to Lyn's conversation or strike up one with the person on his right. He didn't like parties, being distracted repeatedly for the sake of politeness. Like a dog under the table waiting for a morsel to fall, he brooded, multiple conversations going around his table, none of them including him. Across the table, Eleanor looked at him and smiled. He knocked back the rest of his wine and raised his glass for a refill by a passing waiter. He should stop drinking the wine, he knew. Imagining sex with Eleanor was something he should also stop doing.

Finally, a platoon of waiters descended on the table, armed with the salad course. Will's moment of misery was broken, if only for a moment, and he lifted his fork to address tangled, parmesan-sprinkled green patches on his plate. New conversations started, but none with him. He ate his salad quietly, thinking he might go home right after the main course.

~

Leaving her salad fork where it lay, Lyn thought to turn back to Will but held off. He was out of sorts, that was apparent. Why that was didn't matter. She was only meant to sit next to him, she thought, not make him happy. But she felt sorry for him. Mexico had been happy for her. The week raced through her mind like a time-lapse of a flower blooming. The waves, the wind, the sea air, each an idyllic image. And the sex! Not to forget that! Was it sex that was bothering Will, the come-on from the young woman across the table? She saw Eleanor smile at him. It happened all the time, partners sleeping with associates. She hardly knew Eleanor, but she couldn't picture her doing that. There was something else going on.

"Were you at a resort?"

"What?" She'd been lost in her thoughts.

"Where you stayed in Mexico?"

"Oh no. The man I went to see lives in a house on the beach in Baja, south of San Diego."

"Right. Sorry. You said that earlier. Was it near Cabo?"

"Oh, no. Cabo is almost a thousand miles south, down at the tip of the peninsula."

"I should probably look at a map."

"Oh, there aren't a lot of towns in Baja."

Lyn liked that Will was so guileless. Most men didn't consult maps, or at least they wouldn't admit to it. The man seated on the other side of her was silently inspecting an empty wine glass, his hair combed back, an over-the-hill swashbuckler in a bad pirate movie, with his spongy jowls and a belly that hung over his belt.

"What?" Will had spoken and she hadn't paid attention again.

"I said I don't know more about Mexico than what I've seen in Cabo."

"Baja Norte is a different place. The tourist industry is small, and the tourist places are easy to avoid," she said, but remembering the gringo men, actually more boys than men, probably college students, fraternity guys, in the Los Pelicanos rental houses, standing on balconies at night drunkenly laughing in staccato ha-ha-ha-ha's, the braying of donkeys, rude manners and empty heads. She'd wanted to slap their faces. The pirate next to her had probably been one of them when he was younger.

"And your friend lives there? Is he Mexican?"

"No. He's not, though he fits in quite well there!" she said, and laughed. "I'm sure you've heard of Jay Jackson? He was an energy lawyer at my firm's office in New York before he retired."

"Actually, I met him a long time ago, when I was an associate. And coincidentally, he just recommended me to a prospective client. You probably know Anna Stegineo?"

"Never heard of her."

"That's strange. She's the CFO for a Branoble portfolio company. Why did Jay refer her to me and not you? Don't you do work for Branoble?"

"Not exactly. I only represent companies they own. And portfolio companies always want to go their own way," she said, unsettled at the thought that Jay would refer someone to Will, especially a woman. Jay didn't like Branoble, she thought, although he'd not said so directly. Maybe the woman was difficult, and he was sparing Lyn the aggravation. Or was he thinking that a new client would make it more difficult for her to retire? It made her feel good, in an odd sort of way, that he might see an opportunity to broaden the chances for their relationship.

"That's what she said."

"Anyway, Jay is retired, which is what will happen to me soon. So I don't really need a new client."

"Doesn't Jay live in Austin? I heard he has a ranch there."

"He does, in San Saba, west of Austin, but he's living in Baja at the moment."

"You didn't say who you were going to see. I would've never guessed it was him."

"You didn't ask."

"That wouldn't have been polite."

"Okay. I admit it. I was circumspect about the whole thing," she said, looking around to see if anyone was listening. "I don't like people talking about me."

"I'm not one to gossip."

"Oh, of course not."

"And maybe you shouldn't care what people say. He's not at your firm anymore. He retired. Right?"

"Yeah. Maybe I'm being a little paranoid. And what would the firm do, anyway? Ask me to leave? They're about to make me retire anyway."

"Surely they'll let you stay past the mandatory age. They'll be stupid not to."

"You know, just between us, I'm not sure I want to. My trip to Baja made me wonder whether it's time to make a change in my life," she said, looking around for listeners again. "But don't tell anyone that. Houston can be a small town in some ways."

"Of course. I won't tell a soul."

"I never thought it would happen, but I think I've had enough of my career. I want to do things that are fun and exciting," she said, feeling strange at saying it out loud.

"And, not stressful."

"Well, maybe a little stress is okay if in pursuit of a good cause. Don't you think?"

"Actually, I don't like to be anxious. I sometimes get anxious about being anxious, if that makes any sense."

She laughed. "That sounds dreadful."

"It is," he said, and she saw him glance across the table in Eleanor's direction.

He isn't joking, she thought. His wife had told her that he could sometimes twist himself in a knot about tiny disappointments. She watched him wave to a waiter for another glass of wine. He was lonely, she decided, with his wife out of town.

"When is your wife back?"

"Don't know. Her mother is in a coma, so it may not be soon."

"It must be lonely," she said, and put her hand on top of his, dismissing a thought that she shouldn't, that touching him could be considered inappropriate under the circumstances.

"Thanks," he said. "I'm getting by. My dog is good company. You've met Mason, I think."

"That I have. He's unforgettable."

The waiters barged in with the entrees, a droning speech from the podium accompanying them. Nothing could be said while they were required to listen and to chew the overcooked food. When the ritual was over, she saw that the pirate at her left had little bits of beef fat on his plate, chewed into balls. A button in his shirt was undone, and his beer belly leered out from it, a splotch of salad dressing encrusted on his stomach hair. She swallowed hard, thinking she might gag.

Eleanor's face was flaccid, her gaze directed at nothing. Could she be drunk? Lyn imagined Jay saying, *That woman will be pissin' in her boots before she makes it home.* She liked how he was so free with his cowboy aphorisms. How had he managed at Princeton? The incongruity made him attractive.

Will slouched in his chair, looking comatose. The band began to play. She expected he planned to go home when others left the table to dance. His being home with Mason, watching TV, being too drunk to read, made her sympathetic.

"Qué pasó?" she asked.

"Oh, you know there's a ritual that takes place now," he replied. "One dance is obligatory but everyone wants to see who will go first."

"Really, Will. You have everything sorted out, don't you? Are you so analytical all the time?"

"I guess I am. I can't help it. I like to know what happens next."

"That probably makes you a damn good negotiator. And I should mention that you did a wonderful job in our meeting last Saturday with Gerald."

"Thanks. I don't like being as hard-nosed as I was."

"You can't have it both ways, Will. Gerald's intransigence required a like response, which you did so gracefully. I would've been shouting at him."

"Maybe we shouldn't talk shop," he said. "For me, the office has been difficult. Everyone seems to have an opinion about the stupid ownership guaranty, as if it wasn't hard enough dealing with Gerald."

"Oh, Will," she said. "That's just life in a law firm. Someone is always minding your business, thinking they know better."

"Right. Sometimes I wish I'd chosen a different profession."

"Oh come on, Will. Isn't that like throwing out the baby with the bathwater? Every career has problems. Besides, it's wrong to paint the profession with the bad actions of a few incorrigibles. Isn't it?"

"I don't know that it's only a few. Many lawyers advocate what they don't believe, to keep their clients. We are all complicit by tolerating their bad behavior."

"Surely that's hyperbole, Will. Nothing is so absolutely backward as that," Lyn said. He was getting himself riled up. And for nothing. Too much wine, maybe. Belligerent drunks made her uncomfortable. She thought of that creepy man at Los Pelicanos named Joe.

"Ah, you're just too forgiving. It's like this. You tell a lawyer he can claim five dollars if he flips a coin and it turns up heads. He flips and it turns up tails. So he flips it some more until it turns up heads and then he claims he should get his five dollars. He thinks he isn't cheating because he hasn't lied. Some of my partners don't even flip the coin once. They just demand the five dollars. The numbers are bigger, of course. It's a virus, really, and it's spreading through the profession."

The look on his face made it clear he wasn't kidding. He'd had a lot to drink, and he was still drinking, a blurred edge on his words, his logic distorted. She needed to lighten up the situation.

"Well I hope you can offer me a cure if, as you say, the practice of law is a virus."

"I wish I had one. If I had a pill, I would swallow it immediately."

Now there was resignation in his voice. It disheartened her. She wanted to grab his shoulders and shake him. How could he be so cynical? Broad indictments of lawyers usually struck her as funny, but he was dead serious. "Just don't do anything rash, Will. Maybe Mason has an idea?"

"He does. It's to put his head under the couch, same as I've been doing."

She laughed. "Now that's a smart dog! It's best to just avoid bad people. Right?"

"I know, but it's hard to ignore such things in my own firm. You're probably thinking I should shrug it off, like water off a duck's back."

"I've never liked that expression," she said. "It's another way of saying grin and bear it, and that's not me. But, hey, we're talking shop. I have a better idea."

Music playing louder now, her nerves a bit jangled from having not eaten much, wanting to put an end to this awful conversation, Lyn felt adventurous, pushing back her chair, standing up, looming over him, hands on hips, demanding. "Let's dance, Will."

"Wait," he said. "We'll be the first ones out there."

"Exactly! Someone has to do it."

Lyn walked in the direction of the dance floor, leaving him no alternative but to follow her. Once there, he gingerly took her into a formal dance position. But she grasped his hand tightly and pulled herself toward him, stopping just before their bodies collided. No way she wanted him to think he was dancing with his mother. To her surprise, he didn't freeze up or back away from her. A Lyle Lovett song, an easy two step, making her feel good, and she pulled him closer. Heads turned in their direction, her partners' wives narrowing their eyes, cats looking through a fishbowl's glass. Was she imagining that?

"I don't mean to be personal, Will," she said into his ear. "But you should really lighten up about work. You have many years to go."

"It's okay," he said. "So we can be friends? If we're going to be personal and all."

"Well, of course," she sang. "Good friends."

His innocent request, her laugh too loud, more heads turning in her direction, an encouragement to her defiance, she pulled herself even closer to him, erasing the gap between them. Her hand slid a few inches across the top of his shoulder until it brushed the hair on his neck just above his collar. No conversing needed for now, her breasts against his chest, a pleasurable warmth radiating inside her.

It was only dancing that she intended, maybe sensual, but not necessarily sexual. And what if she was enjoying it? Nothing wrong feeling that way, particularly when it was generated by empathy. Or so she told herself. She just felt so much fondness for him. She wasn't going to drag him up to a room. She saw him turn his head in the direction of several women, and suspected that their glaring threatened him. But it emboldened her.

"Maybe we were a little hasty coming out here first," he said.

"We'll just be the talk of the party," she replied.

"Will that be a problem for you?"

"Not in the least."

"Okay," he said.

They continued to dance, other couples now on the dance floor, the music faster. Suddenly it was if they were going slow in the fast lane, the others younger, dancing wildly, arms and bodies barely avoiding collision. And then he was holding her too close. "Good time to retreat, Will," she said into his ear.

"Gracias por la danza," he said, as he stood back and bowed.

"El gusto es mío."

Back at their table, several of her partners' wives, gathered near the bar, looked her way, one wearing a horrible green dress that was too tight. Should she go over and ask them what they were looking at? Instead, she smiled and waved at them, confronting them with friendliness. It made her feel like she'd just taken a shower after falling in some mud.

Distracted as she'd been by the women, she hadn't noticed that Will was leaning close to her. Their shoulders were actually touching. And then his hand was on her leg. She thought to brush it off, quickly, but she just looked at him instead, hoping he would offer a good explanation, that it wasn't what it seemed.

"Lyn, since we're now good friends, maybe we should get out of here and go somewhere quieter to get to know each other better," he said, his voice tentative and barely audible.

The bleary eyes of a drunk or the confused request of a lonely man, she didn't know which. It didn't matter, of course. She was sympathetic and guilty, for she clearly had encouraged him, pulling him close on the dance floor, confiding in him about her trip to Mexico. Whatever. It was water under the bridge. She gently pushed his hand off her leg.

"Oh Will, don't be silly," she said, sliding away from him, making her voice sound as merry as she could. "They're playing all my favorite songs. Let's stay right here and talk some more over coffee and dessert."

A waiter showed up, as if on cue, with coffee. Will nodded his head for the coffee, a morose look on his face, a small twitch on a cheekbone. Lyn had said no to many men, but she'd never before felt herself responsible for their propositions.

"Sure," Will said. "That sounds great."

His voice was flat, an invitation for her to jump back into her earlier garrulousness. Would that be throwing salt on the wound? Not knowing what to do, she decided they both needed a few minutes in their own space and pushed her chair back. "If you'll excuse me for just a minute, Will, I need to run to the ladies' room," she said.

"Sure. No problem," he said.

Almost sprinting toward the hallway where the restroom was, not waving to friends she passed or stopping to chat like she normally would, she fought back tears. The music was incredibly loud, but she felt her phone buzzing in her clutch bag. Shouting her name over the music, holding the phone to her ear, still moving toward the hallway door, as if she was escaping from a catastrophe, balancing her bag in the other hand, it occurred to her that running in heels could make for a real disaster, but she didn't care.

"Julius Jackson here," the caller said.

"Jay?"

"The very one."

"Hold on a second. I'm going to a quiet place," she said, turned around, and used her back to power through the hallway door. "There. Now we're good."

"You are simply amazing," he said.

"How so?"

"You're not back there a day yet, and you're out having a wild time. I didn't know you were a party girl."

She laughed. "I'm not having a wild time, Jay. It's a charity benefit."

"Ah. Well, I'm sorry to interrupt."

"You're not! I was just on my way to the ladies' room anyway."

"Okay. But you can go ahead if it's urgent and we can talk later."

"Fixing my makeup can always wait for a conversation with you."

"Good, then. I just got a call from my ranch and there are some matters there that I need to attend to right away. So I have to go back, maybe as soon as tomorrow. I'll know more after I make some more calls. And I just got a wild idea that you might want to come up there for the weekend. I know you just got back, and you're probably sick of the likes of me."

"Of course I want to! Are you kidding? How could I ever be sick of you?"

"Oh, I don't know. You seem to have lots of wild parties back in Houston. The ranch will be boring."

"Quit! I can't wait to see it. And already I need some peace and quiet."

"Really?"

Eleanor emerged from the restroom, looked at Lyn, smiled, and turned to the stairs down to the ground floor. Another woman behind her went back to the ballroom, letting out what was now howling from the dance floor. The Macarena. After the doors shut, Lyn said, "It's a long story I can tell you out in a meadow. How's that sound to you?"

"As good as the brisket Rosie will make for us."

"Sounds delicious. When will you know your timing?"

"I'll call you first thing in the morning."

"Can't wait!"

"Okay, go on back to your party then."

"Yeah. I guess I should. Thanks so much for the invite."

"My pleasure. Talk tomorrow," he said, and hung up.

A pause, one more of her difficult decisions, going to his ranch, made without a thought, her shoulders slumped slightly as several people came through the door, accompanied by a blast of music. She went into the ladies' room and looked at herself carefully in the mirror. It was embarrassing, how she'd enticed Will to suggest what he did. To give him a bit more time to get over it, she sat in a stall for about five minutes, looking at email on her phone. Then she went back toward the table, this time stopping on the way to say hello to friends. Will wasn't at the table when she got there. It was an easy decision for her to go home, saying her goodbyes to more friends. At the door, she looked around quickly for Will, thinking it would be rude not to thank him. But she didn't spot him. He'd been quite drunk. As she headed out to the parking garage, she hoped he went home in a taxi.

19.

THE SAME EVENING, THE SECOND of November, 2017, the Four Seasons Hotel, bringing two dark-colored drinks with ice in them, Eleanor sat down in Lyn's chair. When Will didn't notice her presence, she nudged him. It startled him. He turned to her.

"That's a Black Russian," she said, pointing to the drink. "Much better than coffee after dinner. It may perk you up a bit. You're looking a little down."

Feeling woozy the minute before, now his spirits rose after he took a drink, a smooth coffee taste, sweet. "It's good," he said.

"Where'd Ms. Larkin go?"

"The restroom, I think. Or maybe she went home. I don't know."

The past hour swirled in his mind, but he didn't want to remember it. Maybe he could make himself believe it'd never happened. A waiter put desserts on the table, orange sauce over cheesecake with a maraschino cherry.

"Will, I apologize for saying what I did earlier. It was so inappropriate. And I'm ashamed of myself." Eleanor said, her face red in embarrassment, tears welling in her eyes.

His first thought was to say he hadn't even noticed, but thought better. "Not to worry. It was no big deal," he said. Of course, it was a big deal to him, to believe if only for a moment that he was desirable.

"You're being kind. My boyfriend was supposed to fly down from Denver today for a long weekend, and he was supposed to come straight here from the airport. But he texted me right after I got here and told me he wasn't coming. It's no excuse, I know," she said, starting to cry.

"Hey, it's going to be fine," he said, putting his hand on her shoulder.

"Probably not," she said, shaking her head, sobbing slightly.

Will noticed several people glancing in their direction. He worried that Belinda would return and assume he'd also propositioned Eleanor, which had made her cry. "Let's take a walk out to the patio," he said. "It will make you feel better."

She nodded. They took their drinks and went to an adjoining patio space where cocktails had been served. There were a few small tables set up, and they sat down at one. Will found some cocktail napkins for her to use on her eyes. She sighed heavily.

"I'm so sorry," she said. "You've met David. You probably remember that he was supposed to come down last weekend and didn't. So he was coming a day early this weekend. I have another friend who lives in Denver, a law school classmate, same as David. She called me on Monday to tell me she'd seen him at a cocktail party last weekend, when he hadn't come to Houston because he had to work. He's been hanging around with a crowd of analysts from a private equity outfit in Denver. One of the women was hanging all over David, and my friend asked him what was going on. He's been impressed by this one private equity guy who my friend says leads a glamorous life. David told my friend he's tired of dull lawyers like me, that I'm too reserved and don't wear attractive clothes, like the women he's been hanging with."

"That's ridiculous. You're an interesting and attractive young woman."

"You're kind to say so. But evidently, he thinks otherwise. So I decided I would give him something to look at this weekend. I went to Neiman's and bought this dress, which is a bit much.

And I got carried away with the makeup," she said, sobbing. "I'm sure it's a wet mess on my face."

He handed her a few more cocktail napkins. "A little," he said.

"This is so humiliating."

"Nonsense. There is nothing to be ashamed about."

"So I'd come here thinking, 'I'll show him what an exciting girl I can be.' After I got the text, my first thought was to go home. Then I decided I would stay here in this awful dress and prove to myself that David was wrong. I drank a couple of shots of tequila but I couldn't get up the courage to talk to any of the guys. That's when you showed up. It was stupid. I thought you would be safe. I knew your wife had been gone all week, but I'd only intended to flirt with you. Then I just lost control. Thank god Ms. Larkin showed up before I made a complete ass of myself. And now you'll probably have me reassigned to another partner. What was I thinking?"

Eleanor sobbed again and leaned forward so that her hair fell in front of her face and he couldn't see the mascara streaks on her cheeks. He handed her more napkins. It perplexed him, that emotion caused the misplacement of reason. Was he any different? He'd thought it possible that he might see and touch Eleanor's naked body. The same with Lyn. He'd thought a tryst safer with her than with Eleanor. Many people let compulsion push them across a line drawn by reason. His horniness had compelled him to proposition Lyn. And he'd embarrassed himself.

"Eleanor, everything will be fine. If anyone even noticed you were acting strangely, they won't remember it tomorrow. And I certainly won't be telling anyone. But I wouldn't mind giving David a piece of my mind."

"He would only ask you more questions about Global Trading, that's all he seems to care about."

"He's still asking about that?"

"On Tuesday he asked what I thought about Ms. Larkin. He said his new private equity friend is involved somehow with the deal. I didn't answer, like you told me. Just said I couldn't discuss the deal. Maybe that pissed him off," she said, and sighed heavily.

Will shook his head, still feeling the jolt from the Black Russian, which strangely had ameliorated his inebriation. David was a prick. "What private equity company does his friend work for? Did he say?"

"Branoble Partners, I think. His friend's name is Erik. I don't know a last name."

"Branoble owns Global Trading," he said. "Erik shouldn't be talking to David about it."

Eleanor shrugged. "It is so screwed up that he didn't come down. I even reserved a room here. Checked in when I got here. You know, after I had him all hot and bothered with my new dress and my new attitude, I was going to take him upstairs and fuck his lights out," she said, her words a bit unsteady. "Oh, sorry, Will. That was crude."

Will laughed. "I'm not so old that I haven't heard stuff like that before."

"I know, but I don't talk like that, especially to a partner." She took out the card key to her room. "I should probably go upstairs and sober up before I say anything else stupid."

Will stood up when she stood up. They didn't move for a moment while she took a deep breath and pushed her shoulders back, mustering her muscles to walk. Then she leaned over and took off her heels. The movement made the dress over her breasts sparkle dramatically. He closed his eyes, but it was too late.

"I rarely wear shoes like this either," she said, holding up pumps with long heels. "Don't want to fall on my face until I get there."

He laughed nervously. "I can walk up there with you to be sure you make it."

"No, that's really not necessary. I'm sure you want to get home."

"No. Really. It will only take a minute."

"Okay," she said, and led him through a door with an exit sign over it that he hadn't noticed. They walked down a guest-room hallway to an elevator bank. She had to look in her purse for the paperwork.

"They don't put the room number on the card key," she said. "I can't even remember the floor."

"The same thing happens to me," Will said. "Even when I'm sober."

She laughed. The elevator came, and she pushed the number eight on the panel. But the elevator didn't move. "Oh, stupid," she said, and slid the card key into the slot and pushed the eight again. This time the elevator moved. At the room, she held the door open for him to follow her in, which he did, but thought he shouldn't. The room was large, a king-size bed, and a writing desk at one end next to a window through which Will could see the south side of downtown, a view of the Toyota Center. Eleanor threw her shoes on the bed. Then she walked into the bathroom, after saying, "I have to wash my face. I'm sure it's awful. I overdid the makeup."

There was nothing he could do but stand there. He had a full erection now, pushing hard against the front of his pants. His mind swirling with the events of the evening, he could hardly think at all, never mind make any decisions. She came out of the bathroom, her face scrubbed back to the one he was accustomed to.

"Will, I'm mortified to have put all my troubles on you. It was completely wrong."

"I'm happy you thought you could tell me. It was my pleasure to help, Eleanor," he said, shuffling his feet, trying to relieve the pressure in his pants. "I should be going now. Let you get some sleep."

"You look worn out too. Maybe you should take an Uber home."

"I think I've sobered up enough to drive."

"I can't thank you enough for listening to me."

She came forward and hugged him. He worried she might feel his erection. But he didn't care, it felt so good.

"I'm glad I don't have to drive," she said. "I guess I can thank David for that. I'm short enough to sleep on that couch, and you can sleep in the bed, if you don't want to drive home."

He thought he felt her breasts press against him. His lust surged. *Why not?* he asked himself, and his imagination took the dress off her, put her astride him, her breasts swinging elegantly as she pushed her hands through her hair. Then he returned to the present when she moved a tiny bit, only an adjustment of balance, but it caused his penis to rub against the inside of his pants, and he was too stimulated. Every inch of him burned. His control was lost before he could back away, and semen exploded into his underwear as he almost groaned, before releasing her. His embarrassment was immediate with the thought that she'd noticed.

"I really have to get home," he said, worried at how shaky his voice sounded. "The dog is probably in a panic being left alone. He needs a walk. You look fine now."

She laughed. "Poor Mason. You'd better go. I'm feeling fine. I think I'll just raid the minibar and watch some TV."

"Good night," he said, and she closed the door. Then he hurried, almost ran, down the hallway to the elevators. His underwear stuck uncomfortably to his groin and he buttoned his coat, worried that a wet spot was soaking through. One more humiliation. Not wanting to run into Belinda, he moved quickly through the lobby and across the street to his car in the garage. He sat for a minute before starting the engine. When he got home, after he let Mason out to the backyard, he would clean himself up and put on his pajamas. He would never sleep naked. Tonight he might not sleep at all.

Ruben Sanchez had boarded the plane to Houston after Brashner, arriving at the last minute, just before departure. Sanchez passed through first class without acknowledging him. And then he saw him again, checking into the Four Seasons Hotel. Ruben introduced the man with him, Larry Sutter. Brashner asked them to have breakfast in the morning. They declined.

Too early to go to bed, Brashner went to the cocktail lounge just off the reception area, where he saw a sexy woman go to the bar and speak to the bartender. Eleanor had returned to the ballroom to retrieve her phone that she thought she'd left at the bar when she'd bought the Black Russian for Will. It wasn't there, but she ordered another Black Russian. Brashner got to the stool next to her just in time to hear her order the drink and witness her dress sparkle during her mounting of the bar stool.

"Make that two," Brashner said to the bartender. "And put the young lady's on my tab."

"Oh no," she said, and quickly gave the bartender some cash. "I won't be here long. Just waiting for someone."

Her voice didn't match her dress, Brashner thought. And she'd barely looked at him. That made her all the more appealing, a challenge. "Looks like there's a big party going on up there," he said to her, making small talk.

"It's a charity benefit," the bartender said, as he put down the drinks.

"Weren't you having a good time?" Brashner asked Eleanor. "I mean, you're sitting here and not up there."

"How do you know I was up there?" Her voice was hostile.

"I assumed so. The dress you're wearing doesn't look like something you'd wear barhopping."

She shrugged and tossed her hair back. "You're right. But it was too loud, so I decided to come out here to wait for my boyfriend. He'll be here soon to pick me up."

"What a shame the band has to play so loud," he said, and spent a moment for a better assessment, her coral-colored lipstick, her perfect manicure, the Manolos on her feet. "I'm here from New York on business. Ever been there?"

She looked at him now, but her demeanor was hardly friendly, more like he'd insulted her with his question. "No."

Eleanor looked away, and Brashner noted that her hand was clenching her glass. The woman was an ice cube in a sexy dress, he decided, and he wouldn't be persuading her to go upstairs with him, no matter how charming he was. Suddenly the music stopped in the ballroom, and people began emerging from the doorway.

"Too bad the party's over," he said.

"I'm going to find my friends," she said, dismounting the bar stool and leaving most of her drink in the glass.

Brashner shrugged and signed his tab. The beautiful girl was no doubt a prudish Texan, probably working for a second-rate Texas bank, waiting for someone to marry her. He wondered what her boyfriend was like, as he looked at a few men milling about the lobby area, some of them wearing cowboy boots.

Brashner lingered over his drink for a few minutes and then rode the elevator up to the eighth floor, where he was surprised to find Eleanor getting off an adjoining elevator. He couldn't believe his luck, and he quickly went down the hall before her, gambling that the room she was going to was beyond his. She was still behind him as he feigned his card key not working in the lock.

"Lucky to run into you," he said, when she reached him. "I can't seem to get my key to work. Maybe I'm doing it wrong. Could you give it a try?"

Brashner made his voice proper and cordial. Eleanor looked at him skeptically, and he thought she was going to bolt down the hall. But she took the card key and slid it into the lock. It had worked to his advantage that she was a Texan, he thought, probably raised to be polite to an old man in difficulty. The green light flashed and she pushed the door open a bit, turning to him to hand him back the key.

"Let me repay your kindness with a glass of an exquisite brandy I have in my room," he said.

"No thank you," she said, still holding out his keycard.

He saw her look down the hall, and he feared someone would come along and she would call out. She started to back away, but he grabbed her wrist, causing the keycard to fall to the floor. He didn't need it. The door hadn't shut. He pushed her inside and closed the door behind him with his foot. Then he grabbed both her arms just below her shoulders.

"What do you think you're doing? Are you crazy? Let go of me."

He pulled her toward him, thinking he would push his mouth against hers and she would relent. But he saw that the look on her face had become fierce and he feared she would bite into his lips. So he held back.

"I know you want this. That's why you came on to me in the bar," he said, his voice hoarse with desire.

"I did no such thing," she stammered.

"So you want to keep playing the game," he said, walking her backward into the room.

"Let me go," she shouted.

Brashner had to stop her shouting. A guest in a neighboring room might call the front desk. He hurled her onto the bed so abruptly that her shoes fell off, such a small girl, no match for a man like him. She struggled to get off the bed. He yanked one of the pillows free, threw it on the bed, grabbed her arm as she got on her feet, turned her around, and bent her over, her face in the pillow and her feet on the floor.

"Stop," her muffled cry came from the pillow.

After Brashner finished, Eleanor fell to her knees and kept her face buried in the pillow for a moment. He saw her hands trembling, which he took for the great excitement she was still feeling. Bruises on her hips were already showing from how hard he'd grasped them, but he didn't notice. When her breathing slowed a bit, she stood up shakily. "You bastard," she yelled, turning to him and smoothing the front of her dress, finding her shoes and purse, walking out the door, but leaving her panties behind.

Brashner chuckled when he noticed them. A memento, he thought.

20.

THE NEXT MORNING, THE THIRD of November, 2017, Houston, Lyn's phone vibrated as she was about to leave her house for Will's offices. She was sure it was Jay, but the phone had slid down to the bottom of her bag and she couldn't find it amongst all the things she had in there. Frantic, she sat down on the floor and emptied everything in her bag onto the floor next to her.

"Hello," she said, out of breath.

"Catch you at a bad time?" Jay asked.

"I'm sitting on the floor," she said. "I had to pour out everything in my bag to find my phone. Now I'm surrounded by trash. It's embarrassing. Good that you can't see it."

"Why, I'd never think you were trashy, darling," he said.

"Oh, isn't it nice of you to say so."

"My pleasure. So, I'll be at the ranch late tomorrow afternoon. But you can drive up there whenever you like. Or, if you want to fly to Austin, I can have someone go to the airport to get you."

"I'm going to drive. But I might be delayed by these negotiations that start today and go until we finish. I can't see them going longer than the weekend. You know how it is. Lots of posturing and then lots of compromising when the clothes get dirty. I hope you're staying at the ranch for a while."

"For as long as it takes. Whenever you can get there will work. But plan to stay a few days. You can always drive into the Austin office if you need to do some work. It's not too far."

"You don't have internet in your ranch house?"

"Oh, hell. I've got a whole office full of stuff. Internet, fax machines, telephones. Anything you need. I hadn't thought of that. But you can go to Austin for appearances' sake if you need to."

"How could a girl refuse all those amenities?"

"And I also have laundry service."

"You may never get rid of me."

"Fine with me. I'm going to email you directions and the phone number at the ranch. When you call, Rosie will probably answer. She knows you're coming. I hope I wasn't presumptuous."

"Just don't make a habit of it."

"Wouldn't think of it," he said. "Not to push my luck, but I'm also thinking about going up to Raymond's farmhouse in New York next week to start an inventory. Any chance I could talk you into going with me? There is good birdwatching on the property. You can see hawks and owls on the trails."

That was a little presumptuous, she thought. What if she hated the ranch and wanted to return to Houston right away? Somehow their relationship had taken a leap forward without the occurrence of anything but a day's absence. A time of reflection can sometimes have such an effect, like a seedling popping through the soil overnight. But she'd had no such time, dealing with the Global Trading frenzy and then Will's awkward pass the night before. It seemed to her that only an hour had passed since their strained goodbye in the San Diego airport. This telephone conversation was one between longtime lovers, the tone soft, the manner playful, the plans to share a hobby, hawks and owls, and an old-time friend, Raymond. As appealing as it was to her, it was too fast, at least for the time being.

"I don't know," she said. "If we sign this agreement, I'll have a closing to prepare for."

"Get someone to cover. What will they do when you retire?"

"That's a problem for later. For this deal, it's probably impossible."

"Oh, Lyn, you have never thought anything was impossible. Will you at least think about it?"

"I guess it wouldn't be impossible for me to think about it."

"Good. I won't pressure you."

Right. He'd already done that. She associated Raymond's house with Jay's not calling her, a bad memory, and a long way to go in order to confront a demon. Her stuff was like a pool of vomit on the floor, but she began to pile it all back in her bag.

"How about we talk more when I see you? I'm running late. Why don't you text me as soon as you get to the ranch."

"Will do. Looking forward to seeing you."

"Me too," she said, and hung up.

In the car, she considered his New York proposal. She'd not even come to terms with going to San Saba, to tell the truth, a trip that in her mind was two years too late. And there were so many other things to think about today, like how to act with Will when she saw him.

Outside, a typical Houston mist hung in the air, one part humidity and the other petrochemical fog, the same as the day before, and the day before that. She sighed and remembered the glorious weather at Los Pelicanos. The car's air conditioning always chilled her, almost froze her arm from the vent on the dash, but she knew better than to crack the window. She fiddled with the temperature control. It was never right. The Chase Tower garage was crowded, and she had to drive up five floors to find a space. Just last Saturday it had only been two.

The receptionist directed Lyn to a small conference room. Her associate was already there, reading a copy of the revised draft of the agreement Will had left on the table. The plane carrying the Global Trading people was scheduled to land later that morning. Gerald was already in Houston, but she knew he would take his time getting there. He'd been a nuisance the day before with the landmen, badgering them about the process.

Suddenly, Lyn realized she didn't want to be there. She wanted to be driving to San Saba, not suffering through what she knew was coming in the meetings. And she was tired. She couldn't remember having ever felt so lethargic, the draft on the table looking heavy, too heavy even to lift, as she slid it over in front of her.

An hour later, Will came into conference room, wearing a stony face. "Good morning, Will," Lyn called cheerfully. Nothing had happened the night before, as far as she was concerned. He'd been drunk and she incautious. Regretting it would do no good.

"Edward Reid, our managing partner, wants to speak to us, if you have a minute," he said, his voice sounding like a car driving on gravel.

"Of course. I know Ed. We were associates together. Didn't I tell you that?" She was nervous, and talking just to talk, attempting to clean up the mess they'd made together.

"Probably," he said, avoiding eye contact, and then held the door open for her.

"Thanks again for a lovely time last night," she said, as they walked down the hall.

"I had too much to drink," he said. "I apologize for my behavior."

"Nonsense, Will. You were perfectly charming," she said, and then they walked in silence to Reid's office. It wasn't in her nature to demand accountability from a good soul, how she viewed Will. And the fault had been as much hers as his.

In his office, Ed Reid came around the desk and hugged Lyn before saying to Will, "We were associates together here."

"So I heard," Will said, and dropped into a chair at the small conference table.

"It was a very long time ago," Lyn said, sighing.

"Have you seen Jay Jackson recently?" Reid asked her, as he held a chair out for her. "I heard that he retired a few years ago."

"I heard the same," she said.

"Okay, let's get to the matter at hand," Reid said. "Patrick Brashner was in here earlier. He's all worked up because he doesn't think your deal is being handled well. He wants to take part in the negotiations. I'm guessing he's called you, Will."

"He called me too," Lyn said.

"That is odd," Reid said.

"It wasn't a big deal. I hung up on him after he threatened to call my client. He was probably insulted. I suspect he is a man who usually gets his way."

"Did he explain himself?"

"Oh, he thinks I am pushing too hard for a title warranty, and I should be telling my client to give it up to get the deal done. It wasn't clear which party was whose client when he was talking."

"This is bizarre," Will said. "It's one thing for Brashner to call me. But Lyn? He represents Global Trading, Lyn's client in this deal, on a litigation matter in New York. So we had to get a conflict waiver from ERIS in order to represent them in this deal. And in my conversation with Brashner, he told me it would be best for ERIS if they gave the title warranty requested by Global Trading. That's the opposite of what he demanded Lyn do."

"Brashner told me he was the lead partner for ERIS on our deal," Lyn said. "I disputed that as well, which made him angrier."

"This is disturbing," Reid said. "Was a conflict waiver signed by both parties? It should've been."

"I wouldn't know," Lyn said. "And Global Trading didn't mention to me that Stewart Baines was representing them in a litigation. That's not really a big deal to me, as long as it's unrelated and the lawyers don't overlap."

"Stewart Baines also represented them many years ago," Reid said. "Will's father did work for them back in the day. But I didn't know Brashner had a current matter with them."

"You're right," Lyn said. "I forgot that. So I'm sure you have a waiver from Global Trading too. But they were owned by a Japanese company back then, so the Stewart Baines client might have been that company. They are now owned by a company called Branoble. One of Jay Jackson's clients in New York. And I worked on their sale of some LNG terminals a couple of years ago."

"I don't know all the details, but we did get a waiver from them also," Will said. "This is all recited in an exhibit to the waiver document. I can ask my associate to bring it over."

"That would be great," Reid said. "Brashner is coming back here in a few minutes. I don't know how much of this history he knows."

"All of it, I'm sure," Will said.

"What does he want you to do?" Lyn asked.

"He wants me to tell you guys to include him," Reid said.

"Ah, an order from the top," Lyn said. "Poor you."

Reid laughed. "I told him I wouldn't do that. But I did agree to get the four of us together so he can he tell you why he thinks you're screwing up."

"Lovely," Lyn said. "Then he'll go back to New York?"

"I hope so."

"I don't get it," Will said. "He came down from New York to barge into a meeting, unannounced. That seems like a lot of trouble just to impress his friends at ERIS or Global Trading. It'll only piss off the guy from ERIS."

"I suspect he wants to make a big scene. Do you remember that the compensation committee meets next month? Brashner is notorious for claiming credit for matters with which he is only tangentially involved. I can hear him saying that he had to fly to Houston to keep the deal from falling apart."

"Ugh," Lyn said. "It's always about money."

"Yeah. It's unfortunate how that works. But could you two just humor me and let him talk for a few minutes? Maybe then he'll leave me alone and let you go back to your deal."

"Fine with me," Lyn replied. "I wouldn't mind connecting a face with a name. Besides, haranguing us in here may make him stay away from the meeting. I think my client will be pissed if he barges into the negotiations. And they're already being difficult. But I can't promise, Ed, not to challenge him."

"The whole thing is stupid," Will said.

Reid laughed. "No disagreement there. Can you humor me anyway? And Lyn, I've never known you to hold back and don't expect it here."

They took places around Reid's small conference table. Then Brashner came through the door without knocking. Lyn didn't offer to shake his hand, didn't even get up from her seat. That was going too far. She wasn't surprised that he wore a designer suit, and that he had a perfectly folded silk handkerchief in his breast pocket and a Jaeger-Lecoultre rectangular watch peeking out from a shirt cuff with gold cufflinks. He was short, really short. Standing, he was about the same height as Will was, sitting.

"You must be Ms. Larkin," Brashner said to Lyn.

"Yes," she replied. "What gave me away?"

"Okay, Patrick," Reid said. "You told me you wanted to talk to Lyn and Will about the ERIS transaction. Let's get through it so we can all go back to work."

"It's the *ERIS-Global Trading* transaction," Brashner said. "A very good deal for both parties if we can stop the silly posturing and make some compromises."

"Have you been posturing, Will?" Lyn asked.

"I'm not the posturing type."

"We all know that's not true," Brashner said. "You're both being obstinate concerning a silly assurance about ownership of properties. And I don't think your joking attitude here is very professional."

"Patrick, I didn't know you had experience with oil and gas agreements," Reid interrupted. "Or anything in the industry, for that matter. Do you have experience with mineral rights? That's what they call them in the oil business, if you didn't know."

"It doesn't matter what they're called. I know my way around negotiations. And I know what's good for my client, Edward."

"Which client would that be?" Lyn asked. "I don't want to look a gift horse in the mouth, Mr. Brashner, if you're support-ing my client's position to the detriment of your firm's client."

"I have represented both parties for many years, long enough to know when they're both about to mess up a good deal."

"Patrick, there's an ethical problem with your judging what is good for both sides," Reid said. "It sounds like that's what you're doing."

"My clients will consent to my intervention in order to reach a compromise," Brashner said.

"Then you've spoken to them? To both parties?" Lyn asked.

"That's none of your business, Ms. Larkin," Brashner said. "And you seem to think impertinence is going to help you. It's not. You aren't qualified to be representing Global Trading."

"Patrick, whatever your implication, Ms. Larkin is a respected partner at a firm as big as ours and, I might add, a highly regarded alumna of Stewart Baines," Reid said. "And in any case, this isn't germane to our issue. Maybe you could elaborate how you think this title issue should be handled."

"Compromise," Brashner stated. "Rather than simply refusing to give one or demanding a full one."

"We've offered the customary oil and gas title warranty," Will said.

"Obviously, my client doesn't think it is acceptable," Brashner said.

"Actually, your client proposed it, I believe," Lyn said. "Assuming your client and Will's client are one in the same."

"In fact, I wrote it," Will added.

"I'm sorry, Patrick, but I'm concerned with this exchange," Reid interjected. "You seem to think you are acting for both parties. I know I'm repeating myself."

"Your attitude is harming both parties," Brashner said, pointing a finger at Will. "You need to go into the negotiation and agree to Global Trading's full ownership guaranty. If you won't, I will take over the representation."

So the horse has left the stable, Lyn thought. He'd gone from compromise to demanding capitulation. "I should probably keep my mouth shut since what you're demanding is so good for Global Trading," she said. "But it's not making sense to me. Both parties are actively negotiating the point. And the deal isn't about to fall apart. Is it, Will?"

"Nope," Will said.

"You are both going to regret this," Brashner said.

"Patrick, I think you need to tone down the rhetoric," Reid said immediately.

"It's not rhetoric. I am totally justified in this." Brashner was leaning over the table now, pointing his finger at Lyn. She'd been in some difficult negotiations before, but nothing like this. It was going to make a good story.

A knock on the door, and Eleanor entered with a document. She handed it to Will, glanced at Brashner, and then took a step back, as if she'd been pushed. Lyn watched her struggle to keep her face impassive, and wondered whether Brashner had also been making demands to her for drafts.

"Eleanor, this is Patrick Brashner from our New York office," Reid said. "Patrick, this is Eleanor Sorel, one of our excellent young associates."

"Pleased to meet you, Mr. Brashner," Eleanor said, regaining her composure.

"Yes. Of course," Brashner said, not looking at her.

"Is that what you wanted, Mr. Baines?" Eleanor asked, turning to Will.

"Yes, definitely, Eleanor," Will said. "Thank you very much." He handed the document to Reid.

"Gerald and his associates have arrived at the conference room," Eleanor said. "But the other Global Trading people aren't here yet."

"I think we're done here," Reid said, and stood up. "Will, why don't you and Lyn go to the meeting and I will finish up with Mr. Brashner."

Lyn stood up and followed Will and Eleanor to the door. She could tell Ed wasn't happy. He was frowning as he looked at the waiver document. Brashner didn't appear that he was going to even acknowledge their departure. She turned and smiled at him.

"Mr. Brashner, I've heard much about you, and it was very good to put a face with the name," she said. "Adios. And y'all have a nice day."

21.

THE SAME DAY, THE THIRD of November, 2017, Los Pelicanos, Baja California, Jay sat on the bench at the curve of the malecón above the rock beach, the ocean calm, waves lapping the rocks, an eerie change from the customary sound of rocks grinding against each other. Thursday, after leaving Anna at the Sheraton, while driving back to Los Pelicanos, he'd decided. Time to move forward, return to his ranch life. His anonymity of two years had to end right away. He would go to New York. Get the interview done and an inventory of the Hatcher estate.

The first step, the easy one, was to call Lyn, which he did last night and this morning. She was now a part of his going home, as she had to be. Without her he was just a spy, playing at ranching and sometimes wandering the world, wondering why he'd done with his life what he had. It was a bad joke, thinking what might have been. If he'd not gone to Princeton, stayed in Texas, maybe gone to Rice, become a professor, married a nice girl, or just been a happy bachelor. If he'd not agreed to Raymond's proposition to join the CIA. If he'd buried Raymond and let it all be, rather than going to France. The sad truth was that he would do those things again. He had to own up to it and get his ass off the bronco, go home, and ride Patsy in the meadows.

He stood up and walked to the edge of the curve of the malecón that jutted out perpendicularly to the ocean, like a thumb on a hand, the fingers extending along the rock beach, in the distance a sandstone cliff on the top of which was a large area of grass. It reminded him of the ocean cliff in Thomas Hardy's *Far From the Madding Crowd* where the sheep fell to their deaths on the rocks below. Beyond the cliff loomed the big Jesus statue.

Tidal pools were on the left side of the thumb. A dozen birds had gathered there, hopping around the pools of water, snatching crabs and mussels, ignoring him, just as he wanted, so he could enjoy their resplendence. At the ranch, if he was patient and quiet, he saw chapparal birds doing similar things. These ocean birds were not typical oystercatchers. Their bills were orange, not red, with a slight curve, not straight. Were they oystercatchers at all? He'd not been able to find an exact match in his books. His heart twisted in his chest. Raymond would know what they were.

Jay grew tired of brooding and walked back toward his house. A bit farther, where the malecón was higher above another tidal field, he came upon the white egret, la garza blanca, always present when the tide was out, one leg crooked, its neck extended, as if it was pointing the way home. He'd taken solace from its appearance his first few weeks in Los Pelicanos, the bird's stateliness reminding him of Raymond, sitting straight on the edge of a chair on the porch of his farmhouse in Dutchess County, spying a cardinal, its flash of red coming from a tree across the field, while he listened intently to something Jay was saying. Jay had spotted another white egret in Vietnam, near Sa Pa. It was an area so vividly described in Raymond's journal, bloody red, a carnage sprayed in the jungle, where Captain Wright and his wife had died. Jay had rejoiced at the sight of that noble white bird, a symbol, he hoped, that before he died, Raymond had reconciled himself with the murder of the Wrights.

He quickened his pace, looking at his watch again, thinking he must depart soon to make it to Arizona before dark. He wasn't sure why he'd been moping down on the malecón. His phone rang as he stepped onto his patio, and he sat down.

"Julius Jackson," he answered.

"Is the cowboy still chasing dolphins or is he back on his horse where he belongs?" Anna asked.

He laughed. Why was she calling? "I'm an old cowboy and don't travel fast. But I'm about to head east."

"Good news. Can I come visit when you get there?"

"You'll have to give me a little time, like I said. I'm going to have a houseguest this weekend and then I'm going to go up to New York. But I'm sure you know all this. I made the phone calls in the clear."

"Oh, they only send me the transcripts when I ask for them. Cowboy talk bores me."

"Best I can do. I'm leaving shortly and driving to Texas and will probably spend the night near Tucson with an old friend of Raymond's from his OSS days. If I leave his place early tomorrow morning, I'll be in San Saba by dinner time. Easy."

"Sounds much better than hanging around Dallas looking at financial statements and meeting with accountants."

"Sitting on a horse is fun. And I know now that you know how to ride. We could ride out to that big tree I saw you behind."

"Hmmm. Sounds good. For tonight, I think I'll go home with a pizza and watch the horses in a few episodes of Westworld."

Jay thought that was unlikely. "Well, good luck with that," he said.

"Thanks. Drive safely." She hung up.

～

Jay drove east on Corredor Tijuana-Rosarito 2000, a road carved through desolate hills that became dotted with warehouses and small housing communities as it got closer to Tijuana. That city soon spread out in a small dusty valley, houses close together for as far as the eye could see. As he approached the intersection of Mexico Highway 2, which he planned to take to the Andrade Port of Entry not far from Yuma, Arizona, he thought about Ben Lufkin, a bureaucrat's bureaucrat who'd been the one behind the denial of Raymond's request that he continue after retirement from the Agency in an advisory capacity for a few extra years, more than likely because Lufkin saw Raymond as a threat to his authority at the time. It was probably unfair to think these things about Lufkin. The man was just doing his job. And frankly, it was a waste of time to be thinking about Lufkin at all.

An hour later, the dirty air hazy in the sunlight, an old car without a muffler puffing black smoke in front of him, Jay watched a black Ford with South Dakota plates in his rearview mirror follow him onto Highway 2. He'd first seen the car parked under the Cuota underpass near Los Pelicanos, and then noticed it behind him on Avenue 2000, which connected Rosarito with Tijuana, maintaining a good distance until slow traffic brought it closer. A coincidence, he thought, until at the tollbooth just east of Tijuana, the Ford got too close and he saw a familiar man sitting stiffly in the passenger seat, as if posture and sunglasses would disguise him. It was the young man with the white hair with whom he had tried to be friendly the morning he was going to pick up Lyn at the San Diego airport.

That man hadn't struck him as an Agency man, working with a surveillance team. Was Anna using this level of surveillance? Did these guys intend to follow him all the way to Texas? There was no sense in that, and Jay gave some thought to his route. He'd planned to continue on Highway 2 until he was at the border crossing near Yuma, Arizona, a long, winding, and remote stretch of road through desert. If they were Agency guys, that would be fine. But if they were a group with a nefarious purpose, it was a bad idea to expose himself in a remote place. Parnell was no longer a murder suspect in France, Anna had just told him. Were these men in the car behind him sent by Parnell for revenge? It wasn't impossible.

Jay couldn't see if there was a third man in the car, but that didn't matter. He decided that the best bet was to cross the border at Tecate and head for the interstate, find a truck stop, and make himself available in the café. That way, if they followed him in, he could go over, introduce himself, and have a nice friendly chat. He took the turn for the border checkpoint at Tecate, emitting a long breath through his nose, an unvoiced sigh. Spying was a stupid game.

Campo Road in California ran parallel to the border from Tecate to Interstate 8, with many desolate stretches, curves carved through chest-high sandstone, large outcroppings of rock, clumps of trees, and dirt roads through brush that seemed to go nowhere. Around a curve at a turnout to a dirt road, a man, wearing black jeans and a black T-shirt, next to a Chevy Suburban with its hood raised, stood waving his arms. Jay was sure the guy was with the guys following him, and his first thought was to keep driving. But he didn't much care to be followed all the way to San Saba. So he pulled over. When he was out of the truck, walking toward the man, he heard a car roaring up behind him, and looked to see the Ford pulling to a stop. When he turned back, the man who'd waved him down was holding a pistol. And now that he was closer, Jay recognized him as the man on the malecón on Wednesday night, the man named Joe.

"Move over here," Joe said, motioning with the pistol for Jay to go to the rear of the Suburban, behind vegetation and rocks, out of sight from the road.

"Hey, amigo, I'm only stopping to help," Jay said.

"Just move. If you want to be shot, I'm happy to do it," Joe said, pointing the pistol at Jay's knee.

"No need for that," Jay said, and heard the other men come up behind him.

"We meet again, Mr. Jackson," the man with the white hair said. He wore chinos and a blue collared shirt, neatly tucked in, sleeves rolled up to his elbows.

"Long time no see," Jay said. "But I'd prefer we catch up over some coffee. I know a diner up the road." The man smiled, didn't say anything.

"Shut up," Joe said. "You're not funny."

There were two other men, also in the black-shirt-and-jeans uniform. One must have been in the backseat of the Ford. They walked to Jay's truck and searched it. One of them had a tiny hitch in his step, a grimace on his face whenever he bent sideways to look in. After they'd taken Jay's bags out of the truck, one of them got in and started the engine, the other went to the Ford.

"Hey, that baby is brand new," Jay called to them. "Be careful with her."

"Shut up," Joe said again.

Jay turned to the white-haired man, who was clearly the boss. "And what was your name again? I don't think we were properly introduced last Saturday morning."

"Joe," he said, and smiled.

"Now isn't that a funny coincidence. You must be Joe Uno to his Joe Dos," he said, pointing to the man with the gun. "Or have I got that backwards?"

"Just shut the fuck up," Joe Dos said.

Jay's truck and the Ford disappeared down the dirt road. The two Joes tied his wrists and ankles with duct tape and then pushed him into the back of the Suburban, along with the things they'd taken out of Jay's truck. The other two men returned, walking up the dirt road, and once they were in the back seat, the Suburban accelerated onto Campo Road, heading east.

The two men who'd taken his truck joked about setting fire to it then rolling it into a ravine. Jay twisted himself to lay on his back, his head up against the wheel well, and watched the road signs: Campo Creek, Campo, the Campo Indian Reservation, Old Highway 80, and then Interstate 8, toward El Centro.

The loss of his new truck upset Jay more than his captivity. Whoever these men were, his life wasn't in danger yet. Much easier to transport a corpse than a hostage, so they would've killed him by now if that was the plan. After El Centro came Yuma, and then nothing but sand and odd billboards, an RV park ahead, best burgers at Gila Bend, no traffic. They pulled off at a rest area. The two Joes went to the facilities and the other two men stayed with him, unwrapping the tape around his wrist and ankles. His wrists were sore from the tape sticking to his skin. Then, the Joes back, they walked him to the bathroom, walking shoulder to shoulder with him, joking like they were friends. He stood longer than he needed to at the urinal, but no one came in. There were no other cars, only a big truck, idling for the air conditioning, the driver asleep. Back at the Suburban, they rewrapped the same tape on him. He'd brought back a paper towel, hoping to put it between the tape and the skin on his wrists. But they threw it on the ground.

"Sorry to hold you up, boys," Jay said, as they accelerated back onto the interstate. "But I'm an old man with a weak bladder. Can't help it, and I don't want to piss up the back of your car."

"Shut up," Joe Dos said.

"You have a wonderful vocabulary, son. Anyone ever tell you that?"

"You want us to tape your mouth too?" one of the men asked.

South of Phoenix, near Casa Grande, they turned onto Interstate 10 and then passed through Tucson, the signs saying Las Cruces, and sometimes El Paso. It was almost dusk now, a ridiculously long way to drive a hostage. But he'd managed to find a position that kept him from cramping up. The rewound tape was looser, so his wrists no longer stung. This was about as far from an Agency operation as he could imagine, the timing too slow, the risks of being seen too high. And the men didn't appear to be trained, the lazy manner in which they held themselves, one of them noticeably dragging a foot, his breathing labored after a short walk.

Late at night, what time Jay couldn't tell because Joe Dos had taken his watch, they exited to a small road, passed a few broken-down houses, and then drove another half mile on an unpaved strip until they came to an Airstream. They dragged him inside, unwound his wrists so he could use the bathroom—he had to hop in and out of it—sat him down in a chair, and rewound the same tape again on his wrist, but this time in front of him so he could hold the bottle of water they gave him. Some of the tape around his ankles was unwound and then rewrapped around the chair legs. The chair would accompany him if he tried to get up.

"Poland Spring," he said. "Why, that's my favorite. How'd you know?"

There was no response. Joe Dos and the two men flopped onto a couch and put their heads back. Joe Uno paced the room, reading messages on his phone, beyond him a towel on the kitchen counter, a rusty pot on the stove, a loaf of bread on a shelf, green mold visible inside its wrapper.

"Nice little place you got here," Jay said. "Must be nice to take it with you whenever you move. You never have to pack a suitcase, I bet."

"Shut up," Joe Dos said, not opening his eyes.

"Just being social," Jay said.

Joe Uno left in the Chevy. Joe Dos went to sleep in the bedroom area. The other two made themselves comfortable in the corners of the couch. It was going to be a long night, Jay knew, sitting in the chair. But he had to sleep if he was going to be of any use the next day. So he let his chin fall toward his chest and thought about the darkness of the ranch's meadows.

The next he knew, it was morning, and he heard birdsong mixed with a distant whine of big trucks on a highway. Then Joe Dos came out and banged some things around in the kitchen, swearing. "I hope he comes back soon with some food," he said, and ripped open a bag of chips.

It wasn't soon. About five in the afternoon, Joe Uno banged through the door with a pizza and two six-packs of beer. The two others were too hungry to complain, and they grabbed slices like schoolboys. An hour later, Joe Uno pulled the second chair over and sat in front of Jay. "Time to talk," he said. Finally, Jay thought, rotating his stiff neck in a circle, feeling the bones at the top of his spine crackle. He'd been sitting a long time.

22.

THE SAME DAY, THE FOURTH of November, 2017, the offices of Stewart Baines, Houston, the negotiations ended in the late afternoon and the agreement was signed. At noon, Lyn had sent a text to Jay that she planned to see him Sunday. Now six hours later, and no response. She texted again that the deal was signed. Where was he? She'd pictured him at the airport, boarding the flight to Austin, then three hours in the air and driving to San Saba, which she'd found on her maps app during one of the late-night breaks. And then it occurred to her that he'd not said he was flying. She sighed. Did that old cowboy have to drive his truck all the way to Texas?

An older man from Global Trading, the vice chair, had kept Gerald in line. Or they would still be arguing. He told her during one break that they'd met a long time ago, a matter when Global Trading was represented by Will's father, and Lyn had been his associate. She felt bad. She didn't remember. He was a very gracious man. And so it was impossible after the agreement was signed to refuse his invitation for a celebration the next day. His old friend Bennie, Will's father, was going to host a BBQ at his house in River Oaks on Sunday evening. Lyn texted Jay again, *Now I'm arriving Monday, not Sunday. Long story.* On Monday she planned to drive up Interstate 10 toward San Saba before the sun was over the horizon. Again, no response.

On their way to the elevator, Lyn and Will were stopped by Ed Reid. "Have you heard any more from our friend Mr. Brashner?" he asked.

"No," Will said.

"Not a peep," Lyn said. "Maybe you scared him off, Ed."

"Maybe," Reid said. "But it was rather strange. Right after you left, he regained his composure and told me that perhaps he needed to give you all a last shot."

"The agreement has just been signed," Lyn said.

"I know. Bennie just called and invited me to his party tomorrow."

Will didn't say anything. He wasn't in good spirits, Lyn could tell. He'd been curt with everyone except Eleanor during the meeting, even after she'd disappeared for several hours on Friday afternoon. Lyn had warmed up to Eleanor.

"I am hoping that no one invited Mr. Brashner," Lyn said.

"No, no. That won't be happening," Reid said. "He's surely on his way back to New York by now. But I am curious, Will. Your father mentioned Brashner. Did you say something to him?"

"Not a word," Will said. He looked at his feet when he answered, and for a reason she couldn't imagine, Lyn suspected he was lying.

"I'll ask Bennie tomorrow night. My guess is that the vice chair mentioned him to your father, which means that somehow word about Brashner's antics got back to Global Trading."

"Certainly not from me, I wouldn't waste my breath on him," Lyn said. "And the vice chairman didn't say anything to me about it."

"Good. I would like the whole thing to blow over. It isn't good for the firm for something like that to be exposed," Reid said.

"It isn't right to sweep it under the rug," Will said. "That kind of behavior shouldn't be allowed." Lyn saw that he was very angry, more than what was warranted.

"I agree, but there's not a lot to be done about it."

"Sure there is," Will said. "He could be sanctioned by the management committee. Called to the carpet and asked to explain himself. We have an ethics partner, after all. He should be told."

Lyn studied Will's expression. He was right, but that kind of thing just didn't happen in law firms. Surely, he knew that. And it wasn't in the cards here, Lyn was sure. Will shouldn't be so angry, now that it was over.

"Perhaps you're right, Will. In a perfect world, a sanction would be the right course. But it would be an ugly proceeding."

"It's none of my business, but I would drop it," Lyn said. "Everyone who does a good deed is punished. And it would be a terrible distraction for everyone who just wants to do good work for his clients."

"A good point," Reid said.

"I'm just tired," Will said.

"And that is an excellent point," Lyn said. "We were here all night last night, and this girl needs her beauty sleep."

In her car, exiting the garage, the light fading to twilight, Lyn sighed. She had a whole vocabulary of sighs, after this last week. Ones for frustration, anger, disappointment, and several more; she didn't want to think of them just then. This last one was for poor Will. He'd done excellent work for ERIS, his brilliant compromise on the title issue. What a shitty way to end a deal, all of Brashner's nonsense.

Retirement was looking good, she thought, taking the Shepherd Drive exit from Memorial Drive. And then another sigh, because Jay still hadn't responded to her texts.

23.

THAT SAME EVENING, THE FOURTH of November, 2017, the Four Seasons Hotel, Brashner sat alone at the bar that evening, drinking a Penicillin, which, as he'd expected in a Texas venue, he'd had to instruct the bartender how to make. Brashner had just learned in a text from Sanchez that the deal was signed. He felt good. His visit to Houston was a success. During the meeting in Reid's office with Will Baines and the Larkin woman, he'd successfully made his point that the deal was in jeopardy. All the posturing that Baines and Larkin had done was only face-saving, he was sure. Now he would be justified to claim to Ben Lufkin that his intervention had turned the transaction to success instead of failure.

After the meeting with Reid on Friday, he'd returned to the hotel to get his suitcase and go to the airport for a flight back to New York, thinking it best to leave town. The woman associate's appearance in Reid's office had unsettled him. He'd had no idea that she was a lawyer, let alone at his firm, and their little passionate liaison could have unfortunate consequences. Some of his partners, his detractors, should they find out, would certainly use the event against him. Several years before, the legal rag *Above the Law* had run a story about his callous behavior with associates. Brashner's compensation had stayed flat the next year. A similar article about his fucking a woman associate would be worse. His compensation could be reduced. And for nothing, just a little fling. The girl had asked for it. She'd quickly stopped fighting him once he got going. He doubted she would tell anyone. But even if she did, the worst that would happen would be rumors.

And then he'd had an idea. Perhaps Eleanor could be an asset, a person on the inside like Sanchez was. She'd clearly enjoyed what happened in his hotel room, her struggling at the beginning just a part of the game, a way of making their fucking more exciting. And she'd only called him a bastard in order to save face, not wanting him to think she was just a tart, which she certainly was. There was plenty of evidence it was all con-sensual. Why else would a pretty girl go into a hotel room with an older man? And what about the sexy outfit she was wear-ing? It was impossible to prove that he'd forced himself on her. Maybe she would entertain another meeting with him, now that she knew he was an important partner at her firm, not to mention another fuck. Why not? Brashner had looked her up on the firm website. Eleanor Soren, a graduate of Columbia Law School, an undergraduate of the University of Texas, her home-town Houston. A smart girl. No one would believe she'd been tricked into his room.

Brashner had called her office on Friday and her assis-tant said Eleanor was out of the office for an appointment and that she would then be tied up all day in a meeting when she returned. That was understandable, he told the assistant, but he would appreciate it if she would just give Eleanor a note with his name and phone number. She could call him whenever she had a break, which she did, an hour later.

"Hello Eleanor. Thank you for calling back. I have to go back to New York and I just wanted to call and let you know I very much enjoyed getting to know you on Thursday evening," he said, deploying his most charming voice. A pause of a few moments, and he worried she would rebuke him. But that would be fine. She could call him a bastard again. No harm done. And maybe he would have an opportunity to turn the conversation to his plan. But she surprised him, didn't rebuke him in any way.

"How nice of you to call, Patrick," she said.

"Of course, and it would be very nice if we get together when you're in New York next. I know some very good restaurants."

"That would be lovely. But it's too bad you have to go back so soon," she said.

"Yes, it's unfortunate."

"It looks like this deal I'm working on may get wrapped up tomorrow sometime. I'll need some fun and conversation when it's done. You've met Will Baines and Ms. Larkin. They're very uptight. And boring."

"As it turns out, I'm not going back until tomorrow morning. All the evening flights are booked," he lied.

"I doubt I'll be able to get out of the office before Saturday evening," she said.

"I suppose I could manage to stay until Sunday," he said. "I've always wanted to go to the Menil Collection. This would be a good opportunity."

"It's spectacular. You will love it," she said. "Why don't I send you a text tomorrow when I know what time I can get away."

"That's perfect. I am looking forward to seeing you tomorrow."

"Likewise," she said, and hung up.

He'd rebooked his flight to Sunday. The text came at five on Saturday, saying she would meet him in the hotel bar at six. Brashner had been excited most of the day, waiting for the text. He'd had flowers delivered to his room, and a bucket of ice and some seltzer for a nice bottle of cognac he'd ordered. Then he went to the bar a little before six and found a nice table. At seven, she'd not shown, and he was irritated. He hated to be kept waiting. Maybe he'd stayed in Houston for nothing. Tomorrow, the chances were high he'd have to sit next to a Texan on the plane and listen to insufferable witticisms. Most respectable New Yorkers wouldn't be in Houston on a Sunday. A visa should be required for a Texan to visit New York, he thought, or at least some kind of quota should be imposed. He waved over a server and held out his empty glass, a wilted piece of ginger adrift in the dregs at its bottom.

"I'll have another."

"I'm sorry sir, but what is it you're drinking?" the server asked.

"A Penicillin."

"What?"

"A Penicillin. Do you want me to spell it? The bartender will know what it is. I taught him how to make the first one."

"Yes, sir."

How exasperating, he thought, having to tolerate this Texan incompetence, the dimwitted look in her eye, the ill-fitting clothes, her chest as flat as an ironing board. Weren't cocktail waitresses supposed to be busty? They certainly were in a proper bar. His feet hung above the carpet, the chairs in the lounge all too tall, as awkward as the patrons, their pointed-toed boots planted on the floor. His disdain came in waves as he looked around. When she finally arrived, he would have to work hard to be charming, so as for her not to have second thoughts.

A few minutes later, the server scurried back to his table with the cocktail. Brashner studied the messages and emails on his phone. Maybe he'd missed one from her. He jumped, slightly when two men, standing quite close, sought his attention. Had they approached from behind? How long had they stood there?

"Good evening, sir," one of them said.

"I'm waiting for someone," Brashner said curtly.

"I'm Detective James Minte. Houston Police," the taller of the two said politely, holding up a badge attached to a wallet flap. "We would like to talk to you for a minute."

"What about?" Brashner asked, not bothering to look at the detective's badge.

"We're investigating an incident that occurred here at the hotel a couple of nights ago," Detective Minte said. "Your name was mentioned by a person involved. The hotel desk clerk told me you were Patrick Brashner, so I hope we have the right man."

"I don't know anything about any incident. I'm from New York and I'm here on business. And I arrived on Thursday night."

"Right. The incident we're investigating occurred on Thursday night, as it happens. Were you here in the bar that night?"

"I was, but just for a nightcap after my flight. I don't remember anything unusual. There was some large affair going on in the ballroom upstairs. Maybe the incident occurred up there."

"Actually, it didn't. Can we sit down?" Detective Minte asked. "This will only take a few minutes."

"I'm very tired. It's been a long day for me. Can't this wait until tomorrow?"

"It can't, actually. Would you rather that we conduct this interview at our offices?"

Brashner had heard that threat in a movie once, meaning, he recalled, that he should capitulate and grant them an audience here, or expect to be up all night in a windowless room. Eleanor would be here soon. She could tell them she was here also, and there was no incident.

"Fine," he said. "Let's make it quick."

"We'll go as quickly as we can. So you were here in the bar on Thursday night?" Detective Minte asked.

"Yes. I said that already."

"Okay. We understand from the bartender that you spoke to a young woman at the bar," Detective Minte said. "Is that true?"

Brashner looked over at the bartender, who, along with the server, was looking at him and appeared to have a smirk on his face. Had the man reported him for hitting on a woman? "That was certainly none of his business. Or yours," Brashner said.

"Sorry to say, we need to inquire. Do you remember the young woman's name?"

"Why would I know her name? We only had a conversation."

"After your conversation, did she accompany you up to your room?"

Brashner paused, debating whether to continue to deny his meeting Eleanor. "This woman came on to me. For all I know, she was only trying to get me to pay for her drinks. I ended up giving her money for a cab home. She was quite drunk."

"So she did accompany you to your room."

"No, she did not. When I went up to my room later, she was waiting at my door. She must've seen my room number when I signed the tab. And that's also none of your business, frankly."

The other detective with Detective Minte had taken out a notepad and was writing in it with a small pencil like the one golfers use to keep score. Brashner felt like he was in a scene from *The Bonfire of the Vanities*. His heart rate was elevated and he was sweating. Where was Eleanor? Her explanation would make these men go away. Detective Minte was quiet for a few moments and looking at him intensely.

"Mr. Brashner, do you know Eleanor Soren?" Detective Minte asked. "The complaint filed with us about this incident names her as the woman at the bar, and the woman who went into your room with you."

"Yes, I know Eleanor and she will be here any minute to clear this up," Brashner said, looking across the room for Eleanor.

"Mr. Brashner, I don't think that will be happening," Detective Minte said.

~

They told Brashner he was going to the station with them. It was his choice. He could go voluntarily or in handcuffs. That was an easy decision for him. At the station, they put him in an interview room with dark-gray walls and no window, only a mirror on one wall, just like in the movies. They recited the Miranda warning and then Minte loosened his necktie, sat down, and started to ask more questions. Brashner stopped him quickly and demanded a telephone call and a lawyer. They brought him his phone, which they'd taken away, along with the rest of the contents in his pockets, when they'd first arrived. His call wouldn't be recorded, they said, and left the room. He called Lufkin's number and once again was surprised when Lufkin answered.

"Hello again, Patrick," Lufkin said.

"Thank god I reached you, Ben," Brashner said. "I'm in a little trouble and need some help. I'm in Houston, but you probably know that."

"Why would I know that?"

"Because I saw your lawyer, Belinda Larkin, yesterday and confronted her about how she has been doing a bad job for you."

"Her client is Global Trading, not me. To remind you, I rarely talk to any of our lawyers, Patrick. You seem to be the exception. I've not spoken to Ms. Larkin in many years. Branoble has its portfolio companies take care of those things."

"In any case, I just heard that the deal with ERIS was signed, I suspect on account of my calling her on the carpet."

"Nice to hear that, Patrick. But I don't see any trouble in that. You said you had some trouble."

"Right. My trouble is that I've been detained in Houston by the police. They suspect that I molested a woman on Thursday night at my hotel. But it's all a misunderstanding." The line was silent. He couldn't even hear Lufkin breathing. "Ben, are you still there?"

"I am, Patrick. But I'm not sure how I can help."

"I need a lawyer, Ben. You can no doubt arrange that for me. It would be embarrassing for me to call someone at my firm. And it needs to be discreet. I'll also need money for bail."

"This isn't something I do, Patrick."

Lufkin's voice was hard. But Brashner had anticipated that might happen. Lufkin just needed a little motivation, and he had a way to do that.

"Ben, it will be very unfortunate if this isn't handled quietly. I'm very deep in my representation of Global Trading for those securities-fraud claims of two years ago, relating to your secret financing activity. You would have to get a new counsel up to speed and tell him the things you would rather not tell him. It would be, I should say, rather delicate."

The line was silent again for a minute. "Patrick, I will have someone there to help you shortly." And then Lufkin hung up immediately. Brashner hoped it wouldn't be a long wait. Room service would still be available back at the hotel. And there was the bottle of brandy, though most likely the ice would be melted.

24.

THE SAME DAY, THE FOURTH of November, 2017, a town in New Mexico, Joe Uno was even better groomed than when Jay had seen him last, his haircut recent and precise, not too short, and styled, like a picture of a man's head in a beauty salon. His blue button-down oxford-cloth shirt was laundered and pressed. It had been carefully packed, not something pulled out of a duffle bag. He leaned forward, holding his phone lightly with both hands near his lap. Was it recording? "You need to do something for me," he said.

"I'll certainly help if I can," Jay said.

Joe Uno shook his head, slowly. "You're not taking me seriously, Mr. Jackson. And I'm deadly serious."

Jay straightened his back the best he could. "Okay. Why don't you be more specific about what you need from me."

"Money," Joe Uno said. "A lot of it. More than what's in your wallet."

Jay thought a moment. "Joe, I really don't mean to be flippant, but we just drove through several urban areas with banks and ATMs. Why didn't you ask then?"

"Mr. Jackson, I know you're smarter than that. I know a lot about you, actually. Why would I go through all of this trouble to get cash from an ATM? I need ten million dollars."

"That's a lot of money. How would I get that for you? Maybe what you know about me is wrong. I'm a retired lawyer. I own a ranch."

"You have several offshore accounts with deposits exceeding that amount. And you have brokerage accounts with liquid assets that would satisfy the request as well. So, please don't tell me stories about being a lawyer and rancher, Mr. Jackson. You're wasting my time and I'm running out of patience."

Jay stayed quiet and tried to look defeated, how he'd been trained to act in the face of an interrogation, which is what this really was, he knew. The man was well informed; the intelligence he possessed was from very sophisticated research, something the Agency would have the tools for, as little sense as that made. But there had to be more to this. This couldn't possibly be an Agency operation.

"Okay, Joe. I don't want to waste your time. You must know that my retrieving money from those sources isn't simple, and, in case you don't know, it would require my personal involvement. It's not something I can do online. So maybe you're wasting my time. You can threaten to kill me, if that's what you're doing. But killing me won't get you any money. And then you've really wasted your time."

Joe Uno smiled, turned the phone over in his hand a few times, taking his time. "Come now, Mr. Jackson. A man like you, with your financial resources, always provides alternate access, a trusted advisor, a friend, someone with a power of attorney. A second person with a key to a safe."

The last comment was troubling. Was he shooting in the dark or did he know about the safe behind the wall in the ranch house? There were millions in bearer bonds in there, as well as Agency documents he'd kept, insurance if they decided to throw him to the wolves. Did they intend, ultimately, to drive him there, make him open the safe? Joe Uno sat back, a smile of contentment on his face.

"Since you know so much about me, you must know who that person is. Call him and tell him you're holding me. Isn't that how kidnapping works?"

"It doesn't with the safeguards you've built in. You know that. And I can't be sure I know who the person is. Let's stop the games, okay? Why don't I start with Belinda Larkin? I know she's in Houston, and I suspect she can help me, if with nothing else, then your cooperation."

Jay worked hard to suppress his anger, swallow his threats, keep the hatred from his eyes. He laughed. "Ms. Larkin is a girl-friend, Joe, and a recent one at that. Do you expect her to have access to my accounts?"

"No. I expect that if I have her, I will have access to your cooperation. Maybe I'm wrong and you don't care that much about her. But it's easy enough to pick her up and find that out," Joe Uno said, holding his phone up. He would only have to make a call, this was saying, and Lyn would be in his custody.

"She's an innocent person," Jay said, and regretted it.

"Means nothing to me that she's innocent. To you, perhaps, it means her death would be more troubling than your own."

Jay's mind raced. Joe Uno's information, at least what he'd revealed so far, didn't quite add up. He was being smug about Jay's feelings for Lyn, assuming she was more than a casual girl-friend. How would he know that? Wherever the information had come from, it came with conclusions, that a man with millions hidden in offshore accounts might be so sentimental about a lover that he would bend to a threat of killing her. Was the threat a bluff? He feared it wasn't.

"Joe, I'm sorry, but I'm confused. Since you know so much about me, you must know I've been out of the country traveling for two years. How can you expect me to be serious about Ms. Larkin? Or that it would be simple for me to have someone to get funds quickly?"

Joe Uno's smile evaporated. "Mr. Jackson, this is tiresome. You didn't leave the planet."

Maybe he didn't know as much as he suggested. "Okay, Joe. You're right. We should get on with it. But Ms. Larkin won't get you anywhere. You will want to contact the person with my power of attorney. He was a partner of mine at my law firm." He wanted to add, *I'm surprised you didn't know this.*

"And how do I reach him?"

"I'm not sure how to reach him. I haven't spoken to him for two years."

"Mr. Jackson, you are playing games again."

"No. When I left the country, he was working for a private equity concern called Branoble Partners. But he left there to take over a company. I will have to find him and ask him to meet me at the ranch before he agrees to anything. To verify my safety. He is very cautious."

"That would be fine, Mr. Jackson." The look on Joe Uno's face was one of satisfaction, as if he'd known Jay would require that meeting.

"I will also need to call my financial advisor. His name is Ben Lufkin, and I've known him a long time. Surely you know that. He will need some assurances."

It was a ploy, to test whether Joe Uno knew about his past. Evidently he did, because he flinched slightly at Lufkin's name. It was common for agents to have offshore accounts for a rainy day, a part of a bug-out contingency. So Joe Uno could have a source at Langley. But he was too young to be a former agent himself. Something just wasn't right about Joe Uno, but Jay couldn't guess what.

The phone in Joe Uno's hand vibrated. He looked at the caller ID and stood up quickly, walking out the door. Jay strained to hear what he said, but all he could make out before Joe Uno came back through the door was, "Fine. I will go immediately."

Joe Uno stood in front of Jay. "Mr. Jackson, I have to go out again. I will investigate what you've said. I hope for your sake, and Ms. Larkin's, that you are not sending me down a rabbit trail," he said, taking the Suburban keys off the counter, and then looking at a curious Joe Dos. "Joe, we're going for a ride."

Jay leaned his head back after the two Joes went out the door. He heard the Suburban spin its tires on gravel as it accelerated. It wasn't exactly a wrench he'd thrown into their plans by mentioning Ben Lufkin. But he'd bought a little time, and time always created opportunities.

～

The two men left behind in the Airstream began to complain to each other a few hours later, the beer supply exhausted, chips almost gone, no peanuts, no milk for the coffee, no car. One of them limped badly on his way to the bathroom and back. The other searched the kitchen and eventually found a bottle of tequila behind a cereal box in a cabinet. Both had stomachs that hung over their belts and stains on the fronts of their shirts. One of them farted long and loud, raising up a leg, like a dog peeing. It sounded like a roller bag dragged over a rough floor.

The light outside faded. From what he had seen during their drive there, Jay knew they were in New Mexico, not far from El Paso, the topography flat and sandy, a few small mountains in the distance, too small for those around Alamogordo, so maybe the Florida Mountains, and scattered clumps of trees, probably around houses, and general desert brush. The two men watched a spy movie on a small TV, their backs to him, leaning forward to see the screen and interpret the tinny dialogue, their attention strained. The duct tape around Jay's wrists had been unwound and rewound so many times that its adhesive properties were compromised. How many times had he said he was an old man with a weak bladder? They'd been very sloppy wrapping it the last time. Jay twisted his wrists patiently and the tape came loose from his skin, after which he slowly slid one hand free, watching the men carefully. They weren't checking him at all. Then he slowly unwrapped the tape holding his ankles to the chair legs, pulling it free in small increments at the times in the movie when the cars sped in the rain and water sluiced under their tires.

Jay left his chair and positioned himself over them. It was easy then, moving swiftly, surprising them, wrenching an arm behind a back, propelling one head into another, one man dazed and down, and, at last, his arm around the other man, flipping him forward in a circle to the floor, flat on his back, the wind knocked out of him. Jay wedged his boot on the winded man's throat. "You best stay quiet, padner, or you'll make me get rough," he said.

The gun was on the kitchen counter. He put it in his belt, ripped a bedsheet into strips, and made them sit side by side on the couch, tying together their hands and feet. The man with the limp whimpered. Both of them were breathing hard, whether from the struggle or simple humiliation. The surroundings outside the window were painted bright red by the setting sun.

"Boys, I'm right disappointed in you. Did you really burn up my brand-new truck like you said?"

"We was just kidding," the one without the limp said.

"I don't care for anyone making jokes about my truck."

"Just a joke, man."

"And kidnapping me. That a joke too?"

"Those were our orders."

"And what will you do with me after I pay up? Another joke?"

"Joe didn't tell us that. We don't know."

"You have no idea?"

"We don't know much."

"That's no exaggeration, is it? But it'd be right kind of you to tell me what you know."

"We don't know anything."

"How about your boss? He didn't explain what happens next?"

"He didn't tell us squat."

"And me? What he'd tell you about me?"

"Like I said. Squat."

"I'm sure you're not doing this for nothing. How much is he going to pay you?"

The man shook his head, and the man with the limp said, "A few thousand."

"Shut up, dummy," the other man said.

Jay laughed. "What we have here is a horse with no shoes. You boys went out and roped yourselves a stranger who you know nothing about. And you don't even know exactly what you're going to be paid. Is that what you're saying?"

"Okay. Joe said you're a rich guy and we'll get ten thousand each after he gets his share."

"And where does he get his share?"

"From the other Joe."

"So the first Joe, the one with the nice shirt, is the big boss? This is all his idea?"

"You can ask him that. We know nothing about it."

"I hope to do that."

"Good luck with that," the man with the limp said. "He's got friends."

"Will you shut up, stupid?"

"I'm just saying."

Jay shook his head, discouraged suddenly, a languorous feeling coming over him. It was probably time to start walking, dark outside now. His overnight bag was in a corner, his phone and his wallet inside it. He switched the phone on to look at a map, intermittent service, one bar fading in and out, not enough to give him a map, and not much of a charge. The charger had been plugged into his truck. Why hadn't they taken the SIM card out of the phone? Something wasn't right. So he sat down, deciding to wait for the Joes to return. He had the gun.

After an hour, Jay gagged the two men, went outside, the pistol resting against the small of his back, held by his belt, and leaned against the dark side of the Airstream, where the headlights wouldn't find him. It was peaceful, the stars twinkling on the sky's dark palette hanging above the flat New Mexico landscape, the small glow of light from a town off to the east against the horizon, a faint purr from Interstate 10 to the north, a lone truck moving slow, inaudibly, down a road closer to him. He thought for a few minutes about the dark meadows at his ranch, where a night might pass with no mechanical noise, nothing artificial, only rustling sage and owls hooting in the distance.

Just before midnight, the Suburban's headlights approached the Airstream, its movements abrupt, bouncing in the ruts, then stopping. The lights went out quickly. Jay waited. There was only one man in the car, he saw when the door opened, the overhead light illuminating the interior. Joe Uno had not returned with Joe Dos, who struggled with a grocery bag that broke after he'd closed the car door, requiring him to get on his hands and knees to find the contents. When he stood up and moved toward the Airstream, the broken bag and its contents clutched to his chest, Jay stepped out of the shadow. The groceries were dropped again.

"Looks like you escaped from the two idiots," Joe Dos said.

"That's a right clever observation," Jay replied.

"I guess they were no match for a smart lawyer like you."

"Oh, I don't know, padner. I'm not a lawyer anymore. Just a rancher now, as I've been saying."

"Makes no difference to me."

Jay watched Joe Dos slowly advance on him, one arm held flat against his chest, the other bent at the elbow and extended away from his body. It reminded him of a bull pawing the ground with one foreleg before his charge. Joe Dos quickened his pace, and Jay feigned surprise, which made his attacker leap into the air, his foot cocked back for a blow to Jay's chest. But Jay had anticipated the move and stepped to the side, like a matador, the intended blow not connecting, and a quickly rammed fist to the kidney had Jay standing over him. What Jay expected was Joe Dos to continue to lean forward, bending to put his hands on his knees. A mistake then, Jay relaxed his guard for a moment, long enough for Joe Dos to spring up, deliver two retaliatory blows, fast and sharp, making Jay backpedal furiously.

Jay was on the defensive, using both forearms to protect himself as he slid in the loose gravel in the parking area. He should reach for the gun, he thought, his adrenaline pumping fast, like it did when his horse was startled by a rattlesnake and he needed to stick in his saddle to get control. He might win on his own in the end, but he was old and the risk of injury was high. For a moment, his greatness flickered. He knew he should pull out the gun, but he just couldn't admit he'd lost a step. Pivoting, his outstretched hand shooting to the ground, his legs, coupled at the ankle, swinging, levered in a full circle of velocity to strike the man's knees, Jay knocked Joe Dos to the ground. Now extracting the gun from his belt, Jay made the man stand and then pulled his wrist behind his back and walked him hard, headfirst, into the side of the Airstream, pushing the man's face flat against the metal and the gun between his shoulder blades.

"Nice try, amigo," he said, his mouth close to Joe Dos's ear.

"Fuck you."

Breathing hard—fighting the younger man had been stupid—Jay pushed Joe Dos inside, where, not taking any more chances, a flick of the wrist, the pistol handle against the skull, he sent the man to the floor at the feet of the others. While Joe Dos was incapacitated, Jay squeezed him and the other two together on the couch, binding their six ankles all together with a long strip. Then he waited for Joe Dos to regain his wits, pulling a chair over to sit himself in front of them. It was very quiet. The night insects around the Airstream had fled the area during the altercation. But he heard a soft hum of those further away, their sound carried on a breeze. The two men breathed quietly behind their gags, their eyes wide, moving between Jay and the limp Joe Dos between them, his chin on his chest. Finally, his head rose.

"So, with whom do I have the pleasure of visiting?" Jay asked. "I've heard your name is Joe, but I'm a bit skeptical about that."

"None of your business."

"Why, that's right unkind of you. And it's none too clever, unless you figure on sitting here like that for a long time. Seeing as how we've been spending so much time together, I just want to put a name with a face."

"It's Joe."

"Just Joe?"

"Joe Joseph."

Jay laughed. "That's a good one. Joe Joseph."

"Fuck off."

"I'm sorry you think you have to be unfriendly. It looks to me like I'm the best friend you got at this moment."

"Just tell me what you want."

"Now there's some cooperation."

"You're not funny. Fuck off."

"Well, maybe not. You keep repeating yourself. Maybe I should try a different approach?"

"What do you want?"

"There you go. Repeating yourself again.

"I don't know nothing. How's that?"

A good time to pause, Jay went outside and retrieved the contents of the grocery bag on the ground: chips; salsa; bread; canned tuna; condiments; seltzer water, of all things; and a bulging brown envelope. He came back in and lined them up on the counter. Then he sat back down in the chair, ripped open the envelope, and pulled out thirty packs of hundred-dollar bills.

He leaned his head back, looking at the ceiling for a time, remembering for no reason a time when he was a boy. His brothers had locked him in the tack room in the barn. What had they wanted? There was a small crawl space in the corner, beneath some saddles, and he'd escaped that way. And then he'd acted like it hadn't happened, ignoring their smirks. He'd never found out why they'd done it. And now his brothers were dead. Leveling his head, he looked at each man on the couch, one after the other.

"I sure have a lot of questions, Joe. What's this money for?" Jay asked, holding up the envelope.

"It's yours. Just take it and leave us be."

"How kind of you, Joe! But it isn't enough for a new truck like the one you boys burned up back in Campo."

"We didn't burn it. It's still back there where we got you. We were joking."

"I guess I'd still have to go all the way back there to get it. That's a bit inconvenient."

"That's all we got."

"I can see that. But you know, I can leave the cash if you tell me who and why. Let's start with who. The name of the guy you're working for would be a good start. And why didn't he come back with you?"

"His name is Joe."

Jay laughed. "There's a whole lot of Joes running around here. How about where he is now, if you can't tell me his name."

"I don't know anything. A guy picked him up in Deming and they were driving to El Paso."

"That's where we are. Deming. And when will Joe be back?"

"How should I know? He doesn't tell me much."

Jay chuckled. "Of course not. Okay. Then let's get to the why."

"It was just a job, man. The other Joe hired us to help him kidnap you. That's why I went to town with him. To get paid. And I was supposed to come back here, get these two guys, and drive back west."

"This isn't much money compared to what your boss was hoping to get for me. Maybe you didn't get such a good deal."

"I don't know anything about that. It was his business. We were just doing a job."

"Got it. And you were going to leave me here?"

"That's what he said to do."

"So why the groceries?"

"He said to wait a few hours here. I think another guy is coming."

"He didn't say who?"

"No. He didn't talk much. And I don't want to know what he was planning, wanted nothing to do with it."

"So after you got your money, you'd just go home?"

"None of my business, what he's planning for you. Don't want any part of it. Like I said."

"Just a job."

"Right. It's nothing personal."

"And what about last week in Mexico. Was that personal?"

"He wanted us to pick a fight and then take some pictures after I beat you up."

"But that didn't happen."

"I didn't want to get arrested, man. The police came."

"And Joe wasn't upset that you didn't beat me up?"

"No. He didn't care."

This Joe was lying. No fight was intended. Joe Uno had been at Jay's house, looking for something. It was well done, but Jay knew the signs.

"So you were supposed to beat up some guy walking by. How'd you know it would be me?"

"We'd watched you. Every night you did that walk."

"I knew you'd been watching us. Your pals here at Ollie's were conspicuous."

"Idiots."

"And you followed us to Ensenada?" Jay hadn't detected them doing that, which bothered him.

"No. We just hung around the place where you live. Look, like I said, it was nuthin' personal."

Just a job. Nothing personal. A spy's rationalization. Jay had lost his cool on one occasion when he was much younger, just starting out in the game. He'd cut a man's throat in anger, a man who'd murdered another agent's wife. That had been personal. And a bad mistake, as it turned out. Raymond had been patient then. But the same anger was edging toward him again. This was personal to him, Joe Uno's threats about Lyn. He took a breath, calmed himself. "But you see, friend, it's not making sense to me, your boss paying you to pick a fight, then kidnap me, drive me almost a thousand miles, and leave me in a trailer in New Mexico. Does that make sense to you?"

"Hey, I don't care if it makes sense. I get paid, that's all I care about. I don't want to know why. That's his business."

"As simple as that?"

"I like it that way."

"So what happens when I walk out of here and report you to the police? You going to tell them the same thing?"

"Yes. A guy hired us to kidnap you. I don't know his real name. And I don't know what he was planning. It was just a job for us. I'll tell them the same thing you'll tell them. There was another Joe who was the boss."

"Problem is I have passports for the other Joes here. They have real names."

"Idiots."

"And your passport is in the Suburban, I'll bet."

"Good luck with that."

Not much more to be learned here. Joe Dos was bluffing about some of it, that was Jay's instinct. And Jay wasn't interested in the police asking questions about his background. Joe Uno, whoever he was, would get involved with that in some way. He had significant resources, to have the information about Jay that he had. The charges against Joe Dos and his idiot sidekicks would just go away somehow.

Jay retrieved his pocketknife from his bag and stood for a while before them, opening and closing it. There was a way to send a message to Joe Uno, give him pause should he want to take his extortion further. He paused to look down at his feet. His memory of Raymond hung in the air. The killing in his life had to be over, left in France. He'd come back to be a rancher.

Jay placed the knife on the counter, having wiped it carefully. The two other Joes watched him with wide eyes. He knew they weren't killers. Joe Dos, not so much, Jay thought, thinking he might just pick the knife back up. All of it was senseless, as far as these men were concerned. Best to move along. He put the envelope down next to the knife.

"Okay, amigos. I'm right sorry about all this mess, but I have to be moving along. I'm gonna leave you the money for your trouble. But I can't let you go right away. Y'all should be able to hop your way over to that knife before you pee your pants." Jay looked at them one last time and shook his head. They didn't appreciate the danger they were in. Joe Uno was the kind of man who always covered his tracks.

"Guess I'm obliged to take your car," he said, before he turned to the door. "It's nothing personal."

25.

THE NEXT DAY, THE FIFTH of November, 2017, the police station in downtown Houston, where it had turned out that "shortly" didn't mean a few minutes, or even a few hours. At five on Sunday morning, an officer brought two men to the interview room. Several hours before, Detective Minte had said that he was going home. Then Brashner had insisted that he be allowed to wait for his lawyer, thinking that his name would have to be entered into a log if they took him to a cell, something that a reporter might get access to in the morning. He hadn't yet been formally arrested.

The older man introduced himself as John Gluckman, a criminal lawyer. He used a cane to walk and leaned forward over it when standing. The younger man he introduced as his associate. He was tall, with an athletic build, and well groomed, wearing a blue button-down oxford dress shirt that looked like it had just been ironed. His short hair was so light in color it was almost white.

"The good news, Mr. Brashner, if you can call it good news, is that the police have not yet formally filed a criminal complaint and arrested you. But they let me read a draft of the statement they intend to provide the district attorney, a summary of the evidence they have gathered against you. The bad part of that is sworn testimony of a young woman named Eleanor Sorel. It's fairly detailed, and it's accompanied by forensic evidence, as she submitted to a physical exam within twenty-four hours of an alleged rape by you."

"It's nonsense," Brashner said. "That girl is a tart and she came on to me in the hotel bar."

"Then you don't deny having a sexual relation with her."

"It wasn't rape. It was completely consensual."

"Then we should admit that the sex did occur. The forensic evidence will match your DNA. Sadly, the woman's testimony indicates that in her mind she gave no consent whatsoever, and that you physically forced yourself on her. I assume you know by now that she is a lawyer at a prominent Houston law firm. She told her boss what happened. And he reached out to his father for help. The father is a man named Bennie Baines, who is very wealthy and prominent in Houston. He has some very good friends in the police department, the chief of police being one and the district attorney another."

"It doesn't matter," Brashner said. "It's my word against hers and I am a very important partner in that same law firm. I'm sure this is nothing more than a shakedown for money. I refused to give her money, and this is her response. She even called me to induce me to stay in Houston for the weekend and meet her at the hotel bar last night. The police came instead."

Gluckman looked at Brashner for a while. It made Brashner nervous to be studied. He couldn't believe that the little tart had the guts to do something like this. She probably didn't realize that she would have to give a very public testimony of what happened. His lawyers would rip her apart. He still had her panties that she'd left behind. He would testify that she gave them to him to remember her by.

"Yes. It's right that it is your word against hers. We may be able to make a case of entrapment by the police if you go to trial. And normally the police and the district attorney are averse to get into a public case like this. But right now, they are adamant that they will go forward. It's very early and a Sunday, but I have some friends on the force. I may be able to get you released if you agree you will not leave town and indicate that you are considering some kind of a guilty plea to a lesser charge."

"No sir. I will not admit to anything. And you can tell Ben Lufkin he has to do better than this. If he doesn't, my statement to the police will have a lot more in it than just my denial of that woman's claim."

"Okay," Gluckman said, looked over at the mirror, and stood up abruptly, leaning on his cane. "I can only advise you strongly to reconsider that position. Now they will come in and charge you and take you to a holding cell until we can get a judge to entertain bail for you. That will be Monday at the earliest. Maybe much longer." He turned and started a shuffle for the door.

"Wait," Brashner called out. "I can consider something. But only consider. Tell Mr. Lufkin that."

"That's very good. The Four Seasons is a much better place to wait while I look into this further. Let me see if I can get you released to your room there."

Behind the mirror, Detective Minte watched Gluckman and his associate leave the interview room. Bennie Baines was a force in town, and he wouldn't have become involved if the young woman's claim wasn't credible. And Gluckman was powerful also, but his clients were generally drug kingpins and foreign types, in one recent case a foreign diplomat who was trying to bribe a government contractor. Minte's college roommate and good friend was an officer at the CIA. Who was Ben Lufkin? He picked up the phone.

An hour later, a police officer came to the room and brought Brashner to the station desk, where they returned his personal items and made him acknowledge in writing that he wouldn't leave his room at the Four Seasons until he was told he could. A police officer drove him to the hotel, took him upstairs, and watched him enter his room, telling him as he closed the door that someone would be stationed in the lobby. If he needed something, he should call the front desk.

A man wearing a cowboy hat stood by the window, his arms folded across this chest, smiling. He wore a big leather jacket.

"Who the hell are you?"

The man took off the hat to reveal his white hair, and Brashner recognized him.

"Where's Gluckman?"

"Not here."

"So what do you want?"

"I'm here with a solution for your troubles," the man said, reached beneath his coat, and removed a handgun with silencer attached.

26.

THE SAME DAY, THE FIFTH of November, 2017, Houston. What a blessing, Lyn thought, sitting on a lounge chair in her backyard, the Sunday-morning sunshine streaming through tree branches and the air cool and dry, a Houston miracle. The sun flashed off the pool when a breeze rustled the tree leaves. The pool water was clean and sharp when she'd plunged into it minutes before. Water dripped from her hair onto her shoulders. It'd been an extravagance, having the pool put in. She spent so many hours at the office that the pool was like an ornamental shrub. Her plunge just moments before probably cost several hundred dollars. But she had no regrets.

She leaned her head back to face the sun, thinking for a moment to put on her bathrobe, draped on a nearby chair, and deciding not to. It was pleasant not to move, not even to think for a time. She'd been worrying that Jay hadn't called. The dive into the pool had washed the worry away. It was silly. He would call soon enough. Or she wouldn't go to the ranch tomorrow. Why would that be a catastrophe? The tree was reflected in her patio sliding doors, and she watched a cloud slide along the section of sky beyond the tree.

The romantic memories of Mexico perched on her shoulder. Should the recollections fly away today, fine. A happy life was all about attitude. Disappointments didn't require the future to be put out of balance. Forced retirement, a lover's scorn, each were fleeting events, not debilitating setbacks, only a missed step, the journey still ahead, the rest of her life full of promise.

She stood up, put on her bathrobe, but then let it slip off into a lump on the patio. It was warm in the sun and she thought she might just remove her suit and dive naked into the pool. Her skin would become tight from the cold water. She'd stood nude in Jay's bedroom window. Was this any different? Yes. There were boys in the neighboring house, whom she'd spotted once looking over her fence from a tree. Dropping her suit would give them an eyeful of the spinster—Lyn suspected that was how the neighbors referred to her. It would be sweetly rebellious, stripping off her suit, like telling the managing partner of her firm she had no intention of retiring, or maybe even telling her tomorrow that she was retiring immediately. If Jay didn't call, maybe she would do that. The hell with a plan. She would clean out her desk and go on a trip, no return date in mind, the same as Jay had done. And she wouldn't call him, of course, or even send him a postcard.

Her shoulders sagged from the weight of the knowledge that she would most likely do none of these things. She put on her robe and went to the house. Before sliding the door shut, she heard several birds, perched in her tree, chortling, mocking her.

The mirror in her bathroom, reflecting her nudity, wasn't kind. The wrinkled skin on her upper arms, sagging curves to her breasts, lines cracking like ice from the corners of her eyes and mouth, seemed incredibly magnified. She felt unspeakably old, abandoned by a body that had once been smooth and firm. Never again would she slice through life like a knife though a cake. She put on her clothes, turned off the light, and walked out to her bedroom.

Yet after she'd walked into the kitchen, she was spreading frosting on a cake, her optimism roaring into the house like the wind billowing her skirts while she danced all night. It wasn't in her nature to mope. Tomorrow, she would take off her swimsuit. Or the next day. The sun moved higher in the sky as she made lunch. The air conditioning kicked on, an old reliable companion cooling off the house. The day before, she'd stopped on her way home to buy a book about birds. Turning the pages while she ate her sandwich, she located the chapter about South Texas, so much closer than New York and so many interesting-looking birds. One didn't need to travel a thousand miles to discover something new.

She brushed the crumbs into the garbage and opened the dishwasher. It exhilarated her, cleaning up, aligning the plate with the others, filling the soap receptacle, starting the cycle. Walking quickly to find her bag, she took it to the dining room table and dumped out its contents. She sorted out the almost-empty containers of makeup, breath mints, eyedrops, and other pointless paraphernalia. Then she pushed them all into the trash can, the sound of them hitting the bottom so satisfying. She would do the same with her career, her romance, and all the rest of her troubling circumstances, as she thought of them. What had she asked Will? Was he afraid to be naked? She wasn't. Her phone vibrated. Moving sideways on the table, she snatched it up.

"Belinda Larkin," she said. Damn the robocalls if this was one.

"Yes, hello," a man said. "This is UPS. I'm calling about a delivery to you."

"I'm not expecting anything. Who's the sender?"

"Let me look." A few minutes of clicking, the sound of a keyboard. "A Julius Jackson."

"Oh. Okay."

"We plan to deliver it this evening. Will you be home to receive it?"

"Just leave it on the porch if I'm not," she said, not sure when she would be back from the BBQ party.

"It requires a signature for delivery, I'm afraid."

"Can you tell me a time, then?"

"Probably around eight, maybe a little earlier. I know it's late, but we're slammed today."

"Are you sure you can't leave it? I can leave a note on the door."

"Tell you what. There are several packages in the area. The driver can swing back at the end of his deliveries if you're not there when he first tries. And then he can call you if you're still not there and you can tell him to leave it on the porch."

"I so appreciate it."

"No bother. Have a good evening," the man said, and hung up.

His sending a package was odd, when all she'd expected was a text. And since when did UPS call in advance for a delivery? The hell with waiting for him. She called the number of his ranch, but hung up on the voicemail message, remembering herself as a teenager once being a pushy girlfriend, not being able to come to terms with her infatuation and not convinced that she wasn't being ignored.

Why, she didn't know, but satisfaction of her tidying up departed, as if she pulled the stopper in the sink and an earring fell in, whirled away down the drain. The night before was miserable. She'd popped up repeatedly to reach for her phone on the nightstand, poking the screen, hoping in vain for a notification, just a *made it safe, see you Monday.* Finally, she'd taken the phone into bed, hugging it to her chest, waiting for its vibration.

Now, exhausted, she slunk back to the bed, determined to nap while waiting for the time of the BBQ to arrive, wishing she'd not agreed to go. With the pillow over her head, hoping for solace, if only a little, she willed her thoughts to the mundane:

what she would wear that night, what she would pack for tomorrow, did she need to stop at an ATM for cash. Still awake, and a little desperate, she started a mental list of actions needed for the deal's closing. Will knew that she was going to Jay's ranch. Her associates would work on the closing documents. She could text them the list tomorrow. How many days would she stay? The question kept arising, a leak not yet plugged, its drip keeping her awake. It was foolish to leave town before the transaction was closed, so many actions to be taken, so many issues that could arise. She'd never liked this part of doing a deal, the anticlimax after the excitement of signing the agreement, the preparation of mundane drafts of corporate certificates and legal opinions. It was purgatory.

The darkness underneath her pillow seeped into her, and she slid deeper into the bedclothes. Some comfort came back. One way or another, her anxieties about Jay, the closing, retirement, would get sorted out in due course. That was the way to deal with anxiety. Let it run its course, like a rainstorm. The sun would return to dry things out. There was a faint sound of a car passing on her street and the rumble of the fan in the air conditioning apparatus in the attic. Familiarity was soothing. A fleeting memory of round stones sliding down the berm at Los Pelicanos, and she fell into a light sleep.

27.

THE SAME DAY, THE FIFTH of November, 2017, El Paso, Texas, Jay awoke in a motel room, a local place on the highway that took cash in advance for the night, no real services offered besides the bed, and no credit card or driver's license required. He'd waited an hour near the Airstream on the off chance Joe Uno would return. When he didn't, he'd driven to Las Cruces, crossed the Rio Grande, and stopped at a truck stop for gas, coffee, and a phone charger. In El Paso, he'd parked the Suburban in a Marriot parking lot and then walked along several backstreets for a half mile, until he found the motel he was now in. The place was worn out, stains on the bedspread, lumpy pillows, corners peeling back on the bathroom's linoleum floor. But he was an anonymous guest, sheltered for a time from the intelligence-gathering capabilities Joe Uno had demonstrated.

It was time to do something, he decided after a couple of hours of thinking and dozing. The Suburban surely had a tracker on it. He didn't want to find himself kidnapped again on his way to San Saba. He walked to another hotel and got a taxi to a Starbucks downtown. There, he turned off the cellular function and used Wi-Fi calling on his phone, through a VPN app, to call Anna. It wasn't perfect. The VPN would only slow down a trace, not prevent one. Had they tapped Anna's phone? That wouldn't matter if she was working with them.

"I thought you were retired," she said, when she answered. "And besides, estate lawyers don't work on Sundays."

"I know. But my phone battery is about to run out so I need to talk fast. I got carjacked last night at a rest stop on I-10. They took everything—my wallet, my money, and my truck—after they knocked me out and left me behind the facilities. Good thing I had my phone in my boot, where I put it when I'm driving."

"That's terrible. So you're stuck there? Where are you?"

"I hitched a ride with a trucker to El Paso. My housekeeper isn't answering at the ranch. So I was hoping you might be able to get me some money. I'll probably have to take a bus to Austin since I have no ID. Of course, I don't want to call the police."

"Don't do that. I can definitely work out something. Let me call you back."

"No. My phone's gonna die if I leave it on. I'll call you. How long do you need?"

"Play it safe, give me two hours. Can you wait someplace?"

"Yeah. The trucker had pity on me and gave me a few dollars. So I can nurse some coffee in a diner."

"Good. Call me in two hours," she said, and hung up.

Jay walked around an empty downtown for twenty minutes, checking for surveillance, until he came to a nice hotel, where he got a cab to a Denny's close to the highway. While he ate lunch, he thought about the two Joes. They'd left everything in his bag: his wallet and money and phone. That wasn't clever. Yet they'd had detailed information about his bank accounts. It didn't add up.

The club sandwich, greasy as a burger, sat in his stomach like a rock. Traffic on the interstate had picked up, he saw through the Denny's window. The weather was good, the sky blue and the air clear, a few high clouds. He ordered a slice of pecan pie and a coffee. The place wasn't too crowded; the server didn't seem to care he was sitting there as long as he was. He thought again about his abduction. In spy games, it wasn't unusual to stage a situation in order to create an opportunity for another purpose, one that could take place hours, even days, later and in another place, even halfway around the world. These were clever complexities, a type of bobbing and weaving, like a basketball player faking out the defense to get to the basket. Had the kidnapping and extortion demand been a ruse? His escape from the Airstream had been easy, now that he thought about it. Too easy. His going to Austin now could be a part of their plan. He turned his phone on and called Anna.

"Right on time," she said. "I have a friend who will bring you some money. Her name is Megan Mason."

"Where?"

"She has to drive in from a suburb, which will take a little more than an hour. She'll meet you at a café she knows. It's called the Atlantic Grill. I have directions."

"Don't need them," he said, and hung up.

He walked through several parking lots, a La Quinta, a Hilton, an IHOP, until he crossed a road and went into a Hyatt, where he sat for a while, his bag at his feet, looking like a guest waiting to be picked up. Then he took a cab to Atlantic Aviation, a private jet terminal at the El Paso airport. There was no Atlantic Grill, nor anyone named Megan Mason.

"I'm here to be picked up by Megan Mason," he said to the man at the Atlantic Aviation desk.

The man consulted the computer on the desk. "Here it is. She's due to land a little before three o'clock. Help yourself to coffee or soda."

Jay brooded in the waiting room. He was sure now that his abduction had nothing to do with extortion. But whatever the endgame, he'd put Lyn in harm's way by inviting her to Los Pelicanos. Joe Uno wasn't bluffing about that. Why had he called Lyn, broken his resolve to return to his spy's detached existence of so many years? The good spy's life was a choreographed deception, affability without affection, charming engagements but no attachments, a life within a personal fortress. He thought he'd played the role like an expert actor for forty years, and then, in one weak moment, he'd let the drawbridge down. Twice.

The tarmac outside the window was directly off the smaller of the airport's two main runways. Separating the two was a huge pie-shaped expanse of dirt and low-lying scrub grass. Across that were the air-delivery services, and at the point of the pie was the main passenger terminal and the control tower. A small military-jet trainer plane taxied along the tarmac in front of him. The airport hosted NASA's Forward Operating Location, which was around the post office building next to Atlantic Aviation. The sun was high in the sky now, and the expanse in front of Jay was blinding. A commercial airliner took off on the far runway, the sun glinting off its wings when it banked to the east not long after it left the ground.

Growing up on the ranch, Jay hadn't been tough like his brothers. He'd been afraid of snakes and rats and the unbroken horses. His brothers frequently called him a sissy, a mama's boy. They laughed when he balked at learning to fire a rifle, afraid of the noise and what it might do to the animal the bullet hit. It was ironic that he'd chosen the career that he had, one during which he'd often had to be ruthless. When a boy, he squeezed his eyes closed the first time he was forced to witness putting down a sick calf. Years later, on a mission with Raymond in the Canadian wilderness, looking through the scope of a sniper rifle, his eyes were wide open as he lined up a man coming out of a terrorist safe house.

The man at the desk said that the private jet that had just stopped outside was the one with Ms. Mason aboard. Jay bolted up the stairs and found Anna inside. It wasn't a surprise she had come herself. She did things her own way. He'd learned that in France.

"Nice flight from Dallas?" he asked. "Should I call you Megan? And who's Mason?"

She laughed. "I interviewed a lawyer in Houston on Thursday to represent my company. He had a photo on his desk of his dog, whose name is Mason. So it was a good alias. Don't you think?"

"Is all this connected with Raymond?"

"I'll get to that after I recover my strength. I'm still sweating from my sprint to the airport to pick this bird up for the trip here. This clandestine work is very tiring."

"It wasn't necessary for you to come. Or even to send a plane. I only needed a safe way to Austin."

"I know. But I couldn't resist. I'm a hands-on kind of girl."

"I remember. Still, it's quite an expenditure to put on an expense account."

"I'm not sure my career still exists anyway. More on that later also. I liked your story on the phone, but what really happened?"

Jay was reluctantly suspicious. He had to be careful with what he said. Whatever else, it was possible that Joe Uno had used Agency resources, whether authorized or purloined. And Anna was an Agency resource. Through the cabin window, he saw a ground crew loading fuel into the plane's wing. It seemed like an unnecessary delay.

"My car didn't break down," he said. "I crossed the border at Tecate and stopped on my way to the interstate for a man waving at me next to a car with the hood up. A car had been following me since I left my house in Mexico, so I probably shouldn't have stopped, but I wanted to find out what they wanted. I thought they might be part of your surveillance and I wanted to tell them what for. Didn't turn out that way. One guy had a gun. There were four of them, two I recognized from an incident in my community last week." He explained meeting the two Joes.

She looked at him for a minute. "After I surprised you in San Diego, I started to wonder why Lufkin had asked me to keep track of you," she said. "He was uncharacteristically uninterested when I reported back to him. So I used my authorized access to Agency records to dig a little deeper. And then a friend of mine from Langley called me out of the blue this morning, before you called. He'd been one of my instructors at the Farm. But why don't you finish the story before I tell you about that."

He looked at her a moment, fighting his skepticism. He told her about his abduction and escape.

She didn't speak. The ground crew were finished with their work and the pilot started the engines. Facing her, a small aircraft table between them, Jay leaned forward and looked into her eyes. "I'm wondering whether my escape was too easy. And then you show up in a plane, Anna. I'm sorry. I have to ask. Did Lufkin send you again? Did he have something to do with this?" He remembered how Joe Uno had reacted when he'd heard Lufkin's name.

She returned his gaze for a moment. "No, Lufkin doesn't know I'm here. This isn't an Agency aircraft. I chartered it with an alias I just obtained from a source he doesn't know about. Raymond taught me how to do that."

He thought a minute. He wanted to trust her. And at this point, he was out of options. "Okay. I'm sorry. I'm a bit spooked by all this. And worried that somehow Lyn is going to become collateral damage."

"There is more, I'm sorry to say. First, there are no records in the Agency about you after you retired. None. And I looked carefully. There's not even a flag in your file about your failure to cooperate with anyone in New York. And Raymond's files are in the archives, no sign that anything is open."

"A former agent is murdered and there is no active file?"

"No murder in the file. No outstanding request for an interview with you. Raymond's death in the archive files was 'from natural causes.' And it was Lufkin who asked that the files be closed as quickly as they were. He certified that Raymond had not been in possession of any classified information of any importance. Nothing was there about what you two did in Bilbao."

"Bureaucratic sloppiness on Lufkin's part? Maybe he wanted to hide the fact that two of his former agents went rogue."

"No. I did more research. There's an ongoing investigation by the SEC that hasn't been made public. A hedge fund named Danna Partners evidently sold a large amount of the buyer's stock short in the week before the Bilbao closing ceremony. When the terminal didn't explode thanks to you, Danna was almost wiped out. Piquart was an investor in that, as was Parnell and another one of your old law firm partners."

"Raymond and I knew that."

"But you didn't know of Lufkin's involvement."

"What?"

The plane was moving now, a man waving it on with two batons, one strait up and one to the side. Turn left. And then they were on the taxiway parallel to the runway. Anna looked at him intently.

"Jay, you didn't mention Raymond's journal to me," she said.

"How do you know about it? It can't be referred to in the Agency files. Does Lufkin know about it?"

"No. I saw it in Hudson."

"How?"

"I knew where it was. Raymond showed me once."

"I didn't even know you were there. Hell, I knew nothing about you."

"You were upset and not paying attention. I slipped in and out when you went to town."

"I'm sorry. But does it make a difference? I didn't want anyone to know it existed. What's in that journal is best left unknown. I was going to burn it at the ranch on an anniversary of Raymond's death."

"That's where it is now? At the ranch?"

He hesitated. Should he tell her? "I sent it to Rosie, with an instruction and a onetime code to be used to open a hidden safe. It's in the safe."

Anna smiled and then reached into a valise at her feet, pulled out a small pile of papers, and spread them out on the table. They were held together with a rubber band, the same as the journal was held together, and they looked the same as the journal's pages.

"These pages were in the journal before you found it."

"That's too small to be a duplicate," Jay said.

"I carefully cut them out. They're from 1957. Raymond was smart and guessed I would look for an entry about Vera and him in Budapest, when my mother was conceived."

"I didn't even notice the pages were missing. You left the pages that detail why Raymond was in Budapest at the time, something the Agency wouldn't care to have made public. But why would Lufkin care about that?"

"I was only looking for pages about his feelings for my grandmother. And I found that Raymond went back to them the day before he died and wrote a few new entries on those pages for me to find. He knew I would look there. They didn't make any sense to me until I went to Houston."

"Houston?"

"Right after I saw you in San Diego. I flew privately to Houston and talked to a man named Will Baines, the lawyer Lyn is working with on the sale of an oil company. I asked him to represent my company in a separate matter. One of my questions was whether his firm might have a conflict representing an affiliate of Branoble. They did. His New York partner, Patrick Brashner, is representing the defendants in several securities-fraud cases. One of those defendants is Danna Partners and another is Global Oil Trading Corporation, a Branoble affiliate. I told him I was willing to waive that conflict. But he called me the next day to make sure I also knew that his firm had also been asked to represent Danna on an earlier deal. Nothing came of it."

Jay turned the papers over in his hand. The plane was next in line on the runway for takeoff. The cockpit door was open and he could hear radio talk with the tower. "These look much more interesting than the ones I read about espionage, politics, and birds." He didn't know what else to say.

Anna laughed. "Not too much better. The writing is pretty dry. No sex, of course, only romance and guilt while hiding from the Russians and preparing to swim a river into Austria."

The jet made its roll down the runway and lifted into the air. But Jay's heart seemed to stay behind. The time wasn't right to learn these things. The sky they climbed into was blue. Jay looked down at the pages. It should have been cloudy.

Anna took the pages back and pulled one of them out. "Here is the one with the new writing. You need a magnifying glass. It says, 'No telling Jay about the surprise connection with Danna. He needs his cowboy life back. But I've sent a note to the bastard telling him I know.' It didn't make sense to me for a long time. Who was the bastard he was referring to? That was enough to make me search the Branoble files, where I found a calendar entry referring to Lufkin meeting Patrick Brashner two years ago, a couple of months before Bilbao."

The plane banked to turn east, and in doing so, flew back by the airport. Jay could see the cars parked in the Atlantic Aviation lot. He looked for the Suburban but didn't see it.

"Are you saying Lufkin is the bastard Raymond is referring to?"

"Lufkin made an investment in Danna through a line of companies that could only be traced back to him by someone like me. As I've told you before, I'm very good. And maybe I broke the law a little by hacking into Lufkin's personal accounts."

"And Lufkin's company was the one selling the terminals, if I remember right. So Lufkin was involved on both sides of the deal and with Piquart? Is that it? But we killed Piquart. We did Lufkin a favor. Why would he care now about me? Maybe he thinks I learned about his involvement from Piquart?"

"It would be easy for him to think that."

"And he probably also thinks Raymond left evidence that I have, something I found in his house?"

"Which, as it turns out, you probably do. I'm betting that we'll find another interlineation in the journal when we look closely. I was only looking for the Budapest entries. And there may be more hidden in the farmhouse."

"And what does he think I'm going to do? Give it to the Agency? Give it to the Securities and Exchange Commission? Notes in a journal aren't exactly a smoking gun."

"He doesn't know what you have."

"But Lufkin's a smart guy. I'm sure he's aware of the possibilities. And I can't see him ever allowing anything incriminating to be put in writing. We weren't very smart. We should've searched Piquart's house for papers about Bilbao and something that might incriminate Lufkin."

"Jay, you're missing the point. But give me a minute." Anna got up and went forward to the cockpit. She looked like Raymond in every move she made. "The flight plan the pilot filed is to Austin," she said, when she returned. "I told him that we wanted to divert to Houston to pick up a passenger, but not until we were halfway through the flight."

"Okay." The look of concentration on her face, her careful planning, all reminded him of Raymond. He lost track of what they'd been saying.

"You hadn't asked me where we were going," she said. "I had originally planned to drop you in Austin."

"I guess I was distracted."

She looked at him intently. "We should go make Lyn safe. Don't you think?"

"Yes. Thank you."

"They'll figure out that you're on a plane as soon as they figure out the Atlantic Grill reference after you don't show up at Greyhound or whatever. And they'll know on account of our phone call that I've arranged it. So, they'll be waiting in Austin, and Lufkin probably has guessed that I'm with you. But I'm sure they already had a plan for Lyn. What I hope is that they don't expect we've figured that out. And we can get to Houston before they do something. Still, we have to be prepared that they've figured out my ruse and will be waiting for us at the Houston airport."

"I'm still not sure why they're taking all this trouble. I can see that they were looking for the evidence I might be carrying, and when I didn't have it, they wanted to follow me to Austin in case I had it stashed near there. How did they know about my bank accounts, anyway?"

"Lufkin was your handler after Raymond retired. I'm sure he monitored your trips closely and knew everything else about you. That's not important, and it's not the point."

"It is to me."

"Jay, you need to focus. The point is that Piquart didn't kill Raymond. Lufkin did. Lufkin played us like a fiddle. Our killing Piquart was his good fortune and he was happy to let us be mistaken. He used me to verify that Piquart was killed. And then he got suspicious when you didn't return to the ranch soon after."

Jay wanted to bang his head on the table. Of course. Raymond, being Raymond, would've told Lufkin the particulars of what he'd found. Did he disguise those in the journal also? Jay leaned his back against the seat and closed his eyes. He and Anna had killed Piquart for murdering Raymond, but Piquart hadn't done it.

"It was me he duped, not you. I wanted revenge."

"So did I, but it makes no difference. He's still playing us. He's desperate to find out what we have."

"Which is only a cryptic note in a journal."

"Oh, I'm sure there's more in the journal about other operations that Lufkin never recorded in the Agency's files as he should have, and that you and Raymond assumed he had. We'll find a code, I'm sure."

"So you're guessing also that Lufkin knows Raymond wrote stuff down?"

"We have to assume so, particularly in light of everything that's happened to you since you reappeared in Mexico six months ago. I was stupid not to take the entire journal from the farmhouse. And I was stupid not to realize that Lufkin was sending me to France only to find out what were in Raymond's belongings. You killing Piquart or Piquart killing you didn't matter to him. And I was certainly expendable. My friend from Langley told me that Patrick Brashner was arrested in Houston. It doesn't matter why. But during the interrogation he was overheard instructing his lawyer to tell Ben Lufkin that if he didn't get him out of there, there would be a lot more in his statement than the reason he was arrested. So Brashner knew about Lufkin's involvement with Danna."

"My god. It's all a cover-up. And for what? Money?"

"As usual. But we'll find more when we read the journal in this context. For now, we need to assume that Lufkin won't be satisfied only to get his hands on whatever evidence we have.

There are too many loose ends that are beginning to unravel. And, sorry to say, Lufkin isn't going to take the chance that Lyn doesn't know something."

Jay couldn't think, so many new things all at once, so much guilt, acting in anger, killing Piquart, and now endangering Lyn.

"I need to think. And I'm too tired to do that, so I'm going to sleep a bit. Or try to," he said. He was buying time to rethink, behind closed eyelids, his conviction that Anna was in fact his ally. There were so many loose ends.

"Okay. Before you do, I should tell you, my grandmother believed that Lufkin killed Raymond. I should've listened to her."

"Did she say how she knew?"

"Her Croatian gut, she told me."

28

THAT SAME DAY, THE FIFTH of November, 2017, River Oaks, Houston, the sun was about to slip below the horizon, but cool air remained from the passage of the recent front. It was the last place on earth Lyn wanted to be, standing in the entry foyer of the Baines mansion, a ridiculously elegant space, with its adjacent long, winding, semicircled marble staircases bordered by tapestries and lighted by an enormous chandelier. A formal living room was to the left, where politicians and lawyers rubbed elbows, clinked together their stemware, watched bubbles in champagne flutes, and slapped backs. Lyn had been there several times, and she could slap backs with the best of them, slide her pumps over the oriental carpets next to their wingtips, and listen, with a neutral smile, to jokes about the president, no matter who it was at the time. The room was so pretentious she thought it must be a joke, a private one Will's father had with himself. The rest of the house was entirely different.

She walked between the staircases to an enormous great room, its floor-to-ceiling glass doors rolled aside to give access to a patio and a pool. The furniture was informal, big couches on two sides of a large rectangular coffee table, glass centered on the top of a round pine log pedestal, western art on the walls, and photos of Texas landscapes, many from Big Bend. The outside air pushed in and out of the great room's climate-controlled atmosphere. It was unusual to keep doors open in Houston, and the opportunity wasn't being missed that night. A smell of BBQ came from the kitchen, not the outside. The party was being catered.

As she was about to walk onto the patio, Will came toward her, walking fast. As he was about to pass her—without a word, she was sure—she held up a hand. "Hey, Will. Good to see you."

"Yes. Sorry, but I have to leave."

"So soon? I just got here. They haven't even served the food yet."

"I know. But it can't be helped. Maybe I will come back," he said, and walked around her in the direction of the front door.

"Okay then. I hope to see you later."

He was an awkward man, she thought. Out on the patio she saw Eleanor, dressed conservatively, standing with a group around Ed Reid and his wife. The male associates on the deal were in a group on the other side of the pool. Their wives had formed their own group, which had been joined by Will's mother. Gerald, not to miss an opportunity, was glued to the Global Trading vice chair, who was talking to Bennie Baines. Lyn couldn't decide which group to join, thinking she fell between the cracks, an outsider to each of them. She walked over to the male associates, deciding they would be the easiest to blend in to. The men didn't miss a beat when she joined them, continuing a conversation that was somehow blending politics with baseball. In a nearby tree, several birds hopped around the branches, searching for night insects, which were loud and plentiful, as was customary in Houston. A mosquito buzzed by her ear, and she waved it away with her hand, causing a pause in the conversation.

"The bugs aren't too bad tonight," Nick said. "Probably the cool weather keeps them down."

"Not to mention that thing," another man said, pointing to a blue light glowing in a far corner.

"Bug zapper," a third man said. "Never have a BBQ without one. Bugs can be such a nuisance."

"We need something similar at the office," Nick said. "A partner zapper."

"Quit. How rude!" Lyn said, all of them laughing. And then the baseball topic resumed.

After a time of adding her two cents to the baseball issue and then to Oklahoma's rout of Oklahoma State on the gridiron the day before, she thought how to extract herself from the conversation without seeming rude. There was the woman's ploy she could use, excusing herself for the bathroom. She thought it was reprehensible to do that, so culturally conventional. Men just slipped away when they had to pee, as if they were going behind a tree. Where was equality of the sexes when it made a real difference? Finally, she turned and walked directly to the bathroom without excusing herself.

Alone, she took out her phone. No text from Jay. She washed her hands and then checked again. Nothing. So she fired off another text to him: "What's up, cowboy? Are you dead?" After another minute and no response, not even time for him to type a response, she called the ranch. A woman answered, a brusque tone to her voice.

"Hi. May I speak to Jay?"

"Not here. Who's this?"

"Lyn Larkin. I'm a friend of his from Houston."

"Oh, Lyn. I know who you are," the voice said, warm now. "You coming up here or not?"

"Is this Rosie?"

"Sure is."

"I was supposed to be there today, but I had to delay a day. I sent Jay a message, but I haven't heard from him. And he's not answering his phone."

"I know. He was supposed to be here yesterday. Driving from Mexico."

"Driving?"

"Jay sure likes his truck, if you didn't know. And he's not been here for two years, so I think he was taking it slow. There's an old man in a facility near Tucson who was a war buddy of Raymond. Jay tell you about him?"

"He told me about Raymond."

"Yeah. Well, Louie was in the war with Raymond. So he's pretty old, and dementia is slipping into him. I think Jay wanted to see him before it was too late. But I called there this morning. Louie was sharp as a tack. And Jay hadn't shown up there like he was supposed to."

"Maybe his truck broke down," Lyn said, wanting to feel positive.

"I suppose. But it's brand new."

"Maybe his phone broke?"

"Hell, that's probably new too."

"Anyone else we can call?"

"You're worried, aren't you?"

"Yes. I talked to him Friday morning and I thought he was going to keep me posted."

"It's sweet that you're worried. Jay needs someone besides me to worry about him. But you don't know Jay like I do. Letting people know where he is isn't something he's good at."

Lyn looked at herself in the mirror. The woman reflected there looked guilty. She'd been angrier earlier, thinking that Jay was going to jilt her again, take off on another world excursion, a man on the run from romantic commitment. It made no sense, of course. He'd sounded sincere when he'd called her. But he had two years ago also. Her anger somehow made her complicit with his new disappearance.

"Do you know that he even left Los Pelicanos?"

"Yes, he called just after crossing the border. Said he wanted to remind me you were coming and to make a brisket, which I did do, by the way."

"I'm sorry. I wish I was there to eat it."

"It'll keep. He'll show up sooner or later. He always does. I'll make that man call you as soon as he gets here, no matter what time. I can tell you're worried."

Lyn's thoughts became disjointed, her confusion spilling over the lip of a fancy vase on a nearby shelf. It seemed appropriate that there were no flowers in it. The air in the bathroom was dead still. She reached over to turn on the lights over the mirror, to make the shadows depart, to generate some optimism. But the despondency welling up in her wasn't giving up. Her cheeks flushed and one hand gripped the side of the sink cabinet.

She'd not properly taken care of her hair after her earlier plunge into the pool, she saw. Her damp head had dried under the pillow during her nap. Now, there were kinks where there shouldn't be, and frizzy ends, some of which were invading her eyebrows. Shaking her head didn't help. Neither did brushing them aside with her fingers. Her face reminded her of an unhappy looking puppy, an unshorn poodle.

"Are you still there, Lyn?" Rosie asked.

"Yes. Yes. Sorry. I guess I just feel so helpless."

"Go have a drink. Watch TV. That's what I do. Unless you like to make pies."

Lyn laughed. "I have no idea how to make a pie. And I'm really not good at waiting. Even if he hasn't shown up, I think that tomorrow morning I will go ahead and drive up there. We can eat brisket and wait together, if that's okay with you."

A pause. "Of course it is, darling. I love company when I'm waiting. See you tomorrow."

Lyn leaned her back against the door and blew air through her mouth, one of her broad repertoire of sighs. But her sighs were usually from exasperation; worrying about a person was foreign to her. As far as she could remember, it hadn't happened since her mother was dying from cancer. When was that? More than twenty years ago. She'd been fond of some people, a few friends, several clients. But she'd never worried about them for any reason. Her worries were only for her law practice, and for her client's transactions, not the people. She didn't worry for her sister's troubles, of which there were many. If she told the truth, worrying for her sister was a bother. And so it perplexed her now, how she was feeling about Jay. There was no logic to it.

When she went out the door, she saw that she could easily turn right and slip out, back between the staircases, through the front door to her car, the way Will had gone earlier. But she didn't. Back on the patio she joined Ed Reid and his wife, who were watching the other guests line up at the food table. Gerald joined them after a minute. Small talk was an antidote for worry, a good alternative to sitting on her couch at home. The ribs were piled high on a platter, wisps of steam rising around from the heated water beneath the surrounding serving dishes. She got into line. The comfort of strangers felt good. Everyone was a stranger when she wasn't lawyering with them. Or so it had been before she went to Mexico. Jay had become a stranger again, it seemed, and she would just have to hang out here, getting her fingers greasy, listening to frivolous talk, distracting herself.

A tug at her arm made Lyn back out of line before she could pick up a plate at the food table. "Ms. Larkin, sorry to bother, but can we speak for a minute?" Eleanor asked.

Lyn thought to reprimand the young woman about calling her Ms. Larkin, but held back when she saw the tears welling at the bottom of her eyes. "Of course," she said, and watched

Eleanor's eyes dart to the people near them, which dislodged a tear that ran down her cheek. "Come with me, Eleanor," she said, taking her arm. They walked back into the house through the main staircases and then into the formal living room. On the way, Lyn stopped at the bathroom and grabbed the box of Kleenex.

"I don't know that we should be in here," Eleanor said, as Lyn directed her to a couch deep in the room.

Lyn laughed. "No one will mind. I'm sure of that."

After they sat down, close enough that their knees almost touched when they turned toward each other, Lyn saw that Eleanor's eyes were becoming puffy as more tears emerged. It was a good thing she wasn't wearing all that mascara she'd been wearing at the benefit, Lyn thought. Then she scolded herself, thinking she'd made an unfair judgment about the young woman, remembering that she'd not worn any makeup at any of the meetings they'd been in.

"I made a fool of myself, flirting with Mr. Baines on Thursday night," Eleanor said.

Lyn didn't allow herself to laugh. "Oh Eleanor, that was nothing. I'm sure Will was flattered that a beautiful woman was flirting with him, although he'd never admit it." She took Eleanor's hands in hers.

"I apologized to him right after you left that night, and he was very understanding." Then she told the story about her boyfriend in Denver. "It was humiliating, being at the benefit dressed like I was. I can't believe I did that."

"Nonsense," Lyn said. "Your dress was beautiful and you looked spectacular. I was envious and wished I could still wear a dress like that. Nothing wrong with looking good and stretching your wings a little." Wasn't she being impractical? In the law firm world, there was a prejudice against women lawyers who wore clothes like Eleanor's dress. She'd always worried that men wouldn't take her seriously as a lawyer if she wore such clothes. A stunning outfit would feel good, but the cost was high. All the eyes undressing her, the men not listening to a word she said. As for stretching her wings, she'd rarely done so. She'd buttoned up.

"No, wearing that dress was a disaster," Eleanor said, and then proceeded to tell Lyn about Brashner and the hotel room, stopping to sob uncontrollably on several occasions.

Lyn was stunned and gripped Eleanor's hand tightly during the story, sometimes taking the young woman in her arms in order to bring the sobbing under control. Of course, in Jay's phraseology, she didn't know squat about mothering. But her empathy came naturally. What also came naturally was her outrage when, at the end of her story, Eleanor said it was her own fault for dressing as she had.

"Wait. You can't blame yourself for that horrible man raping you. I'm sure you didn't encourage him. Is a woman required to wear body armor to protect herself? No!"

"That's exactly what Mr. Baines said."

It was hard for Lyn to picture those words coming out of Will's mouth. He would be sympathetic, of course, being a parent with daughters. But Lyn thought he would also be tongue-tied by the surprise and being unable to know how to fix it. "I'm so glad you told him, Eleanor. At the least, your firm's management also needs to be told."

"Oh, I was referring to Will's father," Eleanor said. "I'm not sure what to call him. Maybe 'Mr. Baines Senior?'"

Lyn laughed. "Everyone calls him Bennie. Even his granddaughters call him Bennie."

"Will called him right after I told him. Bennie was so kind to me. He insisted that I file a complaint with the police. He even called the police chief and then drove me down there and waited while I made my statement and they did a rape kit. And then he personally drove over to my apartment tonight and brought me over here. He insisted. I don't know if he has told Mr. Reid."

"Well I'm going to tell Ed if Bennie hasn't. Brashner cannot get away with this."

"It will be so embarrassing when everyone finds out. I don't know how I will face it. How am I going to tell my parents? And if he's arrested and there's a trial. It will be awful."

"I'll be right there with you, dear," Lyn said, hugging her and feeling again like a mother. How strange the feeling was. The whole week had been an avalanche of new emotions. At this minute, she felt herself teeter on the edge of the couch between screaming in anger and rolling up into a ball of despondency.

"I am so sorry, Ms. Larkin, to burden you like this. But I needed to talk to a woman. As nice as Will and Bennie were about everything, I don't think they understand why I'm afraid and blaming myself."

"I'm honored that you trusted me, Eleanor. And you must call me Lyn. I am going to be your best friend as you go through this."

Eleanor nodded her head, and tears began again, but without the sobs. Lyn looked around. It was such a formal room and had probably never witnessed such a discussion like this before. It was time to leave.

"I'm going to drive you home," Lyn said. "Let's go back and retrieve our stuff. I will let Bennie know. You don't have to go back into the party or talk to anyone."

As Lyn drove to Eleanor's apartment, they were quiet, and Lyn realized that her worry about Jay had gone. But the night seemed too dark and the streets too empty.

29.

THAT SAME DAY, THE FIFTH of November, 2017, Hobby Airport, Houston, in the waiting room of a private terminal, Will sat looking through a window at a dark expanse, red lights blinking now and then as a breeze moved shrubs that partially obscured the runway. The man at the desk said Ms. Mason's plane was soon to land. No one else was waiting, and Will didn't know who Ms. Mason was, only that his new client, Anna Stegineo, was on the plane and had asked him to come to the airport on a matter that she said was urgent without saying what that meant, except that she had papers for him. He didn't mind, in any case; actually, he'd jumped at the opportunity to get out of his father's house. Watching Eleanor try to mingle after everything she'd been through was breaking his heart.

Ten minutes later, he heard the whine of a jet approaching and saw a man with light sticks guiding it to a space. Then Anna came through the door, wearing a baggy sweater over black tights, her hair in a braid, curved over her shoulder onto her chest, nothing like how she'd looked in his office on Thursday. Behind her, a tall man in a cowboy hat strolled in.

"Will, you are such a dear to come out here like this," Anna said, and hugged him before he would protect himself with an outstretched hand to shake, making him blush.

"It was really not a problem," he said.

"Let me introduce you. This cowboy with me is Jay Jackson. Don't let him fool you. He was once a lawyer like you."

"Howdy, Will," Jay said, shaking Will's hand. "You know, I'm pretty sure we met once a long time ago on a deal."

"Yes sir, we did."

"And how's your father? He's an old friend of mine."

"I didn't know that," Anna said.

"Oh yeah," Jay said. "Big oil man. Baines Resources. He sold it to some New York private equity suckers for several billion dollars several years ago."

"He's well. Thanks for asking. He's having a party tonight, in fact. That's where Belinda is."

Jay chuckled. "So Lyn told you she was with me in Mexico last week."

"Yes sir. Sorry if she wasn't supposed to tell me."

"Not a problem, son. She's the one keeping the secret, not me. But don't tell her you've seen me. I want to surprise her later."

"Okay, we have to get going," Anna said. "Will, I'm going to make a very strange request of you. There's a rental car outside I had delivered here. I want you to put on Mr. Jackson's hat and coat here and drive the car back to your father's house. We're going to take your car to an appointment and then we'll bring it over there and switch back."

It was nothing like what she'd said when she'd called. "I thought you had papers for me. I don't know about switching cars."

"Not to worry, Will. The papers will be delivered to your office. Here's the deal. I think there are some reporters outside the gate. Someone has tipped them off that Mr. Jackson is going to discuss a deal for the Branoble company I retained you to represent. As you know, the company is in Chapter 11, and any hint of discussions with another company could be a disaster. The creditors are being difficult. The reporters will figure out who we're talking to if they follow us. It would be best for them to think you are Mr. Jackson and follow you to River Oaks."

"I thought you retired," Will said to Jay.

"Yeah. I have. This is an encore as a dealmaker for some old friends. Ben Lufkin has got me in the middle of it. You know him?"

"Never met him, but I have heard the name."

"I know it's strange, Will," Anna said. "But these guys have been a complete nuisance to me for months. This will really help. Not your usual legal assignment, I guess."

Will shrugged. Why not? Otherwise, all he had to look forward to was going home and sitting on the couch with Mason, watching TV. He put on Jay's hat and coat and exchanged keys with Anna.

"By the way, Anna, do you know a guy named Erik who works in Denver? Can't remember his last name."

"You probably mean Erik Lawson. Why?"

"He's friends with a guy who was dating an associate who works for me, and he's been asking her boyfriend to ask questions about a deal I'm working on," Will said, looking at Jay for a moment. He didn't want to say it was the Global Trading deal.

"He was wrong to do that. I hope you ignored the questions," Anna said.

"I did."

"You should keep doing that," she said.

"I don't think she's seeing her boyfriend anymore, so the guy won't be getting any information in the future."

"I will speak to Mr. Lufkin about him."

"Okay," Will said, thinking he could go back to the party and tell Eleanor that David and his friend would get their due. But it was probably best to drop it, with all that'd happened to her. He turned back before he went out the door. "My father's party tonight is a BBQ to celebrate the signing of that deal yesterday. Come in when you get there. My father won't mind."

"A BBQ is my kind of party. Thanks for the invitation," Jay said. "And don't worry, we won't dent up your car."

Anna didn't believe anyone was waiting for them, but caution was needed. Hacking into air traffic control wasn't a risk Lufkin would want to take. Tracking domestic air travel always required a domestic authority to make the request, like the Department of Homeland Security. That would leave a trail. So his guys would rely on the flight plan on file in El Paso, and they wouldn't know that a change had been made until the plane landed in Austin—it had already departed from Houston. They watched from a window of the terminal. No one followed Will in the rental car out to Airport Boulevard.

They drove Will's Audi to Lyn's house, where Anna picked the lock easily, leaving the lights turned off, closing the blinds, then going through the rooms quietly with penlights, ensuring that no one was inside yet, checking for points of access from the outside. Satisfied, Anna went out to move the Audi into the garage. Jay hadn't been in Lyn's house before, and he walked around with the lights on. The colors of the walls were the same as the colors of the lipsticks she wore. The comforter on her bed had a pattern like one of her beach shirts. In the bathroom, a damp bathing suit hung on a hook over the tub, a small patch of water where it had dripped. Everything was tidy. The kitchen counters were spotless. Jay shook his head. She hadn't known anyone was coming. He had run around his house in Mexico cleaning up before she arrived.

They waited on the couch, making small talk. Jay looked at his watch. It was after eight. He was surprised Lyn wasn't home yet. If she showed up before the expected intruder, they would have to improvise. There was a risk that she'd be taken between the Baines house and here. He and Lyn had gambled that it would be too public on the roads for them to risk that. But they had no idea how Lufkin's men would try to gain entry. That didn't matter. They were prepared. And Jay was confident that Lufkin planned to hold her in her home, use video of her when they came for Jay in Austin. So if his men did nab her on the road, they would bring her here.

"So who is this Erik Lawson fellow at Branoble?" Jay asked.

"He's a Lufkin acolyte. Not a particularly nice person. But none of them are. He was recruited by Lufkin soon after your departure."

When the doorbell rang, they walked quietly to the entry foyer. Jay positioned himself in the space that the opened door would conceal.

"Who is it?" Anna sang through the door, a woman offstage delivering a line in a musical.

"Package delivery," a voice said.

"Just leave it on the porch," she said.

"Sorry, ma'am. I need a signature. Didn't we tell you that when we called earlier?"

"Did you? Oh yes, I remember. What's the sender's name on the label? Can you confirm that for me so I know you're who you say you are? A woman can't be too cautious at night." Her voice now had the cadence and tone of an older woman, very different from what he'd heard from her before. He was sure he wouldn't recognize it if she wasn't standing there next to him.

"Of course. The sender is Julius Jackson," the man said.

Anna looked at Jay and smiled. She fiddled with the locks and cracked the door slowly. Jay couldn't see the man, and he wasn't sure why Anna hadn't fully opened the door yet.

"Sorry for the trouble," the man called through the cracked door. "If you could just sign on my pad here."

Jay guessed the man was planning to push her back into the house once she opened the door another inch. That didn't happen. He should've known it wouldn't, after the scene in Piquart's bedroom in France. Anna flung the door open suddenly, grabbed the man's forearm and pulled him into the house. The pad had barely hit the floor before Anna's gun, pulled from the holster in the small of her back, slammed the back of his head.

"Idiot," Anna said, as she kicked the man's feet aside so Jay could close the door. "He wasn't even carrying a package."

Jay squatted and turned the man over. It was Joe Uno, not looking as confident as he'd looked the last time Jay had seen him. A trickle of blood made its way across his forehead.

"What do you know! It's one of those Joes I told you about."

"No, this one's not a Joe," Anna said. "That's Erik Lawson, the shit." She wasn't even breathing hard.

"I guess that confirms the Lufkin connection," he said.

"No time to celebrate. We need to hustle him out of here."

There was a door to the garage off a hallway from the kitchen. Anna had backed the Audi into the garage earlier. They dragged Erik Lawson down the hall and loaded him into the trunk. Jay found some rope in the garage and tied him up. Then he put a strip of duct tape over his mouth.

"Now, that there is a proper use of duct tape," he said, before he closed the trunk. What would Will Baines think if he knew this man was tied up in his trunk? Anna got behind the wheel, and Jay looked at her through the passenger side window.

"I'm going to switch cars, and our friend in the trunk, at the Baines house," she said.

"Okay. After that?"

"I'm going to ask Mr. Lawson a few questions," she said. "And they won't be friendly. I'm right angry, as you might put it."

"And then?"

"You're such a nosy man, Jay. You don't need to know that," she said, put the car in gear, and drove away.

Jay cleaned up carefully, making sure nothing from the incident remained. In his travel bag, he had a nice change of clothes. He had planned to wear them the night he was going to visit Raymond's friend in Arizona. Will had taken his cowboy hat, the one he'd been wearing when he was abducted. He was attached to his old hat. It had buffalo nickels on the hatband. It bothered him to be hatless, so he put on an Astros hat he found hanging on a hook in the garage. And his truck? It aggravated him that it was parked down a dusty road in the middle of nowhere. He'd had it washed on the way back from taking Lyn to the airport. That was only three days ago, but it seemed like a month. He would have to send someone out there to get it.

He got a sticky note in a kitchen drawer and wrote on it in big capital letters, "I'm on the back patio—Jay." This he affixed to the garage door before he walked around the house, through a gate, and sat down on a lounge chair next to the pool. It was a beautiful night, a light breeze, the moon rising over a treetop, reflected in the pool. The full moon at the ranch would be beautiful. Soon enough, something would have to be done about Ben Lufkin.

30.

LATER THAT EVENING, THE FIFTH of November, 2017, Houston, Lyn was weary as she drove up Kirby Drive. She checked her phone at a stop light. Nothing. She threw it on the passenger seat. It wasn't going to do any good looking at it every minute. Her worry had slipped out of sight while she was consoling Eleanor. But it had returned within two blocks of her departure from Eleanor's apartment. Her intentions were set, and she would march forward. In the morning, she was driving to San Saba. On the way, she would call Ed Reid, although she suspected Bennie had already told him.

In her driveway, she noticed a note stuck on her garage door as it was rolling up, and she pushed the remote to roll the door back down. She read it in the car's headlights. Then she jumped from the car and ran to the front door, dropped her keys on the ground, swore, got it open on the second try, ran through the house to the patio, and slid back the sliding door.

There he was, lounging in a chair like he lived here, wearing blue jeans, a bright-red shirt, and an Astros hat. It was impossible to miss her entrance, she'd made so much noise. But he didn't jump to his feet, which annoyed her. Finally, he stood up slowly and performed a polite bow.

"Howdy. I heard that you were at a big party at the Baines mansion, so I had to sneak around back to your patio," he said. "You know, if you lived at the ranch, you wouldn't be locking all the doors."

The smile on his face, the way his eyes gazed at her, the moonlight reflecting on the pool, all made her heart soar. Here he was, full of his cowboy persona, as if he was a neighbor just come by for a visit. But she couldn't even summon up a polite laugh. All of her anxiety and fears of the past hours, and now his surprise appearance, were so twisted inside her that she was frozen.

A frown fell over his face when she hadn't moved. "Why, you look like you've just seen a ghost."

"Not funny," she said.

Relief exploded inside her. As if shot from a cannon, she leaped into his arms and wrapped her legs around his waist and hugged him hard. She wasn't her old self, this grand display of emotion, as unusual for her as the worry that had gripped her in the Baines powder room and the motherly empathy that had poured out of her for Eleanor. She let out a long breath, like she'd just smashed an object with a hammer to rid herself of frustration. No, it wasn't a hammer. She'd hurled the 10th edition of *Black's Law Dictionary* and all of its dialectics onto the floor. She spoke into Jay's ear. "What the fuck, cowboy? I thought you were dead." Then she unsaddled herself and stepped back, gripped his hands and said, "So lovely you could visit, Señor Jackson."

"I'm right sorry I'm late," he said. "But I had a little trouble on the highway to Mexicali. Some banditos forced me off the road, then took my money and my truck. Good thing they didn't look in my boots. My passport was in one. I had to hitchhike all the way to Juarez near El Paso. Then I made my way to the Stanton House. Do you know that place? I was there a few times over the years and I know the concierge. But good luck found me first. I ran into Jim Daniel in the lobby. You know, that rich Houston guy we did a deal for in Indonesia. He had his plane at the airport and I flew with him to Houston and he had a guy drop me here. Nice pool, by the way."

"You could've called, you know." *And stop babbling*, she wanted to say. "But we know you're not very good at that."

"The banditos took my phone. And then I got to El Paso and it all happened so fast that I was on my way to Houston and I thought I'd just surprise you."

"I could be in Austin already."

"Yeah, I called Rosie when we landed and she told me you called her and said that you wouldn't arrive until tomorrow. And, by the way, she was little put out with me that I hadn't shown up Saturday night and hadn't called her either. You got her all riled up. Just made it worse. She'd made a brisket and all. Boy, did she light into me."

"You deserved it, Jay. I'm sure there was a phone at the Stanton."

"Just wanted to surprise you. And it was no big deal. I was only a day late."

"A day! No big deal?"

"I'm sorry. I guess I'm not so good at checking in. As you already know."

No big deal! It was what you said after you dropped a plate, before you swept up the pieces. For her, the week before had been an emotional hurricane. It was a big deal. And now she faced alternatives. Go on as before or do something new?

"It doesn't matter now. You're here," she said, and embraced him again.

"I hope you're not too put out. I was planning on catching a ride to the ranch with you tomorrow. But I could always get a Southwest flight from Hobby. That had been my original plan, before I called Rosie."

She stood back and dropped his hands. The night air was cold now and she crossed her arms across her chest, regretting that she'd not worn a sweater. Refusing to be distracted from the moment, she looked at him and forgot the sweater.

Tomorrow night she would be at the Jackson Ranch, enjoying the warmth and safety of his bed, the quiet of the prairie around them. Would the horses in the barn make noises at night? As a girl, she used her imagination as an anesthetic, in her room under her comforter, a story for her troubles, an explanation for the unexplainable, why a misfortune was an aberration, how she'd really reacted in a manner opposite from the way she had, a fantastic rewriting of history. A good time to do the same. "Are there crickets at the ranch?" she asked.

"If you want there to be, I'm sure they'll be there," he said. "Whatever you want."

She looked into his eyes. It wouldn't be that simple, choosing an alternative. An outline might help, like she'd done in law school, preparing to write a brief. The law was not quite done with her, it appeared. And what would happen if, for now, she temporarily foreswore any decision about her future, putting all of her decisions aside? She could start a new life with this rancher, if he really did produce the crickets. Or she could return to Houston and the law, until she was forced to give it up. Or she could simply retire early with no plan whatsoever. Whatever she chose, she would be there for Eleanor. And she had no doubt that she would find something rewarding to do with herself. There they were, her alternatives laid out like an issues list on her desk. She unclasped her arms and pushed her chest forward, her body warm now. The delay of a decision was alluring, the sweet expectation of something new, an accomplishment yet to be achieved. She kicked off her shoes and unbuttoned her blouse.

"How about a swim?" she asked, dropping her skirt. "The pool water is warm," she lied.

She took off the rest of her clothing and dove into the pool. When she came to the surface, she looked at him. He stood right as she'd left him.

"Can't swim, cowboy?"

"Hell, let me catch my breath first," he said, and sat down to take off his boots.

The water felt safe. She swam to the other side of the pool and leaned back against the wall, her elbows up above the lip, the water on her chest sparkling in the moonlight. He was taking a long time taking off his clothes. It made her laugh. She was doing the same thing with her indecisions. And how should she presume? She didn't know. The naked cowboy dove into the pool. No need to worry. There was all the time in the world ahead of her, enough for a hundred decisions and revisions.

THE END

A NOVEL

A LI**O**N IN THE GRASS

MARK ZVONKOVIC

Set over the course of six decades, *A Lion in the Grass* documents the despair and hope of a spy who suffers the murder of friends and enjoys the success of mentoring protégés.

"Fans of Ludlum, Clancy, and other writers who hold the ability to craft high-impact spy scenarios within the broader scope of world events and interpersonal relationships will relish the attention to detail and the realistic action and perceptions cultivated in *A Lion in the Grass*."
— Midwest Book Review

"*A Lion in the Grass* has strong historical hints, a story with realistic characters, and elements of style that deepen the suspense and the overall entertaining quality of the story." — Readers' Favorite

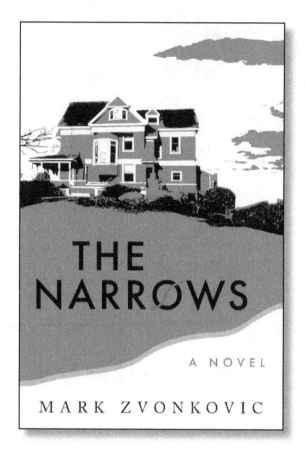

THE
NARROWS

A NOVEL

MARK ZVONKOVIC

The Narrows is an engaging story concerning the personal and social challenges that bedeviled baby boomers coming of age during the cultural transformation of the 1970's.

"...the different path individuals take to find their niche in the world. With Larry it's about maintaining the status quo—a respectable job, a nice apartment and a girlfriend—while Bradley is more open to exploring other avenues to find his nirvana."   —*Foreword* Magazine

"*The Narrows* powerfully employs dialogue, philosophical and psychological reflection, and a slice-of-life feel so expansive that it's hard to believe the timeline embraces only ten pivotal days in the narrator's life."   —Midwest Book Review

"Compelling characters and poignant philosophical questions drive *The Narrows*, where narrator Larry Brown struggles to find his place in the turbulent early '70s. An excellent family drama with suspense and heart."   —IndieReader

About the Author

Author Photograph by Rebecca Westerveld

MARK ZVONKOVIC IS A WRITER who lives in Rosarito Beach, Baja California, Mexico with his wife Nancy and their two dogs, Finn and Cooper. He has written two other novels, *A Lion In The Grass* and *The Narrows*.

CPSIA information can be obtained
at www.ICGtesting.com
Printed in the USA
BVHW040749120722
640641BV00013B/38/J